T0369061

A Dark Mystery in the
WHITE MOUNTAINS

The Unforgettable Story
of an Online Encounter

Kristina Sarkisyan

Based on a True Story

iUniverse, Inc.
Bloomington

A Dark Mystery in the White Mountains
The Unforgettable Story of an Online Encounter

iUniverse books may be ordered through booksellers or by contacting:

iUniverse
1663 Liberty Drive
Bloomington, IN 47403
www.iuniverse.com
1-800-Authors (1-800-288-4677)

ISBN: 978-1-4620-0715-8 (sc)
ISBN: 978-1-4620-0716-5 (ebk)

Printed in the United States of America

iUniverse rev. date: 07/18/2011

This book is dedicated
to everyone who uses dating websites
and
to those who abuse them

To all those who are honest and decent people:

"Please try to avoid online predators.
Be Happy and Good Luck!"

- Kristi

Important Characters

Rebecca Wilson (Becky)
Research Assistant; Philosophy Teacher
She lives in Lynn, MA
She is 23 when the story begins

Aaron Thoreau (A. Thoreau)
Business Owner; Rebecca's Love
He lives in Nashua, NH
He is 35 when the story begins

Jeffrey Jones (Jeff)
Mechanic; Rebecca's Former Friend
He lives in Brooklyn, NY
He is 26 when the story begins

Elizabeth Wilson
Psychology Professor; Rebecca's Mother
She lives in Lynn, MA
She is 47 when the story begins

Kevin Wilson
Manager; Rebecca's Father
He lives in Lynn, MA
He is 50 when the story begins

Caroline Thoreau
Former History Teacher; Aaron's Mother
She is 73 when the story begins

TABLE OF CONTENTS

CHAPTER 1

EXTRAORDINARY CLASSROOM

September 22, 2010: Boston, Massachusetts (MA) – Boston University

It is a sunny and beautiful morning in Boston. The fall in New England is fantastic. The days are warm and bright; the nights are cool and dark, and the leaves change their colors from green to yellow, orange, brown, and red. New England is full of amazing cultural attractions, important historic sites, fascinating cities and towns, breathtaking fall foliage, remarkable sand beaches, wonderful lakes and ponds, expansive and impressive forests, unforgettable mountain views, beautiful landscapes, and restaurants with delicious seafood. New England is also famous for its outstanding colleges and universities, where hundreds of thousands of students receive an incomparable education every year. Thousands of tourists from all over the world visit New England in the fall, and thousands of students dream to study in New England.

The big classroom at Boston University is full of students, who are waiting for their favorite psychology professor. Elizabeth Wilson is their professor this semester. She is a little late today. The title of the course that she teaches this term is *Psychology of Trauma*. All of the students prepared their homework, and they are ready to hand in their papers. Their assignment was to write a paper about trauma. The students had to define trauma and try to explain the different types of trauma. At that time, nobody could imagine that this class would not be like the rest of their classes. At that time, no one could think that this class would leave a very deep impression in their hearts and minds that they would never be able to forget. At that time, nobody knew the real definition of trauma.

ELIZABETH

Good morning students!
Today's class will not be an ordinary class.
Many of you will remember this class forever,
and for some of you this will be an unforgettable lesson,
which may help prevent some of the worst suffering
in the future.
I would like to tell you a story.
I would like to share with you something very personal,
something that happened to me and my family
one year ago.
It was also a very beautiful morning in Boston,
just like the morning today.
I have never told this story to anyone before because
it was too painful for me to even think about it.
However, the time has come for everyone to know...

ELIZABETH (CONT'D)

September 22 is a special day in my life.
This day has changed my life forever.
It has been one year since the day it happened;
however, I remember everything as if
it happened yesterday.
My heart is still full of excruciating pain,
and my head is still full of indelible memories.
I know that I will never be able to forget this.
By telling this story,
I do not hope to end my unending pain, and
I do not intend to erase my indelible memories.
I want to help you live a beautiful and wonderful life.
I want to help you be happy and turn your dreams into reality.
I want to help you find your true love and avoid suffering.
By telling this story, I want to bring more justice into this world.
I feel it is my responsibility now to tell this
story to as many people as possible.

I want to help at least one person avoid the
tragedy that happened to my family.
Only then, it will be less painful for me to continue my life.
Only then, I may be happy again.
Some people say that time is the best doctor,
and that even the worst events and
the most painful memories pass after a reasonable period of time.
However, time does not always heal.
Sometimes it cannot resist the harsh reality of our everyday life.
Time becomes helpless and hopeless in the face of evil.
There are certain events in our life that even time cannot erase.
There are certain events in our life that stay
in human minds and hearts forever.
However, now is the time for me to tell you this story.
I want everyone to know. I cannot be silent anymore.
Silence makes us more vulnerable to becoming
a victim of evil and injustice.
I want as many people as possible to know
what can happen when someone does not take
all the necessary precautions for self-protection.
The time has come for me to tell you this story.
The time has come to tell you the story of my daughter and
to try to prevent other families from suffering.

Elizabeth asks one of the students to respond to her question.

ELIZABETH (CONT'D)
Kathy, do you remember the day when you asked
why I never go to New Hampshire (NH) for a vacation?
Please tell me if you remember.

KATHY
Yes, I remember, Professor Wilson.

ELIZABETH
Kathy, I used to go to New Hampshire several times a year.

This was one of my favorite vacation places in the country.
New Hampshire is famous for some of the most spectacular
views in the world.
The state of New Hampshire offers its visitors wonderful and
unforgettable mountain views from many different locations.
It also has a lot of interesting cultural attractions and
historic sites, which attract thousands of people every year.
The beautiful state of New Hampshire with its mountains,
forests, lakes, and foliage is a natural attraction for everyone.
In wintertime, visitors from all over the world enjoy skiing
and learning to ski on spectacular mountainous terrains.
In summertime, those who like to swim and boat,
enjoy the sparkling, clear, blue lakes and rivers;
those who like to hike and camp,
enjoy the incredible beauty of the mountains,
and those who like beaches, enjoy the ocean.
In the fall, NH is especially beautiful.
The fall foliage colors are full of reds, greens,
yellows, oranges, and browns.
The days are clear and warm with beautiful sunshine,
the skies are deep blue with white clouds,
and the lakes sparkle with unforgettable, brilliant sunlight.
There is usually an incredible sunset over
the lakes and ponds in NH.
The changing foliage, the amazing lakes and ponds,
and the fantastic mountain views attract visitors
from all over the world.
NH can offer something wonderful and amazing
to anyone who goes there.

One of the most famous tourist destinations in NH
is the White Mountains.
The White Mountains cover a large portion
of the state of NH.
The White Mountains is the most favorite
vacation destination in NH for a lot of people.

They include the White Mountain National Forest
(WMNF) and other wonderful state parks.
WMNF has some of the most beautiful landscapes in the world.
The incomparable beauty of the White Mountains
can impress anyone who sees it.
The White Mountains are one of the most
beautiful mountains in the world.
I used to admire the beauty of New Hampshire too.
However, New Hampshire, its beauty, its tourist attractions
and vacation destinations do not impress me anymore…

ELIZABETH (CONT'D)
We all want to meet the person of our dreams in real life.
We want to meet an honest, decent, caring, understanding,
compassionate, and trustworthy person with good manners,
who will always be supportive, and who will never betray,
disappoint, or hurt us.
We all want to find a special person, who will always love us,
and who will always provide emotional comfort and strength.
We need someone to comfort our soul and to rejoice our heart.
Loneliness is one of the most terrible misfortunes, and
we do not want to be lonely.
The one thing that all human beings are afraid of is loneliness.
We want to have a family, and we want to be happy
and enjoy our lives with our loved ones.
When we meet our loved one, we are
definitely afraid to lose him/her.

ELIZABETH (CONT'D)
My daughter had the same dreams and wishes, and
she did not want to be lonely.
She wanted to find a good person,
to marry him and have children.
Rebecca wanted to find a special person and
spend the whole life with him.
My daughter always had an idea

about the person she wanted to meet,
and she wanted that person to become a reality.
My daughter loved art very much, especially music, and
she always thought that the person of her dreams
would be either a musician or a painter.
She thought that her husband would be an artist
because she admired art very much.
However, it was not her destiny to meet an artist.
In the beginning of November 2008,
my daughter did meet the person of her dreams, and
he did become her reality.
Rebecca met Aaron on one of the dating websites,
when she was 23 years old.
Aaron was not an artist; he was an ordinary person
without extraordinary talents.

ELIZABETH (CONT'D)
We all have dreams, and we want our dreams to come true.
We should definitely pursue our dreams
and try to turn them into reality.
As one of the greatest American philosophers
Henry David Thoreau says,
"Go confidently in the direction of your dreams.
Live the life you have imagined."
I just want to rephrase a little this wonderful quotation:
"Go confidently in the direction of your dreams,
but remember, not all dreams come true,
and some of our dreams can be very detrimental
if we do not take all the necessary precautions."
In addition, I would like to say the following:
"Live the life you have imagined, but remember,
you must never hurt others."
My daughter helped Aaron live the life he had imagined,
but he…

This is the unforgettable story of my daughter,

who was full of hopes and dreams, and
who wanted to find her true love and happiness,
but who became a victim of the harsh reality
of our everyday life – a reality that can
become your reality any time.
I want to prevent such realities from happening in the future.
I want to help you all avoid certain life-threatening mistakes.
I want as many people as possible to know
what happened to my daughter.
Now it is a matter of justice for me to tell
you this truly shocking story.
This is the story with an important message,
which can be very beneficial
to humanity in general and to many people in particular.

This is an extraordinary story of one ordinary girl...

As Elizabeth is getting ready to start telling her daughter's story, there is complete silence in the classroom. It looks like there is no movement inside or outside the classroom, even the trees outside stand still. The only interruption is a very sad song that is playing in a car parked on the street next to the University. The name of the song is "Flowers" by Rozz Williams, an American rock musician.

The students hear these words as they
prepare to listen to Elizabeth:

"This is my favorite sad story,
Forget me not or I will forget myself.
I have got quite a few things that I am afraid of.
Sometimes I just can't face myself..."

Elizabeth tells the story of her daughter from the very beginning...

CHAPTER 2

FIRST ONLINE EXPERIENCE

Rebecca has recently turned 23. She graduated from Northeastern University Summa Cum Laude. She has a Bachelor's Degree in Philosophy and Criminal Justice and a Master's Degree in Philosophy. Rebecca plans to apply to a PhD Program in Philosophy. Currently, she works as a research assistant at Northeastern University. She helps one of her former professors with research on juvenile crime and delinquency. In the future, Rebecca wants to teach philosophy to University students.

Rebecca is very young, but she is a very mature and serious person. She is not interested in going to bars and night clubs; she does not drink at all. Rebecca prefers to read books, especially philosophy books. She has read hundreds of philosophy books. Her favorite philosopher is Henry David Thoreau. In her free time, Rebecca enjoys reading books, going to museums and theaters, listening to music, watching interesting movies, walking on the beach, and helping her friends improve their writing skills by proofreading their college essays. Rebecca also volunteers in the local center for immigrant services. She teaches English as a Second Language (ESL) classes to those who want to learn or improve their English speaking and writing skills. Rebecca is a very honest, decent, and kind-hearted person, who likes to help everyone who has a problem.

Rebecca is tired of being alone, and she wants to improve her personal life. Rebecca wants to meet someone special, someone who will always love her, and who will make her dreams come true. Rebecca's mother heard about a successful dating website, and she suggested that her daughter create an account on that website. With the help of her mother, Rebecca registers on one of the dating websites, and she is looking forward to meeting new people and finding that special person, who will help her realize her dreams. However, Rebecca's first online experience turns into a very upsetting and frustrating event in her life. Rebecca has a very bad experience with one person that she meets on the website. His name is Jeff, he is 26 years old, and he is from Brooklyn, New York (NY).

Jeff worked in a car dealership. He worked as a mechanic, and he liked fixing cars. Jeff wanted to become a mechanical engineer; he studied mechanical engineering in college. Jeff also enjoyed driving sports cars. Jeff's passion was fast driving and cars. His favorite car was Lexus Sedan and SUV. He thought that Lexus cars had the highest quality. In addition, Jeff liked street racing, but he had been in a car accident twice. Rebecca told Jeff that street racing was too dangerous, and he should not risk his life. Jeff promised to be careful. He told Rebecca so many interesting stories about cars and driving. Jeff could talk about different cars for hours. He also liked to talk about the different customers that would come to the car dealership where he worked. Jeff always told Rebecca funny stories about his customers. He knew how to make her laugh.

Like Rebecca, Jeff was looking for a special person in his life. Jeff told Rebecca that he wanted to marry a good girl and have children. He said that he would love and respect his wife very much because he believed that a woman deserves a lot of respect and special treatment. He told Rebecca that when he was in a bus or in a train or subway, he would always stand up in order to provide a seat to a woman. Jeff said that he did not understand those men who would not give up their seat for a standing woman. Rebecca really liked Jeff's life principles.

Jeff seemed to be a very nice person. Once he told Rebecca that his best friend died in a motorcycle accident. When that happened, Jeff was very upset. He helped a lot the family of his best friend. He provided moral support and monetary support to that family. When the parents of that boy decided to sell their son's car, Jeff bought his best friend's car. He wanted to keep that car in memory of his best friend. Rebecca really liked what he did. Jeff said that he would never ride a motorcycle because it was too dangerous, and he advised Rebecca not to ride a motorcycle as well.

Jeff told Rebecca that she was very smart, and in a couple of years, she would definitely become a professor. As an inspirational story, Jeff told her that one of his good friends, whose name is Greg, became the vice president of a big company. However, when he started working in that company, he was a regular employee. Because of his determination and hard work, Greg was promoted to a very high position in the company. Jeff would always tell Rebecca that she could achieve everything she wanted given enough determination and hard work.

Rebecca and Jeff talked to each other on the phone for two weeks, and they decided to meet in real life. Rebecca liked Jeff because he seemed to be a very interesting, intelligent, nice, and well-mannered person. She was looking forward to their meeting in real life. Rebecca was sure that there was nothing bad to expect from Jeff given his life principles that he talked about.

At first, Jeff was very nice on the phone. He wanted to come to Boston one of the weekends and meet Rebecca in real life. However, two weeks later, Jeff disappointed her. Rebecca wanted to meet Jeff in the daytime on Saturday or Sunday. A couple of days before the weekend they were supposed to meet, he called her at 7:00 PM. Rebecca could feel that Jeff was a little drunk. Jeff said that he was going to come to Boston and see her. Rebecca responded that it would be too late for them to meet, and she would not want to go out and meet a total stranger at night.

Jeff became very upset and rude. He insulted Rebecca and accused her of being dishonest. Jeff said that she did not want to meet him because she was dishonest about everything, and that she did not even live in Boston. Then Rebecca told him that it was too dangerous to drive drunk, especially at night from NY to Boston. However, Jeff did not want to listen to her; he made a lot of deeply offensive and accusing statements about Rebecca and hung up on her.

To prove her honesty, Rebecca called him back and agreed to meet with Jeff. She said that she would come out for a few minutes if he wanted to meet her so badly that night. Rebecca did not want Jeff to think that she was not real or dishonest about something. When Jeff came to Boston, it was about 11:30 PM. He called Rebecca, and she came down. When Jeff and Rebecca talked on the phone, he assured her that there was nothing to be afraid of, and that he only wanted to say "hello" to her and see her in real life to make sure that she did not lie to him. Jeff said that he just wanted to make sure that Rebecca was who she was saying she was. Rebecca believed him.

Rebecca and Jeff met in her back yard; the condominium where she lived had a beautiful back yard. When they sat down on a bench to talk, all of a sudden, Jeff said that he wanted to kiss Rebecca. She was very surprised at that outrageous statement. Rebecca said that he could not do that because they did not know each other, and to kiss a stranger on the first date was absolutely against her life principles. Rebecca said that she was a decent girl, and she would never kiss a stranger.

However, Jeff became very upset, and he lost control over himself. In seconds, he became a completely different person. He started yelling at her and insulting her. Then he took out a knife from under his coat and ripped off Rebecca's clothes. Jeff tried to rape her. Rebecca screamed in pain. Some of the neighbors heard her and ran out to their bench. When Jeff saw two men approaching them, he disappeared. Rebecca never saw or talked to Jeff again.

This was the worst and the scariest experience of Rebecca's entire life. This was the most terrible experience she has ever had. She could never imagine that such a "nice" person Jeff would want to rape her. He promised that he would only look at her, talk to her for ten minutes to prove her honesty and leave. He said that he just wanted to make sure that Rebecca was honest with him. How could someone say that women deserve respect and special treatment and then try to rape an innocent girl? Rebecca could not find an answer to that question.

That incident left an indelible mark in Rebecca's heart, a mark that she thought nobody would be able to erase. Rebecca was very upset because of that incident, but she did not lose hope to find the person of her dreams, someone who would help her forget that terrible experience with Jeff. Rebecca still hoped to find the person who would help her live the life she had imagined. She did find the person who made her forget what happened. Several weeks later, Rebecca met her ideal person on the same dating website, the person who helped her forget Jeff and his immoral behavior.

CHAPTER 3

IT IS A MIRACLE

November 12, 2008: Lynn, Massachusetts (MA) – Rebecca's Apartment

It is 4:20 PM. Rebecca is in her apartment. She is sitting in a comfortable black leather armchair with her laptop, and she is surfing the dating website. She has recently registered on this website.

Elizabeth is watching a TV program. Suddenly, Rebecca sees a very interesting profile that she has never seen before. It is a man whose last name is Thoreau. His first name is abbreviated – "A." That famous last name captures Rebecca's attention.

Rebecca is very surprised.

BECKY
Mom, this is unbelievable!
I found a very interesting person on this website!
This person's last name is Thoreau.
It is a miracle!

Rebecca smiles.

BECKY (CONT'D)
He must be related to Henry David Thoreau,
my favorite philosopher.
H. D. Thoreau is an amazing author,
Transcendentalist, and naturalist.
I really like H. D. Thoreau.

ELIZABETH
That is very interesting, Becky.
I know that Thoreau is your favorite philosopher.

BECKY
I wonder if this is his real last name.
Maybe Henry David Thoreau is indeed his relative.

ELIZABETH
What is his first name?

BECKY
I do not know his first name.
It is an abbreviated "A."
I wonder what his full first name is...

Elizabeth gets up from the sofa and comes closer to the computer.

ELIZABETH
Becky, look at the picture that is attached to his profile.
It does not show his full face; it only shows his eyes.
This is probably not his real photo.
It looks like some actor's picture.

BECKY
Mom, I know…
His eyes are so beautiful and so mysterious.
I have never seen such a beautiful and
interesting picture; it only shows half of his face.

ELIZABETH
How old is he? Where does he live?

BECKY
He is 35 years old, and he lives in Riverside,
New Hampshire (NH).
I have never heard about Riverside in New Hampshire (NH).

BECKY (CONT'D)
I want to write him "Hello" and see where it goes.
I am interested in talking to this person.

ELIZABETH
Well, you can send him a message.
Go ahead, say "Hi" to him if you want.

Rebecca sends her first message to A. Thoreau.

BECKY
Hi.

A. THOREAU
Hello. How are you?

Rebecca smiles.

BECKY
Oh my God, mom! He responded to me!

Rebecca replies to A. Thoreau.

BECKY (CONT'D)
I am good. How are you?

A. THOREAU
Everything is good too.
Are you in Boston?

Rebecca's profile says that she lives in Boston, but she actually lives
in Lynn. Lynn is about 30 minutes away from Boston.

BECKY
I live 30 minutes away from Boston.
I live in a city called Lynn.

BECKY (CONT'D)
What about you?

A. THOREAU
You live very close to me.

Rebecca smiles again.

BECKY
Wow, mom!
He said that we live very close to each other.

BECKY (CONT'D)
I would like to know more about you.

A. THOREAU
Why are you so interested in me?
What did catch your attention?

BECKY
You have a very famous last name.
I think that you may be an interesting person.
I would like to talk to you.

A. THOREAU
Are you not afraid to fall in love with me?

Rebecca laughs, thinking that it was a joke.

BECKY
Oh my God, mom!
He is asking if I am afraid to fall in love with him.
I will tell him that, of course, I am not afraid.
I liked very few people in my life, but
I do not think that I ever loved anybody.
The person that I thought I could have a relationship with…

Rebecca stops talking for a moment and becomes very sad.

BECKY (CONT'D)
I do not even want to remember what happened to me.

ELIZABETH
We talked about this many times.
Becky, my dear, please try to forget Jeff.
You are so young and so smart, and
you will definitely find your happiness.

BECKY
Mom, it is very hard to forget about Jeff.
However, I still believe that I will find my true love,
and I will be happy.
I will not stop searching for that special person,
who will help me forget what happened.

Rebecca replies to A. Thoreau.

BECKY (CONT'D)
Oh no, I do not fall in love so easily.
I do not really like anybody, especially
on these dating websites.

BECKY (CONT'D)
So where do you live?

A. THOREAU
I live in Nashua, New Hampshire.
I live 35 miles away from downtown Boston.

BECKY
How long have you lived in NH?
Are you originally from NH?
What do you do there?

A. THOREAU
I have lived in the United States of America for 20 years.
Before I moved here, I lived in Europe.
I lived in NY for 18 years, and the last two years,
I have been living here, in Nashua, NH.
I have my own trucking company in Nashua.
It is a small company now, but I am planning to grow.
Currently, I only have two big trucks.
I also work with my friend in NY,
and we ship and sell luxury cars in Europe.
We are partners in this car business.

BECKY
That is very interesting…

A. THOREAU
How long have you lived in Boston?

BECKY
I have lived in Boston all my life.
I was born here.
I went to school here, and then
I decided to go to college.
I went to Northeastern University
to get my education.

BECKY (CONT'D)
I graduated from Northeastern University
with the highest honor;
I was a straight A student for six years.
I studied Philosophy and Criminal Justice in my
undergraduate school.
Then I went to a graduate school to study Philosophy.
Now I work as a research assistant at my University.
I help one of my former professors with research.
However, I plan to apply to a PhD program in Philosophy.
It is my work related dream to become a University professor

and educate students in the subject of Philosophy.

A. THOREAU
That is very impressive! You are very smart.
I like intelligent people.
You will definitely become a professor.
You are very young; you have all your life...
I am sure you have a very bright future.
I think that you will have the brightest future,
and you will achieve all your goals.

A. THOREAU (CONT'D)
Hard work, determination, and motivation
will help you achieve all your goals.
Please remember, "Success usually comes to those
who are too busy to be looking for it."
I am sure you know who made that famous statement.

Rebecca smiles.

BECKY
Thank you very much!
I appreciate your wonderful words.
Of course, I know who said that.
You just mentioned one of my favorite quotes
by Henry David Thoreau.

Rebecca responds to A. Thoreau.

BECKY (COTN'D)
Please remember, "There is no value in life except
what you choose to place upon it and no happiness
except what you bring to it yourself."
I am sure you know who said that.

A. Thoreau smiles too.

A. THOREAU
Of course, I know...
By the way, you write very well.
I do not meet people who write so well very often.
I can tell that you know English grammar very well.

Rebecca smiles again.

BECKY
Thank you very much again!
I really like writing and reading books.
When I was a student, my professors
used my college papers as an example for
other students.
Students always asked me to proofread their papers,
and I was always happy to help them.
In addition to working as a research assistant, I also
volunteer in the center for immigrant services;
I teach English as a second language.

A. THOREAU
Becky, that is very impressive.
What you do is very important; you help many people.
I also like helping people.

BECKY
What do you like to do
in your free time?

A. THOREAU
I know how to fly an airplane.
I like to fly airplanes.
My father used to teach me how to fly
when I was younger. It was a long time ago.
My father is a pilot; he knows how to fly
military and civil airplanes.

A. THOREAU (CONT'D)
I was supposed to become a pilot too.
Unfortunately, not everything that we want comes true.
Not everything happens the way you want it to happen.
I have a flight instructor here, and I like to fly with him
when I have free time.
To fly is my weakness; I really like to fly.
This is how I spend a lot of my free time.

Rebecca smiles.

BECKY
Wow! You know how to fly airplanes.
I think it is amazing that you can fly.

A. THOREAU
If you motivate yourself, you can do everything you want.

BECKY
This is actually funny…
When I was a child, I wanted to become a pilot too.
I still admire pilots a lot; they are very smart people.
Can I please be your passenger some day?

A. THOREAU
Well, everything is possible in this life…

A. THOREAU (CONT'D)
How do you spend your free time?

BECKY
I usually read books. I like reading a lot, especially
philosophy books.
There are other things that I like to do, but
I do not like to go to night clubs and bars.
I never went to those places.
I do not drink at all, and I do not smoke.

I know that the majority of young people
like to drink, and they prefer to spend their
time at clubs and bars, and they like to get drunk.
I am not like them; I am different.

A. THOREAU
That is very good!
It is wonderful that you like reading books.
As the great philosopher Henry David Thoreau says,
"Books are the treasured wealth of the world and
the fit inheritance of generations and nations."
I like reading philosophy books too.
You are not like the majority of young people.
I do not drink or smoke too.
I do not drink at all, and I never liked
bars and night clubs.
Trust me, I do not spend my free time at bars and clubs.

Rebecca smiles.

BECKY
Well, then you are not like the majority
of people too.
It is very rare these days to meet a man who
does not drink alcohol at all.
It is also great that you like philosophy.
I have not met anyone, except for my philosophy
professors, who likes philosophy.
We already have a lot in common.

A. Thoreau smiles.

A. THOREAU
That is true.

BECKY
Are you related to H. D. Thoreau?

A. THOREAU
Yes, H. D. Thoreau is my relative.
I will tell you this story when I know you better.
I need to know you better first, then
I will tell you everything.

Rebecca is surprised.

BECKY
Oh my God! Wow!
H. D. Thoreau is my favorite philosopher.
I enjoy reading his books very much!
I did not know that H. D. Thoreau has relatives in Europe.

A. THOREAU
Did you know that there are some streets in Europe,
which are named after H. D. Thoreau?

BECKY
Wow! I did not know that.

Aaron continues to talk about H. D. Thoreau.

A. THOREAU
H. D. Thoreau says, "I have learned that if one
advances confidently in the direction of his dreams and
endeavors to live the life he has imagined, he will meet
with a success unexpected in common hours."
I live according to his greatest quote,
"Go confidently in the direction of your dreams.
Live the life you have imagined. Live the life you have dreamed."

BECKY
This is my favorite quote too!
I try to live according to that quote as well.
I cannot believe I met a relative of this
great man on a dating website.

I could not even dream about meeting Thoreau's relative.

Rebecca tells Elizabeth that A. Thoreau is real.

BECKY (CONT'D)
Mom, he says he is a relative of H.D. Thoreau.
Can you believe this? This is incredible!

Elizabeth laughs ironically.

ELIZABETH
Congratulations to you!
You finally met a famous person!

BECKY
I know, mom, it is very difficult to
believe that this is the truth, that
someone like that would be on a dating website.

Rebecca continues her online conversation with A. Thoreau.

BECKY (CONT'D)
I cannot believe that H. D. Thoreau
is your relative.
You are so lucky! He was a great man!

A. THOREAU
Thank you, Becky!
H. D. Thoreau was indeed a very intelligent person.
I like his life principles a lot.

A. THOREAU (CONT'D)
What do you like to do on the weekends?

BECKY
I like to listen to music, watch interesting movies,
walk on the beach when the weather is nice,

go to movie theaters, theaters, museums,
restaurants with live music, and different concerts.
As you already know, I also like reading books,
especially philosophy books.
I have read so many philosophy books.
I especially enjoy reading books
by Henry David Thoreau and Ralph Waldo Emerson.
I enjoy reading about American Transcendentalism.
I really like the concept of metaphysical reality -
the idea of going above and beyond the immediate physical reality,
the idea that one should transcend, rise above
and go beyond what is physical;
one should try to be above and beyond the universe and time.

BECKY (CONT'D)
As I mentioned before, I do not go to night clubs and bars
because I do not drink at all, and I do not smoke.
To be honest, I do not like when drunk people
are around me, or when people smoke near me.
Unfortunately, nobody understands me...

A. THOREAU
I understand you.
Please remember, "To be great is to be
misunderstood." These are not my words.
A great American Transcendentalist and H. D.
Thoreau's friend R. W. Emerson said that.
Maybe it is not a bad thing when people do not
understand you or misunderstand you.
By the way, I like reading about American Transcendentalism too.
I enjoy reading books written by Transcendentalist writers.
I think there is an ideal spiritual state that
transcends the physical reality,
and that can be realized only through the individual's intuition.

A. THOREAU (CONT'D)
I believe there is a higher meaning and purpose
to our existence than the physical world.
The spiritual things should always be above the empirical things.
I think the spiritual world is much bigger
and richer than the physical world.
Please remember, our life consists of physical
reality and metaphysical reality.
Our life consists of two realities, which make up one whole.

BECKY
I absolutely agree with you.
I know that there are two realities in our life – one
is physical and the other is metaphysical.

A. THOREAU
You know, I do not go to bars and night clubs too.
I do not drink at all, and I do not smoke.
Even some of my friends do not understand me
because of that.
That is the reason why I sometimes refuse to be in
their company.
Some people think that something is wrong with me
because I do not drink alcohol.

BECKY
I think it is wonderful that you do not drink alcohol!
Do you like to eat sweets?

A. THOREAU
Yes, I do. I like sweets a lot.
What about you?

BECKY
Not really...
I used to like sweets when I was a little child.
I really liked chocolate, but I do not like it anymore.

BECKY (CONT'D)
What else do you like besides eating sweets?

A. Thoreau smiles.

A. THOREAU
Do you want to know all my weaknesses?
I need to know you well in order to tell you
about all the weaknesses that I have.
I need to know you well before I can talk to you
about all the weaknesses of life.

BECKY
Okay, I will be happy to get to know you better.
However, I already know one of your weaknesses –
you like to eat sweets.

A. Thoreau smiles again.

A. THOREAU
This is not a terrible weakness.

A. THOREAU (CONT'D)
If you are not afraid, I would like to invite you to a
beautiful place. You are a very smart girl, and
I like intelligent people.

Rebecca laughs.

BECKY
Oh my God, mom! The mysterious A. Thoreau
wants to invite me to a beautiful place.
He thinks that I am very smart.

Elizabeth gets angry.

ELIZABETH
Where is that "beautiful place" located?
Where does he want to invite you?
Is this a joke? You do not know each other.
You do not even know his real name and
how he looks in real life.
Please do not make the same mistake as with Jeff.
I told you not to meet him at night...

BECKY
Mom, please let us not talk about this again.
I realized my mistake, and I am much smarter now.
We all make mistakes, and we learn from our mistakes.
I will never make the same mistake again.
I am much more careful now, especially
with people on dating websites.

ELIZABETH
Tell your new friend from NH that you do not
go out with total strangers.

Rebecca responds to A. Thoreau.

BECKY
Thank you very much for inviting me!
I am sorry, but I do not know you.
I cannot go out with you until I know you better.
Please do not take it personally, and
please do not be mad at me.

A. THOREAU
Why should I be mad at you? I understand...
You are a decent girl, and I like decent girls.
If you are interested in getting to know me better,
please let me know.

BECKY

Yes, I would like to know you better before we meet.
In addition, I would like to let you know that
I am interested only in a serious relationship.
You know how most people these days do not
want anything serious.
Some people are happy to have a new boyfriend
or a new girlfriend every week.
I do not understand that!
I am not like them, and I will never be like them.
I believe in finding true love, and spending the rest
of your life with that person.

A. THOREAU

I understand that you are a very intelligent and
decent girl.
I do not understand people like that too.
I also believe in finding one true love and
being with that person all your life.
You are definitely different.
I like how you think about life.

A. THOREAU (CONT'D)

If you need anything, please let me know.
Please do not be shy.
I will always be happy to help you.

BECKY

Thank you very much!

A. THOREAU

Please do not thank me. I have not done anything yet.
I will be very happy if I can help you with anything.
Of course, I hope that everything will be
wonderful with you,
and that you will never need my help.
However, anything can happen in this life.

Our life is the most unidentified science in the world.

BECKY
Yes, I absolutely agree with you.
Our life is full of uncertainty and mystery.
You never know what will happen to you tomorrow.
Our life is not only full of uncertainty and mystery,
it is also full of evil and injustice.
Unfortunately, there are a lot of bad people in this world,
who enjoy hurting good people.

BECKY (CONT'D)
I am very happy that there are people like you in this world.
I am very happy that there are still people who offer to help, and
and who do not ask for anything in return.
I am so happy that there are still good people out there
who like to help others.

A. THOREAU
It is good that you understand this.
I find the meaning of my life in helping people.
Everything else that you said is a different story...
Unfortunately, there is a lot of evil and injustice in this world.
It is a pleasure to talk to such a young and smart girl.
You are a very mature and intelligent person.
You differ a lot from the majority of young people today.

A. THOREAU (CONT'D)
If you want, I will give you my phone number.
You can call me when you have a problem.
Please do not be shy. You can call me any time.
I will always be happy to help you.
I will always be happy to do something good for you.

BECKY
Thank you very much!
I really appreciate your willingness to help.

I have never met anybody like you.
You are a very nice and intelligent person.
You are very different too.

BECKY (CONT'D)
There were people in my life who disappointed me, and
it is very hard for me to trust somebody again.
However, I think you are not like them.
I feel that you are different.
I think you will not disappoint me.

A. THOREAU
Thank you very much for your understanding!
You will never be disappointed in what you just said.
Please remember, if anything happens,
I will always be there for you.
All you need to do is just call me, and I will come to help you.

A. THOREAU (CONT'D)
Also, please remember one important thing.
I never say anything just for the sake of saying it.
If I say something, I mean it.
If I promise something, I do it.
As H. D. Thoreau says, "Be true to your word, be
true to your friend, and be true to your work." I
absolutely agree with this wonderful statement.
I believe if a person says something, he or she must be true to that.
Trust me, I will never hurt you. I will never disappoint you.
I will always be honest with you.

BECKY
I hope so...

A. THOREAU
I will always help you. You can always count on me.
I will never leave you alone in a difficult situation.
I feel you are a very honest and decent person.

Please trust me, I will never hurt you or
disappoint you in any other way.
I will be your friend forever.

BECKY
Okay, we will see…
I am just still afraid to trust someone.

BECKY (CONT'D)
I have always been honest; I just never lie.
I do not even know how to lie.
I do not understand the point in lying. The truth will come
out sooner or later; the truth will be revealed eventually.
Friedrich Nietzsche, one of my favorite philosophers says, "On
the mountains of truth you can never climb in vain: either you
will reach a point higher up today, or you will be training your
powers so that you will be able to climb higher tomorrow."
I believe one should always pursue the truth,
and one should always tell the truth.

A. THOREAU
Becky, I absolutely agree with you.
A morally good person always tells the
truth and nothing but the truth.
All human beings should strive for something higher, for
something that is called truthfulness – always telling the truth.

Next Day

Rebecca and Elizabeth are discussing A. Thoreau.

ELIZABETH
So, how did your conversation end
with the mysterious A. Thoreau yesterday?
Is he a very interesting man?
What do you think about him?

BECKY
Mom, it is impossible to describe in words
how happy I am that I met this person.
He is a very nice, polite, intelligent, caring,
understanding, compassionate, and mature person.
He is unlike anybody else that I have
ever talked to before.
I think he is very kind-hearted. He offered to help me, and
I did not ask for any help.
He is a very interesting person; he knows how to fly airplanes.
He does not drink at all, he does not smoke, and
he is interested in a serious relationship too.
I think he has a lot of life experience, and there are
definitely a lot of things that he can teach me.
It is very interesting to talk to him, and we have a lot in common.
He offered his help several times without
asking anything in return.
He will give me his phone number so that I can call him
in case I need help.
He told me that he would always be there for me.

BECKY (CONT'D)
I could not even imagine that I would meet
someone like him online.
Thank you so much for helping me register
on that website!
I will never forget what you did for me!

ELIZABETH
What is his first name?
Why is it an abbreviated A?

BECKY
Oh my God, mom!
It was so interesting to talk to him that I did not even
have a chance to ask about his first name.

I will ask him today.
A. Thoreau seems to be such a wonderful person.

ELIZABETH
Becky, my dear, everything that he said
sounds very good. However, please be careful.
He may not be honest with you.
You know, there are a lot of dishonest
and evil people on these dating websites.
You already had a very bad experience
with one of them.
First, your mysterious friend from New Hampshire
will have to pass the test of time,
and then we will see if he is indeed
a virtuous and trustworthy person
that he seems to be.
The first thing that you have to do is request his real pictures.
I told you, it is not him on that profile picture...

Rebecca happily enters the living room and turns on her laptop. A.
Thoreau is online.

A. THOREAU
Hello. How are you doing today?

BECKY
Hi. I am doing well, thanks.
What about you?

A. THOREAU
I am doing well too.
I just finished some of
my work related matters.

Aaron sees Rebecca's new picture.

A. THOREAU (CONT'D)
Your dog is wonderful!

BECKY
Unfortunately, the lab that you see in
my picture is not my dog.
I really like dogs, especially labs,
and when I was walking on the beach,
I just asked a woman if I could take a picture
with her dog, and she allowed.
I love dogs; I think dogs are people's best friends.
Unfortunately, I cannot have dogs because
there is no one who can take care of that dog.
I am at work almost all day.

A. THOREAU
I understand... This is my favorite breed too,
and I cannot have this dog for the same
reasons as you have.
As one great man Sergey Mavrodi said, "I used to have
two cats, but I do not have any pets now. You should
take care of any pet. A pet requires time and attention. I
never have enough time, and I need to do so much. Time
is the most precious thing in life." Mavrodi is a man of
extraordinary intellectual abilities and artistic talents.
As he says about himself, "I am not a Genius, I am the only one."

BECKY
Who is Sergey Mavrodi?

A. THOREAU
I will tell you about Mavrodi later...
He is one of the very few people that I admire a lot.

A. THOREAU (CONT'D)
By the way, you have very long and
beautiful hair.

BECKY
Thank you, Aaron!
Do you like girls/women with long hair?

A. THOREAU
Yes, of course.

Rebecca smiles.

BECKY
Almost all guys like when girls
have long hair.
I like my long hair too.

A. THOREAU
I really like when a woman has long hair.
I think it is very beautiful.

A. THOREAU (CONT'D)
You are a very beautiful girl.
A lot of guys probably write you.
You must receive many messages from them
every day.

Rebecca smiles.

BECKY
Yes, a lot of people write me.
However, I do not talk to all of them.
I do not even have time to respond to all their messages.

A. THOREAU
Do you live with your parents?

BECKY
Yes, I do. What about you?

A. THOREAU
I live with my mom in Nashua.
My mother is a wonderful woman.
She is very kind-hearted and very smart.
She is a history teacher.
She worked as a history teacher all her life.
She used to teach in a school. She is 73 years old now.

A. THOREAU (CONT'D)
Unfortunately, my mom is sick; she has cancer.
I do everything in my power to fight this disease.
I love my mom so much, and I cannot see her suffering.
It breaks my heart to see that my dear mom is in pain.

BECKY
I am so sorry to hear that.
Please do not worry.
The United States has the best
medical services in the world.
We have the best doctors and the best
hospitals in the world. The doctors
here will definitely help your mom.

A. THOREAU
I really hope so...
If something happens to my mom,
I do not know what I am going to do.
I cannot imagine my life without her.
I love her so much, and she loves me
very much too. She did so much for me.

A. THOREAU (CONT'D)
I just cannot understand the people who
do not take care of their old parents, and
who send their parents to live in nursing homes.
These people are inhumane; they have no hearts.
I would never be able to do anything like that to my dear mom.

BECKY
I absolutely agree with you.

Rebecca decides to change the subject of their conversation.

BECKY (CONT'D)
By the way, what is your name?
I forgot to ask your name the first day we met online.

A. THOREAU
My name is Aaron.

BECKY
That is a very beautiful name.
I really like it.

A. THOREAU
Thank you, Becky.
I do not understand much in the beauty of names.

A. THOREAU (CONT'D)
My name has a very special meaning for me.
When I know you better, I will tell you the meaning
of my name.

BECKY
What is your most favorite female name?

A. THOREAU
I have never thought about this question…

BECKY
Aaron is one of my favorite male names.
I really like your name.

Aaron jokes.

A. THOREAU
What else do you like except for the name Aaron?

Rebecca smiles.

BECKY
I like your last name, and I like your profile picture.

BECKY (CONT'D)
By the way, where is your real picture?

A. THOREAU
My picture is the one that you see - half of the face.
I do not talk to everybody on this website,
although a lot of people write me.
If someone has a pure soul, and if she wants to
talk to me, then I do not mind.
I like people who have a soul. Even R. W. Emerson says,
"The one thing in the world, of value, is the active soul."
I think it is very important to have a pure soul.
A famous American Congregationalist Charles Finney
once said, "If we attend to the soul, eternity is secure; if
we neglect the soul, eternity is lost. Eternity is longer than
time, in just so much is the soul more valuable than all."

BECKY
I also like people who have a pure soul.

A. THOREAU
Given your beauty and intelligence,
you probably get a lot of messages from men
on a daily basis.

BECKY
Yes, a lot of people write me every day, but
I do not really like talking to them.
I need to be interested in a person in order

to talk to him.
Unfortunately, most people on these dating websites
are either dishonest or very limited in their knowledge.
I am not interested in people like that.

BECKY (CON'D)
Do you like Boston?

A. THOREAU
I do not know Boston well.
However, what I saw in Boston,
I liked very much.
Boston is similar to Europe.

A. THOREAU (CONT'D)
If you have time, could you please show me Boston?
I will be very grateful to you.
I just do not want to ask anybody else for this favor.

BECKY
Of course, Aaron!
I will be happy to show you Boston,
when I have time, and when we know
each other better.

A. THOREAU
Well, thank you very much in advance!
I would really appreciate that.
For the past two years that I live here,
I always go to NY and visit my friends.
By the way, if you need anything from NY,
please feel free to ask me whatever you want.

BECKY
Okay, thank you very much!
What do you like to do in your free time
except for flying airplanes with your flight instructor?

A. THOREAU
I like to do whatever my spirit tells me to do.
I can do anything I want.

Fascinated by Aaron's answer, Rebecca continues to ask more questions.

BECKY
Why did you come to the United States?

A. THOREAU
Can I please answer this question when we meet?
It happened this way. I never thought about that.

BECKY
Are you a citizen of the United States?

A. THOREAU
Yes, is this a bad thing that I am a US citizen?

BECKY
Oh no, I asked because I was curious.
How long have you been a US citizen?

A. THOREAU
A long time...

BECKY
Have you been in Europe during the past 20 years?

A. THOREAU
You know, it happened so that I have not.
I wanted to visit Europe, but I did not...

BECKY
Do you have many relatives in the United States?

A. THOREAU
No, I only have my mom here.

BECKY
Do you have brothers or sisters?

A. THOREAU
No, I do not have any brothers or sisters.
What about you?
Do you have any brothers or sisters?

BECKY
I do not have any brothers or sisters too.
I live with my parents.

A. THOREAU
We can talk on the phone if you want.

BECKY
Thank you! It is a little late right now,
and I am going to sleep. We can definitely talk
on the phone some other day.

BECKY (CONT'D)
Have a good night!

A. THOREAU
Have a good night as well and sweet dreams!
Have a wonderful day tomorrow!

BECKY
Thank you, you too!

For the next two weeks, Rebecca and Aaron talk online. They have almost daily conversations.

November 26, 2008: The Day before Thanksgiving Day

Rebecca comes back from work and checks the dating website. Aaron is online.

BECKY
Happy Thanksgiving to you!

A. THOREAU
The same to you! Where did you disappear?

BECKY
I was very busy at work for the last two days,
and when I came home, I was very tired,
and I went to sleep very early.

A. THOREAU
I understand... I have a lot of work too.

BECKY
Did anybody invite you to come and celebrate the
Thanksgiving Day?

A. THOREAU
Yes, several people invited me.
What about you?

BECKY
Yes, my grandmother invited everyone.
We may go to my grandma's place...

A. THOREAU
We should meet some day if you do not mind.

BECKY
I am sorry, but I need some time before I can meet you.
I was very disappointed not long ago.

I just need to overcome the fear of being disappointed again.
Please do not take it personally.

A. THOREAU
Becky, no problem.
Please take your time.

Rebecca changes the subject of their conversation.

BECKY
Aaron, I am sorry for asking,
but could you please send me your real pictures?
I think that your profile picture is not your real picture.

A. THOREAU
Okay, I will send you my pictures.
Please write your email address.

Rebecca writes her email address, and Aaron sends his
real pictures. Rebecca looks at Aaron's pictures.

BECKY
Thank you, Aaron.
Your pictures are very beautiful.
I really like the picture where you stand next to
the mountains.

A. THOREAU
Thank you, Becky.
I like that picture too.

BECKY
By the way, you are a very handsome guy.

A. THOREAU
Thank you, my mom is a very beautiful woman.
Everyone says that I look like her.

However, please remember that in real life, a person is
usually a little different than in pictures.

BECKY
You have a very beautiful hair color.
It is golden brown, and your hair is straight.

A. THOREAU
Thank you. When I was a little boy,
I used to have golden blond hair.

BECKY
Why don't you post these pictures on the website?

A. THOREAU
I will tell you some day...
I just need to know you better.

Rebecca changes the subject of their conversation.

BECKY
Have you ever had a bad experience in real life
or online?

A. THOREAU
Yes, of course. Did you have a bad experience?

BECKY
Yes, I did have a very bad experience with one person.
I met him online; he lived in NY. I liked that guy, and
we were going to meet one of the weekends.
However, one day, he got drunk and decided to come
to Boston at night.
When I asked him not to do that, he insulted me and
blamed me for being dishonest.
However, I was always honest with him.
I would never lie to him or to anybody else.

I would never hurt anyone.
That guy made me very upset.
He refused to understand that I am a decent girl,
and I cannot go out with strangers at night.
I just wanted to meet him in the daytime on
Saturday or Sunday, and we agreed to do that, but...

BECKY (CONT'D)
I believed that he wanted to see me
in real life and nothing else.
In order to prove my honesty,
I agreed to come out at night for ten minutes.
That guy disappointed me so badly...
He mistreated me in the worst possible way.
I could not even work for several days because of him.
I could never think that he would mistreat me that way.
Now I am very afraid to trust somebody again.
I cannot even say what he tried to do to me that night...

A. THOREAU
Rebecca, you do not have to tell me what happened.
I can only say that I will never do anything like that.
I am a man of honor, and my words
have more value for me than my life.
I will never lie to you.
I will always tell you the truth. I will always
be honest about everything.
As H. D. Thoreau says, "Rather than love, than
money, than fame, give me truth."
Truth is the most important thing for me too.
I will never hurt you or mistreat you.
There is nothing else to be said further.

A. THOREAU (CONT'D)
I will never hurt you because I know very well
what it feels when somebody hurts you.

I know how unbearable emotional pain can be,
and I know that emotional pain is much worse
than physical pain.
Emotional pain is the most painful.
Emotional pain is the most terrible.
Emotional pain can even kill.

BECKY
I am very afraid to be disappointed again.
Aaron, are you not afraid of anything?

A. THOREAU
Becky, you should try to overcome your fear.
You must not be afraid of anything and anyone.
As Mavrodi says, "You must never be afraid of anything,
not in this life and not in the next life. Fear humiliates you."

A. THOREAU (CONT'D)
I would never hurt anybody without a reason.
I do not understand how some people hurt others
and then continue to live their lives.
If I hurt a good person, I would never be able to continue my life.
I have nothing else to add.
Time will show what kind of a person I am, and God is my Judge.
You are smart, and you will understand everything yourself.

BECKY
Thank you very much for all the wonderful words,
and thank you for being so supportive and understanding!
There were many people in my life who hurt me before we met,
and it is very difficult for me to trust someone again.
I still cannot believe that I met someone like you online.
I have never talked to anybody like you.

A. THOREAU
Well, regarding the people who hurt you,
let us do the following...

I will hurt them even more if you want.
They will definitely not forget it in this life and
in the next life too.
After that, we will be learning how to trust
each other.
There were a lot of people who tried to hurt and
deceive me too.
Unfortunately, our world is like this.
I do not trust people anymore… As Mavrodi says, "You
must rely only on yourself and nobody else. It is important
to remember this rule." Unfortunately, our life is like this.
However, if your inner world and soul is like mine,
we should definitely keep together.

A. THOREAU (CONT'D)
People like us should be together. Only this way,
we will be able to fight against all the evil and
injustice in this world.

BECKY
Aaron, thank you very much for everything!
I really appreciate all your help!

A. THOREAU
Please, do not thank me yet.
I have not done anything for you yet.
In this world, honest and decent people
should keep together.
I have not lived in Nashua for a long time, and
I need a decent person that I can trust.
I think you need such a person too.
We can definitely help each other.

A. THOREAU (CONT'D)
We will be punishing bad people together.
You are smart, and this is the most important thing.

BECKY

Thank you, Aaron.
Sometimes I feel that I will never be able to trust
someone again given what happened to me.
Sometimes I feel that I will always be sad and
empty inside.

A. THOREAU

It is okay, Becky. You will definitely learn to
trust again. I will teach you…
I think it is possible to ignite the fire inside you.
As H. D. Thoreau once said, "The fire inside
burns hotter than the fire outside."
You just need to trust someone, and you need to love someone.
Please do not be afraid to fall in love; love can be wonderful.
Love can be the best feeling in the world.

BECKY

I know love can be wonderful, but love can hurt too.
As H. D. Thoreau also says, "Love must be
as much a light as it is a flame."
I am sorry; I cannot trust anyone at this time.
I am just afraid to fall in love and then be disappointed.
I am afraid to get attached to the wrong person.
I need some time in order to forget
everything that happened to me.

A. THOREAU

Becky, you can have as much time as you need.
Please take your time.

CHAPTER 4

THE TEST OF TIME

Two Days Later

Rebecca and Aaron meet online. Rebecca
continues to ask Aaron more questions.

BECKY
So you have lived in the United States for 20 years.

A. THOREAU
Yes, I have lived here for 20 years – 18 years in NY and
2 years in Nashua, NH.

BECKY
Do you like it here?

A. THOREAU
I am sorry, but I cannot answer this question now.
In order to answer this question, I need to know you well, and
you need to know me well too.
It will be a long conversation...
I am used to the life in the United States.

BECKY
What qualities do you appreciate in people?
What are the most important qualities for you?

A. THOREAU
Honesty and decency,
if they exist in the contemporary world.

A. THOREAU (CONT'D)
Becky, I would like to talk to you on the phone.
Please call me. We will talk on the phone.
Please do not be afraid. You can call me.

BECKY
Thank you, but I am very afraid to be disappointed again.
I had a very bad experience with a guy I met online,
and I do not want that to happen again.
I want to get to know you better.

A. THOREAU
What has happened, if it is not a secret?
What can happen if I give you my phone number?
You will be calling me,
and you will be getting to know me better.
We can talk on the phone about everything.
What can I do to you by talking to you on the phone?
Absolutely nothing!
Do not display your phone number when you call me.
If you want, you can block your telephone number from
appearing on my caller ID, and I will not see it.

BECKY
Okay, I will tell you what happened to me.
I will tell you what that guy from NY did.
When I came out to see Jeff that night, he tried to rape me.
Oh my God! It was so terrible and devastating!
I was so afraid; he had a knife. I thought he would kill me.
I trusted him, and he ruined my life.
Now I am very upset and depressed.
I have a feeling that something broke in my life, and
it will never be repaired.
I think I will never forget this terrible experience.
Because of Jeff, I cannot trust anybody again.
I am just very afraid to be hurt and disappointed again.

I do not know what I will do if someone disappoints me again.
I do not even want to think about it…

BECKY (CONT'D)
You know, all I wanted was to find a special person
in my life and be happy.
I was so tired of being alone, and I wanted to have a different life.
I was looking for love and happiness, but
I found misery and injustice.
It is so painful to even remember about what happened to me.
I feel so much pain in my heart. The pain is killing me.
I will never forget Jeff.

A. THOREAU
Well, this is like in a very sad movie.
It will not be easy to forget something like this.
I do not even know what to say…
We should revenge for what he did to you; that is all that I can say.
We must revenge against your enemy; then you will feel better.
As a wonderful German philosopher Friedrich Nietzsche says,
"The best weapon against an enemy is another enemy."

A. THOREAU (CONT'D)
I have all the necessary connections all over the world.
A lot of people come to me if they need help
in retaliating against someone.
If you want, we can definitely find your "friend" from NY,
and he will never forget us…
Please remember, I can be the best friend,
but I can also be the worst enemy.

A. THOREAU (CONT'D)
Becky, I promise that I will do my best, and
I will try to help you forget Jeff and what he did to you.
You should definitely forget him.
You must try to live your life as if nothing
happened, and there was no Jeff.

I am sure everything will be wonderful in your life.
I promise I will help you.
As Mavrodi once said, "Every end of something is
always the beginning of something new."

BECKY
Thank you very much!
I already feel better because I can talk to you,
and I shared this story with you.
I am so happy that I can talk to you.
It helps me a lot.

A. THOREAU
Becky, I am very happy that I can help.
You can talk to me about everything you want.
I will always try to help you.
You know, I really enjoy helping people.
If I can make someone feel better, I feel much better too.
As a great American author Mark Twain says,
"The best way to cheer yourself up
is to try to cheer somebody else up."
I absolutely agree with that statement.

BECKY
Thank you very much, Aaron!
I really appreciate everything you are doing for me.
By the way, that guy from NY is not the only person
who mistreated me.
Before I met him, there were others who
were dishonest with me, and
who probably had evil intentions.
Fortunately, I never met them in real life, but unfortunately,
I met Jeff in real life.

A. THOREAU
Well, I think you are not talking to the
right people online.

There are a lot of fake and dishonest
people on these dating websites, and they have evil intentions.
What can I tell you?
You should be very careful when you meet someone online.
You should be very careful in choosing your online friends.
Online dating can be very dangerous;
you must be extremely careful.
There are a lot of evil people on these sites.
When I know you better, we will find your "friend" in NY and...

BECKY

You know, I trusted Jeff, and I did not
think that he would betray me.
It is probably the worst feeling when
somebody you trust betrays you.
I am so upset and frustrated now.
How could I trust him? How could I
think that he is a good person?

A. THOREAU

Becky, I absolutely agree that it is terrible
when somebody betrays you.
It is very painful. Trust me, I know what it feels.
A lot of people betrayed me too. Such people
do not deserve our attention.
We should try to forget them. These
people do not deserve anything!
I really like what Sergey Mavrodi, a famous
Russian businessman and financier, says
about betrayal: "You can betray only that person who trusts
you." "The betrayer is a fallen person. Once he or she crosses
the line, there is no way back. Betrayal is the worst
sin. Those who betray others are not human beings.
They do not even deserve our hatred."

BECKY

I agree; betrayal is the worst thing in the world!
It is the most painful thing. Nothing is worse than betrayal.

A. THOREAU

Becky, unfortunately, betrayal is a part of our life.
Once Mavrodi said that "I was often betrayed. I was betrayed not
because people are evil but because people are human beings."
Please think about this statement.

BECKY

I think I know what this statement means…
It is a true statement.

BECKY (CONT'D)

Aaron, I wish I was more careful with Jeff.
I wish I did not trust him.
If I could only think that everything he
was telling me was not true,
that he probably had evil intentions from the very beginning.
Sometimes it is so hard to understand that
a person is not honest with you.

A. THOREAU

It can be very difficult to understand that a person is lying to you.
As Mavrodi once said, "Yes, there is truth in this world. However,
it is very hard to tell the difference between the truth and lies.
That is the problem. It is almost impossible to differentiate
the truth from the lies. Unfortunately, such is our world."

A. THOREAU (CONT'D)

Becky, it is not unusual for someone like you not to think about
somebody's evil intentions.
Good and kind-hearted people like you do
not think about evil intentions
when they meet someone who seems to be a good person.

People who have a pure soul and a kind
heart usually trust others, and
they do not think that someone may pretend to be a good person.
It is usually the evil people who are afraid of being deceived, and
they do not trust anybody.
As Mavrodi says, "Evil people are always very careful, and
they expect evil actions from others. Honest and decent people
are never ready for evil. Evil comes to them unexpectedly."

A. THOREAU (CONT'D)
Mavrodi also says, "Yes, people are evil, but you must be
kind" and "This world is bad. Well, make it better."
Becky, you are a wonderful person, and I admire people like you.
You have stayed an honest and kind-
hearted person despite everything.
Your existence in this world makes it a better place to live.

BECKY
Aaron, thank you very much for your support!
You have stayed an honest and kind-hearted
person too despite everything.
Your existence also makes this world a better place to live.

BECKY (CONT'D)
I know, I have made some mistakes...
I probably made the worst mistake in my life when
I trusted Jeff and agreed to meet him in the nighttime.
My mom told me not to do that, but I
wanted to prove my honesty.

A. THOREAU
Becky, please do not worry about your mistakes.
Every person makes mistakes. I made some mistakes too.
It is important to realize soon that
you made a mistake, and you need to correct it.
It is important that you learn from your own mistakes.

Our life is such that we all make mistakes, and we
learn from our or somebody else's mistakes.
Sometimes we become better and more
intelligent because of mistakes.
Mavrodi says the following about mistakes, "When they
arrested me without a reason in 1994, I did not fight back. I
could start a civil war in Russia. My investors supported me,
but I did not start a civil war. I stopped. Maybe that was a
mistake, but it is what it is now. It is all past now. Why should
I remember it now? We are living not in the past but in the
present. A person should learn from his/her mistakes. I never
regret anything, and I do not advise you to regret anything.
Regret is the worst thing." I definitely agree with that! Experience
is the best teacher, and we should not live in the past.

A. THOREAU (CONT'D)
Let us think about it. I will help you,
but I need to know you first.
Please be sure, you will never experience anything
like this with me.
I will never hurt you, and I will not disappoint you.
You can be sure 200% and more.
I guarantee that it will be so.

A. THOREAU (CONT'D)
I can prove every word I say with actions.
I have proof for everything I tell you.
There are certain family related matters,
which I will tell you when I know you better.
I just cannot tell you everything at this time.
However, I am being completely honest with you.
Trust me, I will never lie to you.
The one thing that you can be absolutely sure about and
have no doubt is that I will never hurt you.
You will forget about emotional pain forever.
I will not let anyone hurt you.

BECKY

Thank you very much for everything!
I really appreciate everything that
you are doing for me!
I appreciate your help and honesty!

A. THOREAU

It is too early to say "thank you."
I have not done anything yet.
However, you will never regret trusting me.
You will never regret being my friend.

BECKY

You know, it is just so terrible when someone you trust betrays you.
I know that we have already discussed this,
but I just feel so much pain.
Betrayal is the worst thing in the world!

A. THOREAU

Becky, you are definitely right.
As you know, Mavrodi makes an excellent
statement about betrayal.
I can actually provide you with his detailed analysis of betrayal.
I think that no one has ever provided
such an outstanding response.
This is what he said: "Regarding personal
questions, please remember that
I do not like to talk about personal matters, and I do
not like to answer questions related to personal matters.
However, I will make an exception this time, and I will
provide some explanation regarding this issue.
Please remember this once and forever. Memorize this like
you have memorized the multiplication table. You must
never betray! You must never betray anybody regardless of
any life circumstances. You cannot betray others just like
you cannot eat human beings. You just cannot eat another

human being under any circumstances. Betrayal works
exactly the same way. You just cannot do that! Never!
There can be no excuses for betrayal just like
there can be no excuses for cannibalism.
The person who betrayed another person is not a
human being. The betrayer is inhuman!
He or she cannot go back to other human beings. He
or she cannot be part of humanity again. The betrayer
is a fallen person. He or she is not a person.
The person who has eaten human flesh once, he or she
has crossed the line. That person is not a human being
too. The cannibal is inhuman too! The person who
has betrayed once is not a human being as well!
Regarding betrayal in comparison to all other sins, God did
not forgive Lucifer for betraying him. Later Jesus Christ did not
forgive Judas for betraying him. God did not forgive betrayal,
and Jesus Christ did not forgive betrayal. When Christ was dying
on the cross, he forgave all sins, but He did not forgive betrayal.
Thus, there is nothing more to discuss regarding betrayal."

BECKY
Wow! That is indeed an excellent analysis!
Even my professors did not speak like that.

BECKY (CONT'D)
Aaron, I can call you this weekend.
I am sorry, but I do not want you
to know my phone number. It is too early.
However, I do not know how to block it.
Could you please tell me how to block
my phone number when I call you?

A. THOREAU
You should dial *67 and the telephone number
where you are calling.
Then your phone number will not show up

on the display of my cell phone.

BECKY
Thank you very much for this information,
and thank you for listening to all my depressive stories.
I feel very bad for bothering you with my problems.

A. THOREAU
Please do not say that. You never bother me.
I will be telling you stories too later
and asking for your advice.
So do not worry about anything.

A. THOREAU (CONT'D)
I like to give good advice to people.
If I have a useful advice or suggestion,
why should I not share it with others?
If I have a good suggestion or recommendation,
I will definitely share with others.
As H. D. Thoreau says, "Aim above morality. Be
not simply good, be good for something."
People like to talk to me about their problems.
I have a friend, who is a doctor.
His name is Nathan, and he lives in NY.
Even my friend-doctor says that I should have
become a psychologist because I understand
different people and their problems very well.
You know, I also enjoy helping people.
Sometimes Nathan calls me in order to talk to me about
his problems and issues.
He says that I always help him with my advice.

BECKY
Please give me your phone number.

Aaron writes his NH cell phone number.

A. THOREAU
This is my cell phone number.

BECKY
Thank you! When can I call you?

A. THOREAU
You can call me whenever you want.
You can call me right now if you want.

BECKY
Thank you again! I will call you this weekend.

A. THOREAU
OK. Call me when it is a good time for you.

BECKY
Are you going to sleep now?

A. THOREAU
No, I am not going to sleep yet.
You can call me now.

BECKY
I am sorry; I am going to sleep now.
However, I look forward to talking to you on the phone.
I really want to hear voice.
Have a good night and happy Holiday to you again!
Enjoy tomorrow's Holiday.

A. THOREAU
Have a good night too, and
have a wonderful Holiday tomorrow!
I will go to sleep too.
We will talk tomorrow.

November 27, 2008: Thanksgiving Day

Rebecca talks to Aaron online again.

BECKY
Hi Aaron.
Happy Thanksgiving to you!

A. THOREAU
Hi Becky.
Happy Thanksgiving to you too!

BECKY
Aaron, I have been thinking about us a lot.
I am so happy that I met you.
You are helping me forget that terrible experience
with Jeff, who came from NY to Boston to...
Let the sun shine bright wherever you are!

A. THOREAU
Thank you, Becky!
Let the sun shine bright wherever we are!

BECKY
Thank you, Aaron!
I hope all your dreams come true.
You are a very good person.
I am not sure if my dreams will ever come true,
given everything that happened in my life.

A. THOREAU
If you always think negatively,
then your dreams will never come true.
It is all a matter of time.
You should always try to think positively.
Trust me, positive thinking helps.
Given your intelligence and kindness,

I am sure all your dreams will come true soon.

A. THOREAU (CONT'D)
Everything will be wonderful
if you go in the direction of your dreams and goals.
You should not stop despite any difficulties
you may encounter on your way.
You should always motivate yourself.
You must find motivation from within.
According to H. D. Thoreau, "What lies behind us and what lies
ahead of us are tiny matters compared to what lives within us."
As I said before, everything is possible if you motivate yourself.
You are a very interesting and well-rounded person,
and you will definitely succeed in life.

A. THOREAU (CONT'D)
You must also find inspiration from within.
As Mavrodi says, "Regarding inspiration,
I write as fast as I move my pen.
I can write poems and novels any time during
the day and night. I always have
inspiration. It lives inside me. By the way, I never plan
anything regarding the plot of my novels. I do not know what
will happen to the heroes of my novels. They live their
own independent lives. Sometimes certain events
happen, the events that I did not expect to happen."

A. THOREAU (CONT'D)
Becky, you should forget all the terrible things
that had happened in the past.
Live your life in the present and enjoy every
minute of life while you are alive.
You should be happy that you are alive.
As H. D. Thoreau says, "You must live in the present, launch
yourself on every wave, and find your eternity in each moment."

BECKY
Thank you very much for your support, Aaron!
I will try to do that.

A. THOREAU
Unfortunately, life takes away the most important
things from us.
Our life takes away those who are very near and
dear to our heart,
and we cannot do anything about that.
I lost too many important people in my life,
the most important people.
Nevertheless, we have to think about the future,
and we must enjoy every minute of our life
while we are alive.
You never know what will happen tomorrow.

A. THOREAU (CONT'D)
If I think about everything that I have been through
in my life,
not a single mental hospital in the world will be able
to help me.

BECKY
What exactly happened in your life?

A. THOREAU
I do not want to lie to you, but
I cannot tell you everything at this time.
One day you will know everything.
We just need to know each other better.

BECKY
I am sorry for what happened to you.
I wish I could help you...

A. THOREAU

Well, I am a man, and I should endure everything,
I should be strong, and I must always keep my spirits up.
You should always be yourself.
Nothing in life should break you.
Even if you will have to give up your life for something,
you should do it with a positive attitude.
Even if you need to die,
you should still keep your spirits up.

A. THOREAU (CONT'D)

Life's circumstances should never change you
or break you.
You should always try to overcome these difficulties
and obstacles; be above them.
You should persevere in the face of your
obstacles and disappointments.
As one of the greatest political leaders in
the world Winston Churchill says,
"Success is not final; failure is not fatal: It is
the courage to continue that counts."

Aaron continues to talk about his life principles.

A. THOREAU (CONT'D)

You should always be yourself. You should stay
true to yourself in every situation.
As H. D. Thoreau says, "If I am not I, who will be?"
You must stay true to yourself and your ideas
regardless of the circumstances of life.
As the most famous American Transcendentalist
and writer Ralph Waldo Emerson says,
"To be yourself in a world that is constantly trying to make
you something else is the greatest accomplishment."
You should not depend on life's circumstances.

R. W. Emerson also says, "It is a lesson which all history teaches wise men, to put trust in ideas, and not in circumstances."
In addition, positive thinking helps a lot.
Sometimes you need to laugh at things that make you cry, and which make you very upset and frustrated.

A. THOREAU (CONT'D)
A person should always be honest and decent.
Nothing should change that.
Honesty and decency are the most important qualities in a person.
These are the main qualities that I appreciate in a person.
If someone does not have these two qualities,
I will never talk to that person.

A. THOREAU (CONT'D)
Please remember, you should never change yourself
just because somebody else wants you to change. You
should always stay true to yourself and your ideas.
In addition, please do not get upset if
someone else does not like you.
What other people think about you should never change you.
The most important thing is what you think
about yourself, and that you like yourself.
As H. D. Thoreau says, "Public opinion is a weak tyrant compared
with our own private opinion. What a man thinks of himself,
that is which determines, or rather indicates his fate." One should
never change based on what others think about him or her.

A. THOREAU (CONT'D)
This is what Mavrodi said regarding public opinion: "A lot of
people hate me and curse me. However, I have my own perception
of good and evil, and I think I am right. I absolutely do not
care about what others think about me. They can hate me and
publicly curse me as much as they want. Hatred is negative
love. It is also a complex feeling. It is difficult to deserve public
hatred. If people hate you, you can be proud of that too."

This is what he said regarding God and the Bible: "I am my own destiny, and I create my own life. I do not care whether God exists or not. I will do whatever I think is the right thing to do, regardless of God. What is written in the Bible is not a directive for me."

"For me, it makes no difference whether God exists or not. It has no effect on my actions whatsoever. I am absolutely not afraid of God's punishment. I act according to my own perception and understanding of good and evil. If God exists, and if I commit sin, I will be responsible for myself and my actions at the Final Judgment. Fear of God's punishment does not affect my decisions. Nothing can make me do something that I do not want to do. If I do not think that I should do something, I will never do it. No one and nothing can make me do something that I do not consider the right thing to do or the necessary thing to do. No one and nothing can affect my decisions, not in this life and not in the next life. Some people do not sin not because they are so honest and righteous, but because they are afraid of God's punishment. However, I am not afraid of God or Devil. I am not afraid of anyone or anything. I have always acted according to what I think is the right thing to do, and I will always act that way."

"By the way, there can be no logic regarding God and his actions. If God is everything, then he is logic too. For example, you cannot prove the existence or nonexistence of God using your logic. It is very strange that some people do not understand that, and they try to explain God using their logic."

"Also, if you believe in God, then you should accept the Bible and everything that is written in the Bible without any discussion. If you do not accept the Bible, or if you accept only a part of the Bible, then you cannot consider yourself a faithful person. In that case, you will not belong to the traditional church, you will have your own faith. Thus, either we trust the Bible or we do not trust it at all."

BECKY

Wow! I have never heard anyone talk like this.
Aaron, you are truly amazing!
You are not like anybody else I have ever talked to.
You know so many fantastic and motivational quotes.
I really like how you think about life, and how you talk.
I absolutely agree with everything you are saying.
You are not like everybody else, and I really like that!
You are indeed very different.

A. THOREAU

Thank you, Becky!
You know, I have never hurt anybody in my life
without a reason.
As I said before, If I hurt someone without a reason,
I would never be able to continue living my life.
How can someone hurt a good person?
I just do not understand that!
Regarding being not like everybody else,
everyone who knows me tells me that.
That is why people have been always attracted to me.
There are a lot of people who are attracted to me now.
They all want to be my friends; they want to talk to me.
As Mavrodi once said, "To be honest, I am a withdrawn person.
I do not really like to talk a lot; however, people love talking to
me. I do not like to talk to people, not in person, not online,
and not on the phone. I do not like to talk to anybody."

BECKY

Therefore, you must be a natural-born leader...

Aaron smiles.

A. THOREAU

You know, Mavrodi provides a very
interesting definition of a leader:

"A true leader or a true manager should
not be involved in the day-to-day
operations of a company. He should rest, go
fishing, and think about strategic tasks.
If the leader's presence is required in the office, that
means his business is not organized well."

Rebecca smiles too.

BECKY
I have never heard such an interesting definition of a leader.
That is an interesting management technique.

A. THOREAU
You know, people say that I am a natural-born leader.
The principles, values, and norms according to which I live...
Yes, I know that it is very unlikely that there is anyone else
in the contemporary world who lives according to
my moral standards and principles.
If there is such a person in this world, it is good.
I have not met such a person during my lifetime,
and I am 35 years old.
Everybody thinks about money and
their personal interests.
Their thought processes have become very similar.
They are very similar to each other.

BECKY
I agree; everybody thinks that money is the
most important thing in life. They just do not
understand what true love and happiness are.
Unfortunately, people think that money can buy everything.

A. THOREAU
Our contemporary life is very different, and
our contemporary world is very different too.
It is a different time now, and we live in

a different world.
That is why the new generation will never live
according to the principles of the old generation.
The old generation is almost gone – almost no one is left.
Unfortunately, there are very few people left
from the old generation.

BECKY
Our life and the people have changed so much.
They have made this life appear as if everything
can be bought with money.
They think that happiness can be bought with money.
The way people live their lives in the contemporary
world, and their moral values, or I should say the lack
of moral values, makes it so hard to trust someone
or to believe in true love and friendship.

A. THOREAU
Unfortunately, this is our contemporary life.
In some countries in Europe, even justice
can be bought with money.
I really like what Sergey Mavrodi says about
money and the contemporary life.
Just think about it; maybe he is right given
that our life is very different now.
This is what Mavrodi says regarding money:
"Our life is such that without money, there is no
happiness, no health, no success, and no love.
If you do not have any problems with money, then you
will not have any problems with anything else.
This is the world in which we all live, and such is our life.
If you have a lot of money, then you will have
happiness, health, success, and love.
If you have a lot of money, then everything
will be great in your life."
If a sick person cannot afford medical care, he or she will die.

There are so many women who want to marry wealthy men.
These women will love the person who has a
lot of money just because he is wealthy.
Without money, a person cannot get an education, and he or
she will not be able to have a good and well-paying job.
Unfortunately, this is our contemporary world.

BECKY
I agree. That is why, it is so hard to find true love.
How can you love and trust someone who thinks
that money can buy love and trust?

A. THOREAU
Unfortunately, there are very few trustworthy
people left in this world.
One of the greatest Russian singers Vladimir Visotsky once said,
"I feel very sad because the word "Honor" has been forgotten."

BECKY
I think Visotsky was right...
I do not understand why people think that money is the most
Important thing in the world. Money is not everything!
You cannot buy love and happiness!
It is so sad that so many people do not understand that.

A. THOREAU
Unfortunately, our contemporary life is like this.
Even Mavrodi once said that "To make money
is not the most interesting thing in life."
There are more interesting and important
things in life than making money.
Unfortunately, so many people are only concerned about money.
Mavrodi also once said that "Money does not bring happiness."
You know, so many people just do not
understand that money cannot
buy you happiness. Mavrodi has an excellent quote about this too:
"What can't you buy? Whatever cannot be sold."

BECKY
That is an excellent quote!
True love and true friendship can never be bought or sold.

A. THOREAU
Almost no one understands the meaning
of true love and true friendship.
It appears that everyone is concerned about
money and his or her personal interest.
Sometimes I think that there are no real friends left.
Everyone just wants to use you and to benefit from you.
When there is no benefit, there is no friendship or love.
This is very sad and unfortunate. Our
life was not always like this…
Sometimes I think that there is no love and
no friendship if there is no personal
benefit involved.

BECKY
This is so true…

A. THOREAU
How many people would agree to help you
without asking anything in return?
How many people truly respect and appreciate you?
How many people really love you?
Just think about what Mavrodi said regarding this issue,
"Everything can melt down: friendship, loyalty, love, honesty,
and decency. Sometimes it is better not to test these concepts.
Sometimes it is better not to test the people that you love… In
addition, there are places in the world, where nothing exists
except for betrayal, deception, indecency, and dishonesty."
Sometimes, the people that we love and trust most betray us.
Sometimes, the people that we love most kill us.

A. THOREAU (CONT'D)

Unfortunately, very few people understand what H. D.
Thoreau said about friendship, "True friendship can afford true
knowledge. It does not depend on darkness and ignorance.
The language of friendship is not words but meanings. The
most I can do for my friend is simply be his/her friend."
As R. W. Emerson says, "The only way
to have a friend is to be one."

BECKY

Aaron, I absolutely agree with you.
I know what you mean.
Sometimes best friends become enemies, and
money is the reason why a lot of people marry
each other or have a personal relationship.
This is so wrong! This is so unfair!
I just cannot understand how it is possible to marry someone
without love, to be with that person 24/7 and not love him/her.
Sometimes I think that injustice rules this world.
The contemporary world has become so cruel, cold, and empty.
Very few people care about the problems of others.

A. THOREAU

Unfortunately, almost no one understands
what H. D. Thoreau said about money,
"Most of the luxuries and many of the so-called
comforts of life are not only not indispensable, but
positive hindrances to the elevation of mankind. Money
is not required to buy one necessity of the soul."
He also says, "A man is rich in proportion to the number
of things which he can afford to let alone." The less
material things a person needs, the richer he/she is.
I think a person should have a rich inner world, and
the inner wealth is not measured by money.

BECKY

Aaron, I absolutely agree with you.
I also think that money is not everything, and I do not
understand people who think that money is their happiness.
As a prominent Congregationalist and abolitionist Henry
Ward Beecher says, "He is rich or poor according to
what he is, not according to what he has." That is an
excellent statement! I absolutely agree with that!
I am sure you know what H. D. Thoreau says about money
and wealth, "If a man has spent all his days about some
business, by which he has merely got to be rich, has got much
money and many houses, then his life has been a failure,
I think. But if he has been trying to better his condition
in a higher sense than this, if he has been trying to invent
something and to be somebody so that all may see his
originality, I shall think him comparatively successful."
I absolutely agree that a person should have a
rich inner world and a beautiful soul.

BECKY (CONT'D)

I also do not understand those people who marry each other
or who have a personal relationship just to have sex.
I do not understand people who think that sex
is the most important thing in life.
I believe people should love each other,
and then comes everything else.
As a wonderful American actor and film director
Woody Allen says, "Sex without love is a meaningless
experience." I absolutely agree with him!

A. THOREAU

I also think that sex without love is an
empty and meaningless experience.
A relationship should not only be a sexual
relationship; there must be love.

There must be spiritual, pure, and true
love in addition to physical love.
An English novelist and poet Kingsley Amis says,
"Sex is a momentary itch, love never lets you go."
I definitely agree with that.

BECKY
Aaron, I absolutely agree with you.
We understand each other so well.
This is so amazing!
It is so great to talk to an understanding person.

Aaron smiles.

A. THOREAU
Becky, I know that we understand each other very well.
We are very similar to each other.
Our thought processes are very similar.

Aaron continues to talk about money and happiness.

A. THOREAU (CONT'D)
Some people think that they are happy, but in reality, they are not.
They think that money brings them happiness; they
think that money is the answer to their questions
and problems. However, it is not true...
These people are just afraid to ask the most important questions of
life because they do not want to destroy their imaginary happiness.
They are afraid to accept that they may not be happy although
they have all the luxuries in the world. They may not have
the most important thing, which is true love, I think.
As an American Congregationalist Charles Finney says, "If we
are deprived of happiness, nothing can be a real good to us."

BECKY
I also think that true love is the most important
thing in life; I think true love is happiness.

Why can't people understand that money and
material wealth is not everything?
Material wealth cannot buy spiritual wealth and health.
Unfortunately, too many people forget that human
relationships are more important than money.
Erich Fromm, one of my favorite philosophers
and psychologists, says the following,
"If I am what I have, and if I lose what I have, who then am I?"
He also says, "The danger of the past was that
men became slaves. The danger of the
future is that men may become robots."

BECKY (CONT'D)
By the way, not so long ago, my best friend betrayed me.
I was so upset…
Unfortunately, there is a lot of evil and injustice
in this world, and there are a lot of evil and unfair
people who lost their humanity, and who want
to hurt you just because they are jealous of you.

A. THOREAU
I am not surprised…
Unfortunately, life is like this, and these are its rules.
Everyone can become an enemy, even
the person that you love most.
Sergey Mavrodi provided a very detailed analysis of this subject.
This is what he said: "Everything can melt down – love,
friendship, honor, and dignity. Everything and everyone has
its melting temperature or melting point. If you raise the
temperature enough, everything will melt. I have observed
it many times. If you change the temperature of the person
that you love, appreciate, and respect, you will see that
person's other side. You will see a completely different side
of that person. Unfortunately, human nature is like this.
Thus, please do not even try to test the people that you love.

I advise you not to do that. Do not tempt the destiny. I definitely do not recommend you to test your loved ones."

A. THOREAU (CONT'D)

Becky, please do not be upset and do not give up. Mavrodi also said, "I have not experienced my melting point yet, although I had some hard times in life. I had some very hard times in life. I am not sure if I have a melting point. However, that does not mean that I do not have a melting temperature. Maybe I have it. But I think I would rather commit suicide than give in.

If there is no way out, I would rather end my life. I just cannot imagine that I would ever give in or give up. Although you never know what will happen to you if the temperature is raised more and more. However, you can never know if you will be strong enough to end your life. You can never know this beforehand. No matter how strong, brave, and courageous you are, you have not reached your melting point yet since you are still alive. You should remember this."

BECKY

I agree…

A. THOREAU

Erich Fromm also says, "One cannot be deeply responsive to the world without being saddened very often." Please think about it.
Maybe we need to have bad experiences in order
to appreciate good experiences more.
Maybe we need evil in order to understand what good is.
Maybe we need betrayal in order to be loyal.
Maybe we need hatred in order to love.

A. THOREAU (CONT'D)

If there was no death, there would be no life.
If there was no wrong, there would be no right.
If there was no doubt, there would be no
belief. Please think about all this.

Even H. D. Thoreau once said, "If I could
not doubt, I should not believe."

A. THOREAU (CONT'D)
Maybe sometimes, we need to have frustrating experiences
in our life in order to become better and smarter.
Even Nietzsche once said, "What does not destroy me,
makes me stronger. What does not kill me, makes me
stronger." I am sure that you have heard this before.
Please remember, we learn from our mistakes
and from the mistakes of others.
The terrible experiences of our life can make us
stronger, if they do not break us, and
we should never break.
We should not allow life's circumstances to break us or kill us.

A. THOREAU (CONT'D)
You know how some people say that
everything happens for a reason.
Maybe they are right… Please think about it.
As Nietzsche says, "To live is to suffer, to survive
is to find some meaning in the suffering."
What Jeff did to you is definitely terrible and outrageous, but
the good thing is that now you are much more careful than
before, and nothing like this will happen to you again.
Moreover, now you have me, and I will
always protect you and help you.

BECKY
Aaron, thank you very much for all your support!
You are definitely helping me a lot.
I understand what you mean; however, it makes me
very upset to think about all the evil in the world.
Why do honest, innocent, and kind-
hearted people suffer the most?

It is just very sad when good people suffer.
They do not deserve suffering!

A. THOREAU

Becky, unfortunately, our life is like this.
As Mavrodi says, "Life always gives you what you do not need."
He also says that " I am a trusting person. That is why,
I always suffer. Life teaches me, teaches me, but…"

BECKY

I agree; life always gives good people what
they do not deserve – suffering!
Sometimes I feel that jealousy, evil, hatred, misunderstanding,
disrespect, and injustice rule the contemporary world.
It is so sad to see innocent people suffer for no reason.
Our life can be so unfair.
There are so many people who want to deceive you
and take advantage of you just because you are
kind-hearted, honest, sincere, and naive.
There are so many people, who enjoy hurting others
without a reason.
I cannot understand such people,
and I will never understand them.
I should not even try to understand them
because I will never be able to understand them.

A. THOREAU

Becky, I definitely agree with what you said about
the contemporary world and contemporary life.
We have the correct understanding of
the world around us, and we understand
the people around us very well.
We know that there are a lot of dishonest and
indecent people in this world.
However, we will never be able to understand
their sick minds because we are not like them.

Please do not even try to understand their thought
processes which go in the wrong direction, and
please try to choose more decent friends.
I know it is very hard to find decent friends.
Most people pretend to be honest and decent...
Please be very careful.

BECKY

Just because the majority of people pretend
to be honest and decent,
it is so hard to find those who are indeed honest and decent.
Erich Fromm also says, "Love is the only sane and
satisfactory answer to the problem of human existence." I
agree with his statement; however, it is very difficult
to find love.
We want to find our true love and be happy.
Some people search for their true love
all their life and never find it.
Others find their true love and live a very happy and fulfilled life.
For some people, love causes a special kind of suffering,
which leads to self-destruction.
I wanted to find my true love and be happy,
but instead I found misery and disappointment.
I will never forget what that guy from NY did to me...

BECKY (CONT'D)

Sometimes I even think that life has no meaning.
Maybe my life has no meaning. All I do is suffer.
This is so unfair! What is the meaning of life?
What is the meaning of my life?
Maybe the meaning of my life is to suffer...

A. THOREAU

Becky, please do not say that.
Please do not think that way. Everything will be okay, I promise.

By the way, Mavrodi provides a very
interesting answer to that question:
"There is no meaning in life, fortunately. The problem of
searching for the meaning of life cannot be resolved. If there
was a meaning in life, it would have been found a long time
ago, and everything would have ended at that point. Nothing
is absolute in this life, and nothing is absolutely true."
Maybe the meaning of life is the eternal search for that meaning.
Mavrodi also says, "You can never have a final
answer to a question. At some point,
you just need to stop and accept something as a true answer."

A. THOREAU (CONT'D)
Is the guy from NY the only person who hurt you?
Do you have more enemies?
It does not matter how many enemies you have,
we will retaliate against all of them for
everything they had done to you..
Trust me, I can make your enemies regret
everything they had done.
We can make them regret all their evil actions and intentions.
You cannot even imagine how we will do it.
However, this is a different story...
We should get to know each other better,
and then everything will be okay. I promise.

BECKY
To be honest, I do not like these dating websites.
Most people here are dishonest and indecent.
They either lie to you or offer something inappropriate.
A lot of people here start making improper suggestions.
You are so polite and so well-mannered.
You are definitely an exception.

A. THOREAU
Well, to lie or to offer something inappropriate

is definitely against my worldviews and life principles.

BECKY

I wish there was more justice in this world.
I wish people were more understanding and fair.

A. THOREAU

Becky, this is what Mavrodi said about justice:
"Only God can be just. A human being can only be merciful."
Maybe people need to have more compassion and empathy.

BECKY

Maybe Mavrodi is right.
Aaron, I have a question for you.
I even wrote an essay in College regarding this issue.
Can someone become a leader or do you have to be born a leader?
I think real leaders are born that way.
I think true leaders are natural-born leaders.
There are certain leadership qualities that you get at birth
and which you cannot acquire otherwise.
However, some professors disagreed with me.

A. THOREAU

As always, you are correct.
If you are not born a leader,
you will never become a true leader.
Therefore, you are correct.
If any professor disagrees with that,
it means he or she is not a real professor.

BECKY

Thank you, Aaron.
You are a very intelligent person, and
as always, it is a pleasure to talk to you.
I am very happy that I have a friend like you now.
I am sorry, but I still cannot trust you 100%.
I still cannot tell you everything.

A. THOREAU
Please take your time
I understand everything well.
At least, do not expect anything bad
from our friendship.
Do not expect me to do anything bad to you.
I will never mistreat you, and I will never lie to you.
That is all that I can tell you now.
When you feel comfortable and find
it necessary, then we will get to know each other.

BECKY
I would like to ask you something.
Are you afraid of anything?
If yes, what makes you afraid in this life?

A. THOREAU
Everyone is afraid of something.
To say what you are afraid of is to reveal your weaknesses.
I cannot reveal my weaknesses now.
I do not know you well.

BECKY
How do you deal with your weaknesses?

A. THOREAU
I have different ways for dealing with them.
I usually try to avoid them, my weaknesses.

BECKY
I agree that a person should try to avoid his or her weaknesses.
However, sometimes it is very difficult to avoid
human weaknesses.

A. THOREAU
That is true…

BECKY

By the way, do you have any personality weaknesses?

Aaron smiles.

A. THOREAU

As Mavrodi once said, "Regarding strengths and weaknesses,
I did not understand your question. I do not have any
weaknesses. I have only strengths. Everything I do is right; it
is always right. Thus, I do not need to change anything."

BECKY

You know, I am afraid of loneliness. I do not want to be lonely.
I think all of us want to love and be loved.
Unfortunately, some of us never find true love.
Some of us find terrible suffering instead…

A. THOREAU

I agree that all of us want to love and be loved.
However, it is very difficult to find the right person.
It is very difficult to find someone honest and decent,
someone who will always understand you and accept you
the way you are.

BECKY

I agree…
Unfortunately, so many people do not understand me.
They just do not like my beliefs and life principles.
Just because I prefer reading books over drinking in
clubs, they think that something is wrong with me.
What is wrong with reading books?
I have read hundreds of books.
My apartment is full of books.
They just do not understand me.

A. THOREAU

Becky, it is wonderful that you like to read.

I like to read books too, and I like talking
to people who like reading.
Please remember, as Emerson says, "To be
great is to be misunderstood."
Unfortunately, these people need to grow up.
They are too young and inexperienced.
They do not understand the value of reading books.

A. THOREAU (CONT'D)
By the way, Sergey Mavrodi had read thousands of books.
He is a very smart and educated person.
You know, a lot of people think that he is a Genius.
His apartment in Moscow was full of books.
Unfortunately, the Russian government seized
all of his books, when they arrested him.
The government officials stole all of his books.
That was so inhumane and unfair!
He had been buying and collecting his books for many years.
The government officials seized all of his possessions.
Mavrodi's apartment was completely empty.
There was not a single book left on his bookshelves.

BECKY
Oh my God! That is so terrible!
I cannot believe that the government seized all his books!
Mavrodi must have been very upset.

A. THOREAU
Yes, they seized all his possessions.
I think the Bible was the only thing that the police could not seize.
When a journalist asked Mavrodi what he
regretted the most out of everything
the government had seized, he replied
that he did not regret anything.
I agree; one must not be attached to his/her possessions.
However, it is very sad that Mavrodi lost all of his books.

I think he just has a few books describing his court case – the police provided that to him when he was released from prison.

A. THOREAU (CONT'D)
This is what Mavrodi said about that terrible incident:
"They seized all my books when I was arrested. I do not understand why they seized my books. Books are not related to material things. They are related to spiritual things."

BECKY
I really like all my books, and I have a lot of books.
I would be extremely mad and upset if someone stole my books.
How many years did Mavrodi spend in prison?

A. THOREAU
When he was arrested in 1994, he was released later.
Then he was arrested again in 2003 and
placed under police custody.
He was accused of tax evasion and deceiving his investors.
Mavrodi did not consider himself guilty of any charges.
His company MMM did not pay taxes
because it was a financial pyramid.
However, a financial pyramid must not pay taxes.
Also, I do not think that Mavrodi deceived his investors.
He did not violate the law.
By the way, the police called Mavrodi "the most famous
businessman and financial pyramid builder."
Sergey Mavrodi was sentenced to four and a half years in prison.
In 2007, he was released from prison
after serving the full sentence.
The prison where he served his sentence was terrible.
There were a lot dangerous criminals,
among them were serial killers.
The prison guards and police often
punished Mavrodi for no reason.
He definitely did not deserve that!

Mavrodi did not violate the law, and he
was not supposed to go to prison!
A financial pyramid is not prohibited by Russian law, and
the law does not say that a person who has a financial
pyramid must pay taxes to the government.
Moreover, a financial pyramid is not defined by the law.
By the way, when Mavrodi was imprisoned, he had declared
many hunger strikes. The hunger strikes were in protest of
his unfair treatment by the police and prison guards.
Once Mavrodi did not even drink water
when it was extremely hot.

BECKY
Wow! That is amazing!

A. THOREAU
Sergey Mavrodi was a famous, wealthy, and well-respected
man, but the government made him poor and infamous.
The government not only deprived Mavrodi of everything,
they continue to make false accusations against him.
Mavrodi is not allowed to have anything; even all of his books
were seized by the government. It is so unfair and inhumane!
Mavrodi wanted to help people, but he had become a
victim of government cruelty and inhumanity.
I think the government destroyed the financial
pyramid MMM and stole people's money. Then
they blamed Mavrodi for their crimes.
This is what Mavrodi said about MMM company
and the corrupt Russian government:
"It was an absolutely honest, legal, and lawful way. However,
the government did not like that way because their goal
was to steal people's money, and that is exactly what
happened. The government always steals the money of
defenseless people. Then they started defending themselves
as always and directing the blame towards me."

"By the way, do you remember the most important
principle of my company MMM?
*The principle of mutual trust is above the principle of mutual
responsibilities.* I have always lived according to this life
principle. In addition, you must believe in yourself.
That is the most important quality in a person."

BECKY
Well, our life is very cruel and unfair...

A. THOREAU
Unfortunately, there was a lot of injustice
that Mavrodi had experienced.
I do not even know how he survived...
Regarding being misunderstood, once he
provided a wonderful answer
to the person who misunderstood his life principles.
It was probably a young and inexperienced person.
This is what Mavrodi said: "You must be
very young... What do I teach you?
Do I teach amoralities, negation, and nihilism? What
about goodness and kind-heartedness? Please grow up. The
discussion is over for now. We can talk later, some years
later. I am not sure how many years I will need to wait... It
is not a problem; I can wait. I do not need to rush. I have
eternity in front of me. Eternity is waiting for me. By the way,
regarding writers, you are wrong. Heroes do not write books.
Heroes do great deeds. Yes, I write books. However, I am an
exception. I am the only one. I told you this from the very
beginning. I was being honest. Regarding geniuses, they do
not exist in this world. I mean a Genius is born once every
thousands of years. I am not a Genius; I am the only one."

BECKY
That was a very interesting answer.
It appears that Mavrodi thinks that he is the best.

A. THOREAU

Well, he is probably a Genius.
He has exceptional skills and abilities in Math and Physics.
By the way, Mavrodi studied Applied Mathematics at
his University in Russia, and he also liked physics.
He used to win all math and physics contests.
Mavrodi has an amazing talent to write books and poems.
He is also a very intelligent and skillful businessman.
No one can deny his extraordinary talents and abilities.
Mavrodi also says, "Only a Genius can talk about another Genius.
That means nobody can talk about geniuses, or that may happen
once in every thousands of years. However, if a person feels that
he/she is a Genius, that person is indeed a Genius. It is very simple,
and I am not joking about that. What I just said is the truth! It is
impossible to consider yourself a Genius if life always proves the
opposite. Deep inside the heart, every person knows his/her true
value. There can be no doubt in that. It cannot be otherwise."
"As I said before, I am not a Genius, I am the only one."
Maybe the last quote means that Mavrodi
thinks that he is better than a Genius…

A. THOREAU (CONT'D)

By the way, some people criticize Mavrodi, and
the try to teach him what is right and what is wrong.
I really like how he responded to one of these people: "I
do not need you to teach me how to live my own life. I
do not need your teachings and your moral lecture. I am
not a little child. I am a normal, grown-up person, and
I know how to live my life. You can teach your children
how to live, not me. We are not in a kindergarten."

BECKY

Unfortunately, some people think that they
have a right to criticize and teach others.
I think that before criticizing someone else,
they should examine their own lives.

They should ask themselves if they are doing everything right.

A. THOREAU

I absolutely agree. Unfortunately, very few people understand that.
As Mavrodi once said, "Every person has his or her own
way in life. He or she has to walk that life path. Every
person should live his or her own life. If everyone lived the
same life, there would be no difference in the world."

A. THOREAU (CONT'D)

There are two people that I really admire – Henry
David Thoreau and Sergey Mavrodi.
They both love freedom and nature, and they are
not afraid to go to jail for their beliefs.
Both of them are very intelligent and creative people.
You know, I love the mountains, and Mavrodi
loves fishing. We both enjoy nature.
This is what Mavrodi says about fishing: "The only thing that I
truly love in this life is fishing. Fishing has always been number
one for me. It is like a drug for me. I am addicted to fishing."
By the way, Mavrodi does not drink or smoke, and he likes sports.

Rebecca smiles.

BECKY

Wow! There is one more person who does not drink or smoke.

Aaron smiles too.

A. THOREAU (CONT'D)

Yes, that is true, and Mavrodi likes to read books just like you.
I am sorry; I need to go now.
I will be waiting for your call.
I think we will understand each other very well.
We will definitely find many interesting subjects
for our first telephone conversation.
I am sure this will not be our last telephone conversation.

Have a wonderful Thanksgiving Day!

Rebecca smiles again.

BECKY
Okay, thank you very much!
Have a wonderful Holiday too!
I am sure we will have many telephone conversations.
We can always find something to talk about.
I will definitely call you, maybe this Saturday.

Next Day

Rebecca and Aaron meet online.

BECKY
Hi. How was your Holiday?

A. THOREAU
It was good. I was alone.

BECKY
Why were you alone?
Were you not interested in going anywhere?
It was probably a sad Holiday...

A. THOREAU
I understand... A lot of people invited me,
but I did not really want to go anywhere.
I do not even know why...
Maybe because I do not like being in a company
with drunk people.
You know how drunk people are,
someone will say something to me, and…

BECKY
I understand you very well.

BECKY (CONT'D)
You probably feel bad because you are alone.
You probably feel uncomfortable
because of your loneliness.
Loneliness is not a good thing...

A. THOREAU
I am alone, and I feel wonderful!
I am like a lone wolf now.
As Mavrodi once said, "I do not feel uncomfortable because
of the fact that I do not have any friends. I like my own
company. I do not have anybody. That is why, I have nobody
to love. In addition, I cannot stand events, but they love me."
He also said, "To be honest, I feel great when I am in
solitude, when I am alone. I have freedom, complete
freedom. Attachment makes your life harder even if you
are attached to a cat. Loneliness is the best thing."
I can understand Mavrodi...
You know, when you get attached to
someone, and then she betrays and
disappoints you. It is very hard to break that
attachment and overcome sadness.
I am just very tired of having failed relationships.
I am very tired of having relationships,
where you constantly argue with each other,
and where you have scandals every day.
I am just very tired of relationships, where
there is no respect and no understanding.

A. THOREAU (CONT'D)
I am used to being alone.
It is better to be alone than with someone
who will break your spirit.
It is better to be happy alone
than unhappy with someone.
These are not only my words...

BECKY

Well, I understand...
You have to find the right person,
who will be understanding, respectful,
caring, supportive, and intelligent.
You should have similar worldviews,
and live according to similar values,
norms and principles.
You should have similar understanding of life.
You must also have common interests.
If you find such a person, you will be truly happy.
Otherwise, it is impossible to live with someone,
who is very different from you,
and who does not understand you.
I know that it is very hard to find the right person.

BECKY (CONT'D)

However, I still think that loneliness is a very bad thing.
We all should definitely have someone in our life,
someone that can help us live a better life.
We all need a good family to support us.
I want to get married, and I want to have children.
Only then, I will be truly happy.
I do not want to be alone; I am afraid of loneliness.

A. THOREAU

I agree...
Every man needs a woman in his life, and
every woman needs a man in her life.

A. THOREAU (CONT'D)

You see, we have very similar opinions regarding this matter too.
We see and understand things the same way.

BECKY

It is very difficult to find the right person
in the contemporary world.

You can much easier find disappointment and sorrow
than happiness and joy.
I was unable to find the right person for a long time...

A. THOREAU
Let us put it this way.
I have become used to this already.
Unfortunately, such is our life and its reality.
So we understand this the same way.

A. THOREAU (CONT'D)
We should survive and win wherever we are.
We should try to win despite everything.

BECKY
I agree with you.
By the way, why did you post a picture of the wolf?
Do you like wolves?
Is this your favorite animal?

A. THOREAU
Yes, I like wolves.
I associate myself with the wolf.
It is a very strong, handsome, and proud animal.
The wolf can be very aggressive if his life is
in danger.
It is a very courageous animal, who is not afraid
of pain or death.
The wolf will face any enemy, no matter how
strong that enemy is.

BECKY
I agree that the wolf is a very strong and
handsome animal.

BECKY (CONT'D)
What is your favorite country in the world?

A. THOREAU
Italy. The people in Italy are very nice.
However, this is a different story...
You know, some people say that it is good
everywhere, where we do not live.

BECKY
What is your favorite place in Italy?

A. THOREAU
My favorite place in Italy is Amalfi Coast.
It is one of the most beautiful places in the world.
I really like it. I used to go there every year.
I have a friend in Amalfi, who rents me a
beautiful apartment at an affordable price.
That apartment is located on the beach, and
it has an amazing ocean view.

A. THOREAU (CONT'D)
If it works out between us, we could definitely
go to Amalfi together next time and stay at that place.
By the way, their food and clothing stores are not
open as late as here in the United States.
You will have to get used to their schedule.
Most of them close around 6:00 PM.
Stores and restaurants in Europe have different hours of operation.

A. THOREAU (CONT'D)
By the way, if we go to Italy,
I would like you to try their famous pizza-like bread.
It is like a little pizza, and it is very delicious.
I think you will like it.

BECKY
Thank you very much for the invitation, Aaron.
I am very happy to be invited to Italy by you.
I would love to go there with you.

I am sure our trip to Italy would be great.
I just need more time.
You know I cannot really trust anyone at this time...
However, I really appreciate your offer.
I am sure Amalfi is a wonderful place,
and it will be very interesting to go there
and spend some time with someone like you.

A. THOREAU
As I said before, please take your time.
Time is not a problem for me.
You can have as much time as you need.
Do not worry about that.
I understand that you had a terrible experience in your life.

BECKY
Aaron, thank you for your patience and
understanding.

BECKY (CONT'D)
How many languages do you speak?

A. THOREAU
I speak English, Russian, Ukrainian, Polish,
and Spanish.

BECKY
Wow, you know so many languages.
Where did you learn them?

A. THOREAU
I spoke Russian and Ukrainian, when
I lived in the former Soviet Union.
I learned Polish and Spanish at work, when I
worked as a property manager in NY.
There were a lot of Polish-speaking and
Spanish-speaking people in the company where I worked.

Suddenly, Aaron starts talking about his failed relationships.

A. THOREAU (CONT'D)
You will be surprised, but my Colombian
ex-girlfriend, who I met in NY, never spoke Spanish with me.
I asked her to speak Spanish with me; however,
she did not want me to understand Spanish
so that she could talk to her mother, and
I would not understand them.
I did not like that; I did not like the way she treated me.
However, I have two very good Spanish-speaking
friends in NY, and they helped me learn Spanish.

BECKY
Your Colombian ex-girlfriend was not
nice to you.

BECKY (CONT'D)
Do you know where she is now, and what she is doing?

A. THOREAU
After we broke up, she got married and had a child,
but it did not work out, and she divorced soon.
Now she has a two-year old daughter,
a beautiful girl.
She wanted us to be together again; however,
I explained to her that we could only be friends.
I feel that she still loves me…
Sometimes she calls me and asks me to help her.
I help her when she needs my help, but
we are just friends now.
You know, I like helping people if they need help.
As R. W. Emerson says, "Make yourself necessary to somebody."
"Let man serve law for man. Live for friendship, live for love.
For truth's and harmony's behoof."

A. THOREAU (CONT'D)

Once I got a call at 2:00 AM in the morning from one
of my friends, who was arrested in NY for drunk driving.
She called me from the police station.
She asked me to come to NY and help her.
Her daughter was alone at home.
I felt very bad for the little girl, and I came to NY to help
her mother that night.
By the way, that woman was in love with me too, but
we could never be together since she liked drinking.

BECKY

Aaron, that is wonderful that you like helping people.

BECKY (CONT'D)

I am sorry for asking, but why did you break up
with your Colombian ex-girlfriend?

A. THOREAU

It is okay; please do not be sorry.
We broke up because we did not understand each
other very well.
We had to end our relationship.
Unfortunately, she was not the woman that I
could have a family with.
I felt there was a lack of understanding and respect between us.
She wanted to have a child by me; however,
I did not want her to be the mother of my child.

A. THOREAU (CONT'D)

I also had a very bad experience with my
Russian ex-girlfriend, who had a severe
mood disorder.
I met her when I moved to NH.
We argued with her every day.
It was just impossible to have a normal
conversation with her.

In addition, she did not want to move out
of my townhouse when I decided to end our relationship.
I did so much for her and for her 12-year old son,
who lived with us.
However, she did not appreciate anything.
One day I will tell you what a terrible
experience it was.

A. THOREAU (CONT'D)
For some reason, I just do not have luck
with women.
I had three long-term relationships, and
I was even married once a long time ago.
However, nothing worked out.
Every relationship that I had was a failure.
Everything was a big disappointment for me.
There was a time in my life when I was very
depressed because of that; however,
my friend-psychologist, whose name is Alex, and
who is a very famous doctor in the United States,
told me that I should not be upset because of the
women who hurt me.
I should look at it like this: these women are no longer
part of my life, and I should be happy because of that.
Once I met one of my ex-girlfriends with a new boyfriend
on the street; they were hugging and kissing each other.
I was very upset; however, Alex told me that I should
not be upset about that too since her new boyfriend
will be punished soon because his girlfriend
is not a good person.
Alex is a very intelligent man. He lives in Connecticut (CT) now.
He treats Hollywood stars who have depression.
He is an excellent doctor.

BECKY
Aaron, please do not worry.

You are still very young, and you
will definitely meet a nice woman, who
will appreciate you, and who will accept you the way you are.
You will definitely have children, and
you will be happy.
You just need to find the right person.
You have not met that person yet, but
you will definitely meet her.

A. THOREAU
Becky, thank you very much for your support!

A. THOREAU (CONT'D)
You know, sometimes I wish I could live according to this
life principle of Sergey Mavrodi, "I never have depression. I have
absolute moral and psychological comfort. I feel great without
talking to anybody and without doing anything. I would always
live such a life if I could. I do not even watch TV or read anything
these days. In addition, I almost never go outside. However, I feel
almost perfect. I just wish I had a little money in order to survive."
Mavrodi lost everything and everyone when he was arrested.
A lot of people tried to break him, and a lot of people
betrayed him. However, Mavrodi did not break, and he is
not even depressed now. I think that it is truly amazing!

BECKY
I agree that it is really amazing.
I know that a lot of people commit suicide in prison.
They just cannot take the prison realities.

A. THOREAU
A person must be very strong in order to survive in prison.

BECKY
Aaron, please do not be upset bout anything.
You know, there was a time in my life, before I met you, when
I was deeply depressed.

I was so angry and upset that I did not
even want to continue my life.
However, you helped me overcome my depression.
I am so happy that I have you in my life now.

A. THOREAU
Thank you, Becky.
You helped me too.
I feel much better now because I have you in my life.

CHAPTER 5

LEGENDARY MUSIC AND MOVIES

November 28, 2008: Friday Morning

Rebecca and Aaron meet online again, and they decide to talk about art.

BECKY
Hi Aaron. How are you?

A. THOREAU
I am good. What about you?

BECKY
I am good too.
I want to ask you something.
What is your favorite movie?

A. THOREAU
With Fire and Sword – it is a Polish
historical film, which is based on true events.
It is about the life in Poland in the 17th century.
I really like history related movies, especially that
movie. I watched it multiple times. It is an excellent film.
There is also a historical novel with the same
title, which was published in 1884.
There were several different movies made based
on that book, the most recent in 1999.
I remember I even had a video tape of that film a long time ago.
I would love to watch it again.
You know, my mom is a historian, and

we always watch historical movies.

A. THOREAU (CONT'D)
I also like the film *Scarface* with Al Pacino,
which was made in 1983.
It is a very interesting movie; it is about the
criminal and drug underworld.
You can watch it; it is a good film.

BECKY
Okay, I will definitely buy that DVD.

A. THOREAU
There is also one wonderful film called *A
River of Lies; A River of Tears.*
It is an old Russian film; however, it has
a great meaning even today.
This movie can very well be applied to the
contemporary world and life.
The main point of the film is that we should never live a life full of
lies and illusions because it always takes us to a life full of tears.
The inevitable end of a life full of lies is misery and
desperation, which makes a person deeply depressed.
One should always be honest with oneself and with others.
A person should never lie about anything.

BECKY
Aaron, I absolutely agree with you.
I wish there was no dishonesty in the world.
Unfortunately, many people live in a distorted reality;
they have a distorted understanding of life and
happiness and a distorted sense of moral values.
You know how most people are – they are afraid
to accept the harsh reality of our life.

A. THOREAU
Well, I am not surprised…

This is our contemporary life with contemporary people.
Those who do not have a distorted sense of morality
definitely stand out from the crowd.

A. THOREAU (CONT'D)
Unfortunately, the majority of people prefer
to live a life full of beautiful lies
because they know that the truth is not beautiful.
As Mavrodi once said, "The truth is almost always ugly and
unpleasant. Lies are beautiful, wonderful, and pleasant."

A. THOREAU (CONT'D)
What is your favorite film?

BECKY
My favorite movie is called *The Official Story* (*La Historia Oficial*).
It is a Latin American film, which was made in 1985 in Argentina.
This movie is in Spanish; I watched it with English subtitles.
A wonderful film director and screenplay writer Luis
Puenzo directed this movie, and it has excellent actors.
It is the first Latin American film, which won the
Oscar for the Best Foreign Language Film.
In addition, this film won many different awards.
The music, the actors, and the story – everything is amazing!
It is based on a true story. This movie is
truly amazing and very sad.
It is about what happened in Latin America in the 1970s.
It is about the forced disappearances and
the Dirty War in the 1970s.

BECKY (CONT'D)
This film focuses on the story of one family, and
through the life of that family, it talks about all the horrors
that happened to the people who opposed the government.
Many people were brutally tortured and killed in the
1970s because they opposed the government.

The film discusses how a lot of people "disappeared," and their children were sold to those who supported the government. A woman in the movie (Alicia) is a history teacher, but she does not know the real history of her country. She only knows the official government version; she does not know the truth. It takes her some time to realize that the child she has was sold to her husband, who supported the evil government. Even her husband that she trusted so much lied to her. When this woman finds out the identity of her little daughter's "disappeared" parents, she is emotionally shattered and broken inside. Alicia understands that her life was full of lies.

Norma Aleandro, the amazing actress, who played the role of that history teacher, once said, "Alicia's personal search is also my nation's search for the truth about our history. The film is positive in the way it demonstrates that she can change her life despite all she is losing." For Alicia, the bitter truth was better than the sweet lie. The forced disappearances during Argentina's Dirty War in the 1970s ruined the lives of many people.

A. THOREAU
I am sure you know what H. D. Thoreau
once said about the government,
"I heartily accept the motto – that government
is best which governs least."
Here in the United States of America, we have
a true democracy, where there are human rights
and wonderful laws, which protect people.
We have freedom of speech and expression,
freedom of religion, and equality for all.
Here we can say whatever we want, and we can criticize
our political leaders; we will not be punished for that.
Unfortunately, it is not the case in many other countries.
Unfortunately, many countries still have dictatorship and
discrimination. I really like what Mavrodi once said about

government: "The ideal government is when people live
well." People live well in the United States of America.

BECKY
The United States is indeed a true democracy, where
every person has an opportunity to achieve everything
he/she wants and to realize all his/her dreams.
It is very sad that many countries still have evil governments.
The Official Story, through the life of one family,
discusses one such evil government.
I will never forget that film.
It left a very deep impression in my heart and in my mind.
This film is indeed unforgettable.
However, it has a very sad ending.
I watched it as part of my film course in College, and
I cried so much that even the professor was worried about me.
I remember I did not leave the classroom that day
until 10:00 PM, and the class was over at 5:00 PM.
I will never be able to forget this film.

A. THOREAU
Some films are very sad, and
they make us cry. Unfortunately,
not everything has a happy ending.
This applies to our life as well.
Sometimes our life is very sad...

BECKY
By the way, what is freedom for you?

A. THOREAU
I will answer the same way as Mavrodi answered this question:
"Freedom for me is like the ability to breathe."

Rebecca continues to discuss her favorite movies.

BECKY

You know, I never told you this before; however,
Italy has a special meaning for me.
I know that you like that country too, and Amalfi
Coast is one of your favorite places.
There is one truly amazing Italian film,
which I will never be able to forget.
It also left a very deep impression in my heart.
It is a TV Series (*Telenovela*), which was made in 1992 in Italy.
The name of the movie is *Edera*, and it was directed
by a wonderful film director Fabrizio Costa.
The actors in the film are amazing too.
Agnese Nano (Edera) and Nicola Farron (Andrea)
are truly amazing actors! They are also very beautiful
artists inside and outside. I really liked these two
actors and even wanted to meet them in real life.
I watched this film many years ago. I watched
it in Italian with English subtitles.
I will never forget how I watched this film with my dear,
wonderful grandmother, who I love very much.
Edera was the favorite film of my grandmother.
The film had 44 episodes.
I would watch it with my dearest grandmother every evening.
I will never forget that wonderful time of my life…
I think *Edera* describes the most beautiful love story
in the world; it is a very inspiring love story.
Their relationship passes all the tests of time, and despite
evil and injustice, their love wins in the end.

BECKY (CONT'D)

There is also great music in the film *Edera*.
The name of the unforgettable song is "I Ricordi
Del Cuore" by Amedeo Minghi.
The song can be translated as "The Memories of My Heart."
The music in that song is extremely beautiful;
it has amazing piano melody.

This incredible piano from the song
accompanies the entire film *Edera*.
The song "The Memories of My Heart" can very
well explain the love of Edera and Andrea.
The memories of our heart never go away;
they stay with us forever.
Certain love memories cannot be erased from our heart.
Certain love memories and certain people
stay in our hearts forever.
True love can conquer evil and injustice in the
world; true love can save the world.
I think true love is perfect, and it is invincible.
If two people really love each other, nothing can break
their relationship; they will be together despite everything.
The film *Edera* is a very good example of that.
Andrea betrayed Edera, but she was able to forgive him for
everything because she truly loved him. Deep inside she felt very
hurt, but she was able to overcome her pain because she could
not imagine her life without Andrea, who was her first love.
I think your first love is the most powerful,
and it can never be forgotten.
Your first love lives forever.
I also think that you can forgive someone for
hurting you if you really love him or her.
Edera is probably the most powerful and the
most inspiring love story in the world.
Amedeo Minghi is a very talented musician;
many of his songs are haunting.
He is one of the best singers and songwriters in the world.

BECKY (CONT'D)
I even bought the CD with the song "I Ricordi
Del Cuore" ("The Memories of My Heart").
I think "The Memories of My Heart" is the most beautiful
and the most unforgettable love song in the world.

I feel so incredibly good when I listen to this song.
The music in the song is very beautiful.

This is a part of the song translated into English:

"In the memories, everything is possible.
Even without us, you are inside my heart.
But the memories never disappear, they stay with us.
They are much stronger than us, more lively than us."

A. THOREAU
That is indeed a very beautiful love song;
the words are so powerful.
I agree that the memories of true love stay in your heart forever.
It is impossible to forget someone you love so much,
especially if the love of your life is your first love.
I will be happy to listen to this song too. I
am sure it is incredible if you like it.
By the way, I also like Indian movies and songs from those movies.
Their films always have very beautiful love stories.
Sometimes I like watching beautiful love stories.
I agree that some love stories are very inspiring.

BECKY
I have heard about India's film industry.
I know that some of their movies are very
popular all over the world.

Rebecca changes the subject of their conversation.

BECKY (CONT'D)
What is your favorite song?

A. THOREAU
My most favorite song is the "House of the Rising Sun"
by the Animals.
It is a very old song; it was recorded in 1964, but I still love it.

I used to love this song so much that
my friends asked live musicians at restaurants
to sing it for me.
Every time we went to a restaurant with
live music, they would sing that song for me.
Although it is a very old song, I still enjoy listening to it.

I also like "Losing My Religion" by R.E.M.
Please listen to this song if you have not heard it before.

BECKY
I will be happy to listen to these two songs.

A. THOREAU
In addition, I really like one band that performs in the
former Soviet Union.
The name of the band is *Blatnoy Udar* (Criminal Strike).
I enjoy their music very much.
They have so many incredible songs, and the
music in their songs is very beautiful.
Aziz Kasoyan, the lead singer of the band, is an amazing artist.
He is a very talented person, and his songs are very touching.
Aziz Kasoyan has many songs dedicated to his mother,
and he also sings about his father and about prison.
It appears from some of his songs that his father betrayed him and
his mother, and that his mother died when he was a little child.
The lead singer has many good songs about prison. I think
he was in prison for some time. I am not sure why.
It also appears from some of his songs that
the girl he loved a lot betrayed him.
The songs of *Blatnoy Udar* are very sad, but they are
truly incredible, and they have a special meaning for
me. You know, some songs can be haunting…
One day I will tell you why these songs are
so special and so important for me.

A. THOREAU (CONT'D)
There is a wonderful song about a girl who betrayed
a guy, and the guy killed the girl and went to
prison; it is called "You Said You Loved Me."
I really like the final words from the song:

"Dear friends, I would like to give you an advice:
Do not fall in love when you are young.
Please listen to your dear mothers, and
do not lose your authority."

A. THOREAU (CONT'D)
There is another very good and very meaningful
song called "You Are My First Love."
Aziz Kasoyan is probably singing about his first love.
The music is very beautiful in this song. These
are some of the words from the song:

"You are my first love.
You are my unfortunate love.
I think I will never see you again.
We broke up forever, and you left forever."

A. THOREAU (CONT'D)
There is also a truly wonderful song about a little boy,
who lost his mother at a very young age.
The name of the song is "My Mother Does Not Hear Me."
When I listen to this song, I always cry.

BECKY
I would like to listen to that song too.

A. THOREAU
I can definitely give you their music website; however,
they sing in Russian.

Rebecca smiles.

BECKY
I would like to listen to Russian songs, especially
your favorite band.

Aaron writes the website for Rebecca.

A. THOREAU
Blatnoy Udar is a wonderful band with very talented musicians.
Aziz Kasoyan, the lead singer of the band,
is indeed an amazing musician!
Even my Russian ex-girlfriend cried when she listened to the song
"My Mother Does Not Hear Me."

BECKY
Thank you for the website, Aaron.
I will definitely listen to that song.
I wish I could understand Russian…

A. THOREAU
You are welcome!
If you want, I can translate a part of the song for you.
It is a very sad song.

BECKY
Okay, thank you.

A. THOREAU
These are some of the words from the song
"My Mother Does Not Hear Me" by
Blatnoy Udar:

"They buried my dear mother; they took her away from me.
They drowned my mother in the ground.
I will never see her again. I will never see my dear mother again.
Now I feel so lonely in this cold and cruel world."

BECKY

I have never read such sad and depressing song lyrics.
I wonder if Aziz Kasoyan sings about himself.
If that song is about him, he must have loved his mother a lot.

A. THOREAU

I think Aziz Kasoyan sings about himself.
He is a very talented musician.
I also think that the best and the most inspiring songs are
those songs in which a singer describes his or her own life.
As H. D. Thoreau says, "He is the true
artist whose life is his material."

A. THOREAU (CONT'D)

What about you?
What is your favorite song?

BECKY

I really like "7 Seconds" by Youssou N'Dour and Neneh Cherry,
"Mother Love" by Freddie Mercury, and "The
Show Must Go On" by Queen.
These are truly unforgettable and very beautiful songs.
I cannot even find the right words to
describe the beauty of these songs.

The song "7 Seconds" left a very deep impression in
my heart. The music in this song is fantastic, especially
the violin melody in the middle of the song.
Nothing can be compared to the beauty of this song and its music.
"7 Seconds" was a worldwide hit in 1994;
it was a huge international hit.
This song is against discrimination and evil
people. It is a very meaningful song.
These are some of the words from the song:

"Roughneck and rudeness we should be using

on the ones who practice wicked charms.
For the sword and the stone. Bad to the bone.
Battle is not over, even when it is won."

Aaron, please listen to "7 Seconds" when you have a chance.

A. THOREAU
Becky, I will definitely listen to this song.
Could you please write the name of the website that you once provided to me, where I can listen to high quality music?

Rebecca writes the name of the website again.

BECKY
Of course, Aaron.
Please enjoy, and please let me know if you need anything else.

A. THOREAU
Thank you very much, Becky.

BECKY
Trust me, "7 Seconds" is indeed an incredible song.
If you listen to this song, you will not be able to forget it.
You know, some music leaves an unforgettable impression on you.
Music can make you feel so good.

A. THOREAU
I definitely know that.
You must remember what H. D. Thoreau said about music,
"When I hear music, I fear no danger. I am invulnerable. I see no foe. I am related to the earliest times and to the latest."

BECKY
That is another wonderful quote of my favorite philosopher.
Of course, I remember it.
R. W. Emerson says, "Music causes us to
think eloquently." I absolutely agree.

Rebecca continues to talk about her favorite music.

BECKY (CONT'D)
You know, I also love one truly amazing song by
Eminem; it is a very inspirational song.
I always listen to this song when I need some
inspiration and motivation in my life.
The song's name is "Lose Yourself." This song was released in
2002, and it is part of the soundtrack to the film *8 Mile.*
8 Mile is a wonderful film; I really enjoyed watching it. It is about
Eminem's life, and about the difficulties and disappointments
of his life. He was able to overcome all his difficulties because
of his hard work, determination, and inner motivation.
Almost no one believed in his talent, and look at Eminem now…
His life story and his struggle with injustice really inspired me.
I think I can overcome all my difficulties too,
and I will become a Philosophy Professor.

The movie *8 Mile* and the song "Lose
Yourself" are very inspirational.
These are some of the words from the song:

"Look, if you had one shot, or one opportunity
to seize everything you ever wanted.
Would you capture it or just let it slip?
Success is my only option, failure is not.
Feet fail me not because this may be the
only opportunity that I got."

BECKY (CONT'D)
I think Eminem's song "Sing for the Moment" is also inspirational.
These are some of the words from the song:

"They say music can alter moods and talk to you.
But music is reflection of self, we just explain it.
How we can come from practically nothing

to being able to have anything that we wanted."

BECKY (CONT'D)

Eminem is a wonderful musician, and he is a very talented person!
Some of his songs are so inspirational. They can
definitely inspire a person to go in the direction of his/
her dreams and not be afraid of life's realities.
Eminem is a very good motivation. Our
dreams can become realities.
I especially love when Eminem says, "Success
is my only option, failure is not" and
"You can do anything you set your mind to."
I try to look at life and its difficulties like that
too, although it is very hard sometimes…

A. THOREAU

I agree with your favorite phrase – "Success
is my only option, failure is not."
H. D. Thoreau said, "Men are born to succeed, not to fail."
As I said before, we should always try to win,
despite any difficulties we may encounter.
We should not lose; we cannot lose.
I think everything is possible if you motivate yourself.
You can do everything you want if you motivate yourself.
As Mavrodi says, "Please remember, there are no obstacles to
reaching your goals in this world. There are no unattainable
goals. There are wrong strategies. I hope that you choose the right
strategy. Our life is a game, and you must win in this game."
Our dreams and goals can definitely become realities.
We just need to choose the right strategies for achieving our goals.
Also, we must never give up; we must always win in this life.

A. THOREAU (CONT'D)

As I said before, life should never break you.
You have to be unbreakable in this world.
You must survive and win in every life situation.

You must also motivate yourself in any situation.
Even when you feel lost, confused, betrayed, and alone,
you should motivate yourself and believe in a better future.
Joseph Rudyard Kipling, an English poet
and novelist, has a wonderful poem:

"If you can dream and not make dreams your master.
If you can think and not make thoughts your aim.
If you can meet with Triumph and Disaster,
And treat those two impostors the same.
If you can bear to hear the truth you have spoken.
Twisted by knaves to make a trap for fools.
Or watch the things you gave your life to, broken.
And stoop and build them up with worn-out tools."

BECKY
That is indeed a wonderful poem.
Aaron, I definitely agree with you.
A person must never break, even when
everything and everyone is against him or her.
Some of the greatest people in the world had to go through a lot.
They had experienced so much pain and
injustice before they achieved success.

BECKY (CONT'D)
You are absolutely right that music can be
truly haunting and unforgettable.
Freddie Mercury is another incredible
musician, and his songs are amazing!
These are some of the words from his
song "The Show Must Go On:"

"Whatever happens, I will leave it all to chance.
Another heartache, another failed romance – on and on.
Does anybody know what we are living for?

Outside the dawn is breaking, but inside in
the dark, I am aching to be free."

BECKY (CONT'D)
I just love music very much, and my favorite musicians
are wonderful and very talented people.
I love music so much that I do not imagine my life without music.
I think they are true legends – Freddie Mercury, Eminem, Youssou
N'Dour, Neneh Cherry, Amedeo Minghi, etc. are true legends!
I cannot imagine my life without music.
Even one of the most famous German philosophers
Friedrich Nietzsche said, "Without music, life would be
a mistake. In music the passions enjoy themselves."
He also said, "Art is the proper task of
life." I absolutely agree with him.
Art definitely makes our world a much better
place to live, especially music.

A. THOREAU
I can see that you love music a lot. I also love music
and cannot imagine my life without music.
I agree that your favorite musicians are wonderful artists.
As H. D. Thoreau says, "The Artist is he who detects
and applies the law from observation of the works
of Genius, whether of man or Nature."

BECKY
That is true. I definitely agree with that excellent statement.

BECKY (CONT'D)
You know, I also like paintings. There are so many great painters.
I can actually draw a little. I have taught myself how to draw.
It is not that hard.

Aaron smiles.

A. THOREAU

Becky, I know that it is not hard to draw or paint.
Once Mavrodi said that "You can be taught
how to paint very easily, and you
can actually paint very well. You do not need
to have a talent for that. Trust me,
I know what I am talking about. I went to an art
school, and I was taught how to paint."

BECKY

Unfortunately, not all great people live a happy life.
Many of them are lonely and very unhappy.
I am not sure why. It is very sad.

A. THOREAU

You know, a lot of people consider Mavrodi a Genius
because he is extremely smart and creative.
This is what he said regarding being a Genius: "It is very
boring to be a Genius. It is a curse, it is not a blessing. To be a
Genius is to have eternal loneliness; nothing is interesting."

BECKY

Well, maybe that statement explains why so
many great people are unhappy.

A. THOREAU

Mavrodi also said, "I am not a Genius; I am the only one."
Well, I think to be a Genius and to be the
only one is almost the same thing.

BECKY

I agree with that.

A. THOREAU

By the way, you should know what Nietzsche said about art,
"Art is not merely an imitation of the reality of nature, but in

truth, a metaphysical supplement to the reality of nature." I
think art is part of nature; it cannot exist without nature.

BECKY
Well, nature is definitely the best friend of art.
Many artists are inspired by nature.
As you know, nature inspired my favorite Transcendentalist
philosopher H. D. Thoreau to write *Walden* or *Life in the
Woods* – one of the greatest books in the history of humanity.
Nature also helped him a lot in his spiritual journey.

BECKY (CONT'D)
I wonder if the first draft of that book is as great as the final draft.
I think it would be interesting to read the first draft of that book.

A. THOREAU
You know, once Mavrodi said an interesting thing about
authors and their books. This is what he said: "Regarding
authors, I would like to provide an advice. Please do not read
any drafts of a book except for the final, finished book.
Sometimes when you read an unfinished draft of a
wonderful book, that book does not appear as wonderful
as before. You may be disappointed in that book."

Aaron smiles.

A. THOREAU (CONT'D)
By the way, one day I will definitely do what H. D. Thoreau did.
One day I will fully become part of nature.

Rebecca decides to change the subject of their conversation.

BECKY
You know, Aaron, I cannot understand the people
who hurt others without a reason.
I just do not understand how it is possible to enjoy
when somebody else is in pain.

It is so terrible!
Our life is so unfair! There are so many evil
people who mistreat good people.

A. THOREAU

Rebecca, you are a person with a pure soul.
That is why, it is so difficult for you
to live in this world.
Trust me, it is not so hard for other people.
They are very similar to each other.
That is why they do not care.
However, for people like us,
it is not easy to get used to this life.
However, we should get used to this,
otherwise we will lose, and it will not be fair.
We should always try to win, and life should never break us.
I am sure you understand what I mean...

BECKY

I understand you very well, Aaron.

A. THOREAU

Becky, we must always fight against evil and injustice.
We must fight against indecent and dishonest people.
This is what Mavrodi says about evil and
injustice: "If someone treats you unfairly;
if someone disrespects you, degrades you, and humiliates you;
if someone insults your honor and dignity – you must fight
against that person. You must fight in order to protect your
honor and dignity. You must do whatever it takes to protect
your honor and dignity." I absolutely agree with Mavrodi!

A. THOREAU (CONT'D)

Becky, please call me whenever you can.
We will definitely have many common subjects for a conversation.
We have a lot in common.
We will have an interesting and mutually beneficial conversation.

I think we will find many interesting issues to discuss.

BECKY

Okay, can I call you this Saturday after 2:00 PM?
Are you busy this Saturday after 2:00 PM?

A. THOREAU

Of course, I am not busy.
I will be free after 2:00 PM.

BECKY

Okay, I will call you this Saturday after 2:00 PM.
I look forward to talking to you on the phone.

A. THOREAU

I look forward to our first telephone conversation too.

Aaron smiles.

A. THOREAU (CONT'D)

I am sure it will not be our last telephone conversation.

Rebecca smiles too.

BECKY

I think so too.

CHAPTER 6

THE TEST OF TIME CONTINUED

November 28, 2008: Friday Night

Rebecca and Aaron meet online.

BECKY
Hi, how are you?
I did not expect to see you online now.
For some reason, I cannot fall asleep.
Why don't you sleep?

A. THOREAU
I cannot fall asleep too, and I do not know why.
How are you?

BECKY
I am not so good.

A. THOREAU
Why? Did something happen again?

BECKY
No, nothing new happened.
I am just thinking about the old events.
Whenever I think about everything
that happened to me, I get very upset and frustrated.
I get so depressed.
I cannot even sleep because of that.

A. THOREAU
Well, do not get upset any more.
You should be happy now.
You should start enjoying your life.
You should enjoy every minute of your life, and
you should be happy that you are alive.

A. THOREAU (CONT'D)
Becky, please forget everything bad that
had happened to you in the past.
I really like what Sergey Mavrodi, a Russian businessman,
said about the past: "For me, the past does not exist. I never
remember anything, and I never regret anything. Whatever
happened, happened. Why should we think about the past?
You must always go forward and not think about the past."
That is an excellent statement! A person must live
in the present and think about the future.

BECKY
As always, thank you for your support.
I will try to forget Jeff and what he did to me.
I know that H. D. Thoreau said, "You must live in the present,
launch yourself on every wave, find your eternity in each moment."

A. THOREAU
Even the greatest British crime writer Agatha Christie once
said, "I like living. I have sometimes been wildly, despairingly,
acutely miserable, racked with sorrow, but through it all, I still
know quite certainly that just to be alive is a grand thing."

A. THOREAU (CONT'D)
You know, I lost a lot of very important people in my life.
However, you have to think about the future.
You should continue living and enjoy every minute
of your life while you are alive.
You never know what will happen tomorrow.
Please try to forget everything bad that happened

in the past, and think about the future.

A. THOREAU (CONT'D)
You should forget Jeff. Please try to forget what happened.
Now you have me in your life, and I will
always protect you from evil.
As Agatha Christie says, "Evil is not something
superhuman, it is something less than human." Together
we will fight against evil, and we will win. I promise.

I also like how she says, "There is too much
tendency to attribute to God the evils that man
does of his own free will." This is so true...

A. THOREAU (CONT'D)
I will go to sleep now and try to fall
asleep. You should do the same.
I will be waiting for your call tomorrow.
Have a good night, and have a
wonderful day tomorrow.

BECKY
Thank you again for everything!
I really appreciate all your support; you are helping me a lot.
I will definitely call you tomorrow.
Have a good night!

A. THOREAU
Have a good night!

CHAPTER 7

TELEPHONE CONVERSATION

Next Day – Saturday Morning

It is 10:00 AM. Rebecca and Aaron meet online.

BECKY
Good morning, Aaron.
How are you?
What is new?

A. THOREAU
Good morning. Nothing is new.
Everything is the same.
I am just finishing some of my
work related matters.

A. THOREAU (CONT'D)
How are you?
How did you sleep last night?

BECKY
Everything is okay, thank you.

A. THOREAU
I just want to tell you that I am waiting for your call today.
Unfortunately, I need to go now.
Please call me whenever you want.

BECKY
Okay, I will call you today.

I will call you today after 2:00 PM.
I look forward to talking to you on the phone.

A. THOREAU
I look forward to talking to you too.

Same Day – Saturday Afternoon

It is 4:00 PM. Rebecca calls Aaron.

Rebecca's first telephone conversation with Aaron.

BECKY
Hi. Is this Aaron?

A. THOREAU
Hi. Yes, this is Aaron.

BECKY
This is Rebecca from the dating website.

A. THOREAU
Oh my God, Becky!
Hi my friend, how are you?

BECKY
I am good, thank you.
I hope my phone call did not interrupt you.
Can you talk now?

A. THOREAU
Of course, I can talk now.
Please remember, you never interrupt me.
I have been waiting for your call…
I actually expected you to call earlier.
I have been waiting for your call since 2:00 PM.

BECKY

I am sorry; I just felt a little uncomfortable to call you.
I know that you are very busy with your work.

Aaron smiles.

A. THOREAU

Becky, please never feel uncomfortable to call me.
You can call me any time you want.
Please do not be shy.
You will never interrupt me.
When you call me, I will be free for you.

Rebecca smiles.

BECKY

Okay, Aaron.
Thank you; I will not be shy.
You are so nice and polite.

A. THOREAU

Thank you, Becky.
So, how is your day going so far?

BECKY

My day is going well.
I was actually looking forward to speaking with you.
I wanted to talk to you on the phone so badly.
I wanted to hear your voice, and finally, I can hear your voice.

BECKY (CONT'D)

You have a very beautiful and extraordinary voice.
I have never met anyone with such a beautiful voice.
I have never heard such a beautiful voice before.
It is just a pleasure to hear your voice.
I will not be surprised if you can sing too.

Aaron smiles.

A. THOREAU
Thank you very much, Becky.
No, I cannot sing.

A. THOREAU (CONT'D)
So, how are you today?
How is everything?
I hope everything is okay.

BECKY
Well, I am good except for a few things that bother me.
I think that I told you about all my
frustrations and disappointments.
We have talked online and on the phone for so many months…
You know, unfortunately, nobody understands me.
I know that I told you this before… I do not
drink, and I do not go to night clubs.
I like reading books, especially philosophy books.
I also enjoy helping people. I volunteer in
the center for immigrant services.
I teach English as a Second Language. I really like helping people.

BECKY (CONT'D)
I just have a lot of difficulty finding the
people who would understand me.
I just think that nobody understands me, and
nobody likes me because I am different.
I do not like to do the things that the majority of young people do.
I do not think like the majority of young people think.
I do not believe in the things that the
majority of young people believe.
I live according to certain moral standards and
life principles, and I will never change.
I cannot change myself just because
somebody else wants me to change.

I believe that a person should always be who he/she really is.
A person should never try to be someone else.

Aaron smiles.

A. THOREAU
Well, if you like to read books, it will be very
difficult for you to find friends.
I can definitely understand why it is so difficult for you
to find those who would understand you.
The majority of young people today do not
spend their free time reading books.
You are a very young, intelligent, well-rounded,
interesting, and highly educated person, and you
were properly raised by your parents.
You are very mature and serious at such a young age.

A. THOREAU (CONT'D)
Becky, I like your life principles a lot.
I know I told you this many times…
You must never change yourself and your life principles.
You must always stay yourself regardless of life circumstances.
It is wonderful that you have stayed yourself despite everything.
A person must never pretend to be someone else.

A. THOREAU (CONT'D)
I think that every person is responsible for creating his or her life.
We determine our life by the choices and decisions that we make.
Some people decide to be good, and some people decide to be evil.
As Sergey Mavrodi says, "There is no destiny or predetermination.
You determine your destiny by every moment of life, by your
thoughts and feelings, by your hope and desperation, by pain and
fear, by joy, misery, and love. You and only you can determine
your destiny because you are a human being. No one can
determine your destiny for you. A person is the owner of his or her

destiny. A person always makes his or her choice. You can always stay a virtuous human being, regardless of life circumstances."

BECKY
Thank you very much for understanding, Aaron.
You know, I wanted to find an honest and decent person.
I was interested in having a serious relationship.
I just wanted to have a family and be happy.
I wanted to have children and enjoy my life.
However, I met Jeff, that guy from NY.
I thought that he was honest. I thought that he was a good person.
He disappointed me so bad. He devastated my soul.
He used to tell me all these wonderful things, and then...
Oh my God! I do not even want to remember what he did to me.
However, I know these terrible memories
will always stay in my heart.
Because of him, I could not even go to work for several days.
I was so upset and so shocked.
I wanted to cry all the time. I was so depressed.
I am still very afraid to trust someone again.

A. THOREAU
I know that you have been hurt by that guy.
What he did to you is just terrible!
You know, if you want, we can definitely find him and...

A. THOREAU (CONT'D)
Please tell me something.
Did you like him? Did you like that guy?
Why did you agree to meet him in real life?

BECKY
Well, he just seemed very nice.
I liked the things that he told me.
I thought that he was a very good person.
Also, I was very tired of being alone.
I was so lonely, and that made me very upset.

I just wanted to meet a nice guy, and
I thought that Jeff was that nice guy.
At first, he was very nice with me.
We had known each other for almost one month.
However, you know what he did…

BECKY (CONT'D)
To be honest, I never really liked anybody a lot.
I never loved anybody.
I just thought maybe it could work out between me and Jeff.
You know, I was interested in a serious relationship.

A. THOREAU
Becky, I know that you are a very honest and decent girl.
I told you this many times…
Our life is very unfair, and sometimes good people suffer.
I was betrayed by a lot of people, and
many people disappointed me.
I can tell you one interesting story that happened in my life.
You know, some people like to pretend to
be innocent and kind-hearted;
however, they are not like that in reality.
Once I tried to help a girl, but that girl tried to kill me.
She had a gun, and she shot me with it. I barely survived.

BECKY
Oh my God! You were shot with a gun!
You could have died!

A. THOREAU
I know, it was a miracle that I survived.
Unfortunately, our life is like this –
you try to help someone, and that person can kill you.
You know, nothing surprises me in this life anymore.

BECKY
Yes, our life is very unfair.

Sometimes we suffer because we either
help someone or trust someone.
Should we even have trust in someone?
It is just so hard to trust someone after
being disappointed so many times.
Sometimes I feel that good people will lose
in the end, and evil will win.

A. THOREAU
Becky, I know our life can be very frustrating and very unfair.
However, we should not lose hope, and we must
continue to fight against evil and injustice.
We just need to find the right people and be with the right people.

A. THOREAU (CONT'D)
We have to be strong; we must not break.
Life should not break us!
We must win despite all the evil and injustice!
As Mavrodi once said, "I will not give in; I will not give up, and
I will not break."
That is a great statement!

A. THOREAU (CONT'D)
We should definitely try to find the right people, and
we must be with the right people.
We must fight against evil and injustice until the very end!

Rebecca smiles.

BECKY
I think I found one right person in my life.

Aaron smiles too.

A. THOREAU
Thank you, Becky.
I think I found one right person in my life too.

A. THOREAU (CONT'D)

Please do not be upset about anything.
You have me in your life now...
Although our life is very unfair, we must continue
fighting against evil and injustice.
Please remember, all the greatest people in the world feel sadness.
I would like to read you a wonderful poem by Sergey Mavrodi.
It is about our life being unfair.

This is the English translation of that poem:

"There was a time when I had dreams,
When I wanted something in this life.
Why did my dreams disappear?
Why did I find nothingness?
It is like falling leaves.
It is like dropping rain.
We will not remember those who are left behind.
We will not remember those who are tired.
Faces, tears, smiles.
They are going somewhere.
They are melting down.
I forgive the mistakes, but it is too late.
Beautiful rivers turn into muddy puddles.
Light turns into darkness.
I remember the days...
But my life path is getting shorter and shorter, and
The river water is getting darker and darker.
Inside my heart, it is cold and sad.
Inside my soul, it is cold and sad.
And it is getting worse and worse every day.
There was a time when I had dreams,
When I wanted something.
Why did my dreams disappear?
Why did I find nothingness?"

Two Weeks Later

Aaron and Rebecca are talking online.

A. THOREAU
Hi. How are you?

BECKY
Hi. I am good.
What about you?

A. THOREAU
I am good too. I am sorry about yesterday.
There was a second line calling me.
I had to talk to my relatives from Europe.
Please call me again whenever you can.

BECKY
Do you have any relatives in the United States?

A. THOREAU
No, I do not have any relatives here.
All my relatives betrayed me and my mother.
I will tell you this story one day...

BECKY
I am sorry to hear that.
Do you have any relatives in Europe?

A. THOREAU
My mom has some relatives in Ukraine;
however, I have not seen them for about 30 years.
One day you will now why.

BECKY
Okay, Aaron.
You can tell me everything when you think it is

the right time for me to know.

BECKY (CONT'D)
I will call you tonight.
How are you today?
What is going on?

A. THOREAU
Not much. What about you?
Will you call me today?

BECKY
Yes, I will call you today at 9:00 PM, as always.

A. THOREAU
At 9:00 PM. Okay, I will be waiting for your call.

BECKY
By the way, I will never forget our first telephone conversation.
We talked to each other for almost four hours the very first time.
I have never talked to anybody for so long.

Aaron smiles.

A. THOREAU
I know, we always talk for so many hours on the phone.
We always have very long and interesting conversations.
My phone battery can last up to seven hours.

Rebecca smiles.

BECKY
Sometimes I think even seven hours will not be enough.
I remember the day when we talked to each other for seven hours,
and it was still not enough.

Aaron smiles again.

A. THOREAU
What can we do?
Two very interesting and extraordinary people met,
and they always want to talk to each other.

Rebecca smiles again.

BECKY
Yes, that is true.

CHAPTER 8

NO MORE DOUBT

Two Weeks Later

Aaron went to New York for several days. Rebecca
and Aaron meet online.

A. THOREAU
Hi. How are you?
Why don't you call me?

BECKY
Hi. You said that you went to visit your friends in NY.
You must be with your friends now.

A. THOREAU
I am alone now.
My friends decided to go to a bar.
They invited me to go with them, but I told you that
I do not like bars because I do not drink.
It is better for me to be alone than with them in the bar.

A. THOREAU (CONT'D)
Nobody understands me because I do not drink.
At bars, I always have conflicts with others who
get drunk and start making fun of me.

BECKY
I absolutely agree with you.
If you do not drink and
do not like being around drunk people,

it is better for you to stay at home.

A. THOREAU
You and my friend-doctor that I told you about
say the same thing.
Only you and my friend understand me
regarding drinking alcohol.
You know, it is good that you exist in this world.
I am very happy that I met you, and that
you are my friend now.
Do you know how wonderful it is to talk to people
who understand you?
I think it is the best thing in the world.

BECKY
Thank you very much, Aaron!
I am very happy that I met you too,
and that you understand me so well.

BECKY (CONT'D)
I want to ask you something.
How many days a week did you work in NY
when you were a property manager?

A. THOREAU
I worked 24/7.
I was supposed to answer the phone 24/7.
Sometimes they called me at night;
there were a lot of nights that I did not sleep.
Once they called me on Saturday when I
was in a different state, and they asked me to
come back to NY and fix a plumbing issue.
I was with my ex-girlfriend from Colombia,
and I had to come back to NY and go to work.
I always tried to make the tenants happy.

BECKY

I can imagine how happy and lucky your
tenants were.
I wish you were our condominium
property manager. I would be so happy.
You would be able to fix all our problems.
I always have conflicts with my property manager.
I had a bad experience with him again last week.
It is extremely cold in my apartment in wintertime.
I know I told you this.
I am so unhappy with our property manager
and condominium management.
The property manager does not do anything.
I see him drunk with his friends all the time.
Instead of working, he is drinking with his friends,
and he mistreats all the tenants.
He is very rude and unprofessional.
He does not even want to listen to the problems
that his tenants have.
I really wish you worked instead of him…

A. THOREAU

Becky, as I said before, we can
definitely fix your heating issue.
You should find an appropriate agency,
which handles tenant issues and file a complaint.
If the agency finds that the inside temperature
in your apartment is unacceptable, they will
make the management adjust the temperature.
There should be an agency like that in every state.

BECKY

Okay, as always, thank you very much
for the advice.
I will try to find that agency…

BECKY (CONT'D)
How many people worked in your
company in NY?
I hope you were not the only one.

A. THOREAU
There were other managers; however,
they did not work as hard as I did.
I always worked more than others did.
Even my manager's son, Brian, was always
jealous because his father liked me a lot.

A. THOREAU (CONT'D)
You know, I used to play the table tennis with
Brian, and I always won.
No matter how hard Brian tried, he could never win.
I could feel that he was always jealous of me
because I did everything better than him.
Brian's father knew that, and he appreciated me a lot.

Aaron smiles

A. THOREAU (CONT'D)
Once I even went to a restroom and practiced
some boxing before playing the table tennis
with Brian.
For me it was like a boxing match.
I remember Brian almost won that day;
however, he still couldn't beat me.
I won that day, and he was very upset.

BECKY
Wow! It looks like you had a lot of fun at your
previous company working as a property manager.

A. THOREAU
Yes, we had a lot of good time there.

We often had barbeques outdoors.
My mom and my ex-girlfriend used to
come to these outdoors events.
I will send you some pictures.

Next Day

Aaron sends Rebecca more pictures.

BECKY
Hi Aaron, thank you for the pictures.
Who is that beautiful girl in the pictures?

A. THOREAU
She is a daughter of one of my close friends.
You can see him in one of the pictures.

BECKY
By the way, your Colombian ex-girlfriend
is very beautiful.

Aaron smiles.

A. THOREAU
Becky, you are more beautiful than she is.

Rebecca decides to change the subject of their conversation.

BECKY
By the way, I watched the
boxing tournament yesterday.
You were correct about the results.
You are very good at predictions.

A. THOREAU
Well, good for you.
The boxing tournament did end the way I predicted.

Vladimir Klichko TKO Hasim Rahman in round seven.
TKO means Technical Knockout.

A. THOREAU (CONT'D)
I am being told for a long time that I should bet on
boxing before tournaments and championships start.
I have not done that yet.
However, now I am thinking that I could try to do that.
I have been watching boxing tournaments for 20 years.
I have seen many boxing matches,
and I have seen the best and strongest boxers in the world.
I think I was wrong three or four times in my predictions;
I cannot remember exactly.
I did not make a mistake in all the other predictions.

A. THOREAU (CONT'D)
If I see how one boxer fights and
how another boxer fights,
I can be 99% sure who will win.
If I was betting on boxing all those years,
I would not need to work at all.
What do you think about that?
We can try to bet on boxing together.
It does not take a lot to try.

BECKY
Aaron, do I need to have money in order to bet?
I cannot really afford that right now.
I do not have an opportunity...

A. THOREAU
What opportunity are you talking about?
I will do everything myself.
If we win, we will divide the money 50/50.

BECKY
Should I give you any money?

A. THOREAU
No, you should not give me anything.
It will be a pleasure, if we win, to
divide the money between you and me.
You will be my spiritual mentor.

A. THOREAU (CONT'D)
You will use your intuition and spirituality
to help me win.
Everything else is my responsibility.

BECKY
Aaron, to be honest, I am confused…
It will not be fair if I do not do anything,
and you give me one half of what you win.

A. THOREAU
Do you think that being a spiritual mentor is nothing?
Do you think that it does not mean anything to me?
It means a lot to me!
I think it is one of the most important things.
Trust me, it means much more than money.

A. THOREAU (CONT'D)
For me it means more than even putting down
all the money that you have.
I have already had a lot of people offer me money
for betting on boxing.

A. THOREAU (CONT'D)
Let us do it.

BECKY
OK, thank you! I just really want to help you.

A. THOREAU
You are helping me because you are talking to me.

You have been helping me for a long time already.

BECKY
Aaron, it is always a pleasure to talk to you.
You are helping me a lot too.
The conversations that we have are so helpful.

BECKY (CONT'D)
By the way, what other sports do you like
except for boxing?

A. THOREAU
I like to play and watch football and hockey in
addition to boxing.
You know, my day starts with sports news.
Every morning when I wake up,
the first thing that I do is read the sports news on sports websites.

BECKY
Do you like to watch TV?

A. THOREAU
To be honest, I do not really like watching TV.
By the way, Mavrodi does not like to watch TV too.
He once said, "I do not watch TV, even
the TV programs about me."

BECKY
I agree; there is nothing interesting to watch on TV these days.
Unfortunately, there are very few good movies on TV, and
it is very hard to find them.

BECKY (CONT'D)
By the way, I think that today there is a hockey game
between Czech Republic and Canada.
However, the game will be very late on TV.
You will probably be sleeping.

A. THOREAU

I remember Czech hockey players from
the time when their captain was Ivan Hlinka.
Hlinka was a wonderful ice hockey player and coach.
Czech Republic and Canada have been competitors
for a long time.
I have a feeling that Canada will win.
It will be an interesting game to watch.

A. THOREAU (CONT'D)

At what time does the game start?
Can you please tell me?

BECKY

Yes, of course.
I think it starts at 12:00 AM.

A. THOREAU

Thank you, I will try to watch it.
I go to sleep late anyway.

BECKY

How late do you go to sleep and
when do you wake up?

A. THOREAU

It depends on my mood when I go to sleep.
Sometimes I cannot sleep the whole night…
I usually go to sleep late; however,
I wake up very early, at 5:00 AM.
I like to run in the morning because it gives
me a lot of energy for the day.
As H. D. Thoreau says, "An early-morning
walk is a blessing for the whole day."

BECKY

Wow! To be honest, I do not like to wake up early in the morning.

I wish I could sleep until 10:00 or 11:00 AM in the morning.

Aaron smiles.

A. THOREAU
I Like to wake up early. As H. D. Thoreau
says, "To be awake is to be alive."
By the way, Sergey Mavrodi sleeps very little.
He sleeps from 6:00 AM to 10:00 AM in the morning
and from 6:00 PM to 10:00 PM in the evening.
Mavrodi does not sleep at night at all.
He has lived like this almost all of his life.
Mavrodi started to sleep like this when he was in school.

BECKY
Wow! That is amazing!

Aaron smiles again.

A. THOREAU
Great people do not like to sleep a lot.

A. THOREAU (CONT'D)
By the way, I try to run every morning.
I run even when it is cold outside.

BECKY
You must love sports a lot.
I am sure tomorrow you will tell me
a lot of interesting stories related to sports.
I am going to sleep now. Let us talk tomorrow...

A. THOREAU
OK. Let us talk tomorrow.

Next Day

Rebecca and Aaron talk online.

BECKY

Hi Aaron. I have been thinking about you and
everything we talked about.
I feel so good when I talk to you.
You cannot even imagine how happy
I am that I met you.
I almost forgot all the terrible events
that happened in my life.
I almost forgot all the horrendous things that
happened to me.
You are definitely one of the best people in the world!

BECKY (CONT'D)

I am so sorry that I ever doubted
you and your honesty.
I feel so bad now because I did not trust you
in the beginning.
Now I know for sure that you will never hurt me.
You are just incapable of doing anything bad.
You are too wonderful!
You have become a special person in my life.
I am so attached to you. I cannot even imagine
living a day without talking to you on the phone.
I want to see you in real life so badly, but you know
my parents say that we need more time...

BECKY (CONT'D)

I was always honest with you.
I never lied to you.
I am sorry that I cannot meet you at this time.
I just need more time...

A. THOREAU
I know that you are honest with me, and that
you have always been honest with me.
I can feel that, and I can feel you.
Time is not an issue for me.
As I said before, take your time.
Take as much time as you need before you
are ready to meet with me in real life.
All the time is yours.

BECKY
Aaron, I am so happy that I met you.
You have helped me so much.
You are indeed helping me a lot
just by talking to me.

A. THOREAU
Well, that is just wonderful.
I will always be doing that with
a great pleasure.

BECKY
I will call you tonight.

A. THOREAU
Thank you, I will be waiting for your call.

Two Weeks Later

Rebecca and Aaron meet online.

BECKY
Hi Aaron.
Now I understand very well
why you do not trust anybody, especially women.
You are such a wonderful person!

It is almost unrealistic for you to find someone
who could attract you.
I believe that in addition to physical attraction,
there should be emotional attachment too.

BECKY (CONT'D)
You are so different; you are so unlike anybody else!
You are not only a very handsome person,
you also have a very beautiful soul.
Your inner world is what makes you
so unique, so amazing, and so wonderful.
You are so intelligent, and you know philosophy so well.
I have never talked to anybody like you.
Even my philosophy professors in college did not speak as you do.
Your inner world and your inner beauty is what sets
you apart from everybody else.
That is why it is so difficult for you to find the right person.
I always wanted to find a person who has inner beauty.

Aaron smiles.

A. THOREAU
Thank you, Becky.
As R. W. Emerson says, "He is great who is what he is
from nature, and who never reminds us of others. Insist
on yourself; never imitate. Your own gift you can present
every moment with the cumulative force of a whole
life's cultivation. Do that which is assigned to you."
I believe one should always be original. Every person should
be responsible for his or her actions and thoughts.
Becky, you are not like everybody else too,
and you are very intelligent as well.
We have the proper understanding of this world.

BECKY

One of the greatest Russian writers Fyodor Dostoevsky said,
"Beauty will save the world." I would like to rephrase this
statement and say, "Inner beauty and true love will save the world."

BECKY (CONT'D)

As I told you many times,
for me, the most important thing is a person's inner beauty.
I only care about what is inside.
I like people who are beautiful and wealthy inside.
I like those who have a rich inner world.
I do not care about the person's outer appearance.
I think the inner beauty is more important than the outer beauty.

A. THOREAU

Sometimes the inner beauty is more important
than the outer appearance of a person.
However, the outer appearance is also important.

BECKY

Aaron, you helped me forget all my bad experiences.
Because of you, I forgot everything bad that had
happened to me.
I will never forget what you did for me.
I will always remember all your help!

A. THOREAU

It is good that you understand all this.
Only very few people can understand this.
It did not take a long time for you to understand
everything.
Furthermore, you have all the qualities
which help me.
So we are equally helpful to each other.

Next Day

A. THOREAU
Hi. How are you?
Why don't you call me?

BECKY
I really want to call you,
but I do not want to bother you
or interrupt you from your work.
Are you not busy with your work now?

A. THOREAU
Becky, I told you this many times.
You never bother me, and you never interrupt me.
I am not busy; I have been free for a long time.
I want you to remember that I am always free for you.

A. THOREAU (CONT'D)
As I said, you can call me any time you want.
I am always free for you.
Please do not even ask if you can call me.

BECKY
Thank you very much for being so nice to me!

BECKY (CONT'D)
How are you, how is everything?
Are you still fighting against injustice?

A. THOREAU
Yes, of course.
We should fight until the end,
otherwise we will be lost.

BECKY
I know, I agree with you.

You always keep your spirits up.

A. THOREAU
Yes, I always keep my spirits up.
This is one of my life principles.
You too should always keep your spirits up,
and do not let anybody put you down.

BECKY
Good for you!
I agree that you should always try
to be positive.
Sometimes I get so upset because
there is so much injustice in the world.
Some people have everything and
live a very happy life; others have nothing.
So many people do not even have food to eat.
Our life is so unfair...

A. THOREAU
I know, Becky. I feel the same way.
When I see poor people on the streets,
I get very upset.
Whenever someone asks for money,
I always give them at least a dollar.

BECKY
Aaron, you are so generous.

A. THOREAU
Thank you, Becky.
I like helping people, and
I always do my best to help.

BECKY
It is wonderful that you like helping people.

Kristina Sarkisyan

A. THOREAU
When I was in NY, one of my friends was
having a very difficult time in his life.
His wife betrayed him; she left him because of
a wealthy man.
My friend became very depressed.
He started drinking, and he lost his job and home.
I invited him to live in my apartment
with me, my mother, and my ex-girlfriend.
He lived with us in Brooklyn, NY for one year until
he found a job and a new apartment to live in.
I remember my ex-girlfriend did not like the fact that
he was living with us.
However, I had to help my friend.

A. THOREAU (CONT'D)
I just cannot be a bystander when
I see suffering around me,
especially when that suffering affects
my friends and my family.

BECKY
Wow, Aaron! That is truly amazing!
I have never met such a kind-hearted person
as you are.
You are indeed not like everybody else.
I am so happy that I met you!

A. THOREAU
Thank you, Becky.
I told you that I am not like everybody else...
You are not like everybody else too,
and I am very happy that I have you in my life!

A. THOREAU (CONT'D)
Unfortunately, a lot of women are not loyal,
and I appreciate loyalty in women.

However, I can feel that you are different.
You are not like the majority of women.

BECKY
Yes, I am not like them.
Trust me, I will never betray you or
disappoint you otherwise.
I will do everything I can to make you happy.

A. THOREAU
You know, I start missing our
telephone conversations
if you do not call me one day.
I am used to you calling me every day.
Can you imagine that?

BECKY
I know... I start missing you so much
if I do not talk to you one day.

BECKY (CONT'D)
You know, Aaron, I am just afraid to bother you.
I can talk to you 24/7, and
I call you almost every day.
Sometimes I just think what if you are sleeping,
and I am calling you...
I will wake you up, and I do not want to bother you.

A. THOREAU
Becky, please stop saying that.
Please remember you never bother me.
I do not go to sleep early anyway
because I cannot fall asleep when it is early.
Please do not even say the word "bother" any more.

A. THOREAU (CONT'D)
I think we understand each other very well,

and we feel each other very well.
I am sure we can have a wonderful, long-term
relationship because we are meant to be together.
People like us, such extra-ordinary people,
should definitely be together.
We should do everything together – live a happy life,
realize our dreams, fight against evil and injustice,
and revenge against all our enemies.
I just feel that we can do many things together.

BECKY
Aaron, I have never talked to such a wonderful
and polite person.
You are treating me so well.
No one has ever treated me like this.
You understand me like nobody in my life.
Even my mother does not understand me
like you do.
I know, I told you this many times, but
I have never met anybody like you.
It is like a dream come true.
You are like a dream come true.
I am so happy.
I cannot even find the right words
to express my happiness.
I forgot what sadness and depression is.

BECKY (CONT'D)
I will be completely honest with you,
and I will say that there were times in my life
when I did not want to live...
However, now I am so happy that I am alive,
and I want to continue to live.
I want to continue my life because of you.

A. THOREAU
Well, this is wonderful.
I have never met anybody like you as well.
I have never talked to such a smart, young,
and very wonderful girl like you.
You have so much inner beauty.

A. THOREAU (CONT'D)
As I said before,
we must enjoy every minute of our life
while we are alive.
You never know what will happen tomorrow.
Take everything you can from this life.
Live your life to the fullest, and live your
life in the present moment.
This is one of the principles according to which I live.
As Mavrodi says, "I do not remember anything from my
childhood. I do not even have childhood pictures. For me,
the past does not exist. Life should always start from the very
beginning. Whatever happened cannot be brought back. Why
should we remember the past? We should always go forward."

BECKY
Thank you, Aaron.
I will try to live according to that life
principle too. I will try to forget the past.
Okay, I am going to sleep now.
Have a good night.

A. THOREAU
Have a good night too.
I am going to sleep now too.

Next Day (February 23, 2009)

There is a Holiday in Europe.

BECKY
Happy Holiday to you!
As always, I wish you all the best!
May all your dreams come true!
Good luck with everything you do!
You, more than anybody else,
deserve to be happy!

A. THOREAU
Thank you very much!
I would like to thank you and your parents for raising such a
wonderful, beautiful, kind-hearted, and intelligent daughter.
I would like to thank your grandparents for raising such a
wonderful and exceptionally good granddaughter. I wish you
and your family health, happiness, joy, peace, and prosperity. I
wish you and your family great success and excellent health.
Health is the most important thing.

A. THOREAU (CONT'D)
Becky, I am sure you will be happy.
You should definitely be happy.
Let all the bad things that
happened to you stay in the past.
You deserve to be happy too!

BECKY
Thank you very much!
I am so lucky that I met you.

A. THOREAU
Believe me, everything will be okay.
I can say that I am also very fortunate
because I met you.

I feel very lucky too.

A. THOREAU (CONT'D)
Becky, could you please write
the name of the band that sings the song
from the movie called "The Sandpit Generals?"

Rebecca writes the name of the band and the
website where Aaron can listen to that song.

Next Day

Rebecca and Aaron talk online.

BECKY
Aaron, I want to tell you something.
Ever since I have met you on this website,
my life has become like a fairy tale.
I not only forgot all the bad things that happened
to me, I cannot even think negatively any more.
I am not depressed any more.
I forgot what depression is.

BECKY (CONT'D)
You helped me so much; you cannot even imagine how
much you helped me.
When I think about you, I smile.
You are the only person who can make me
smile and laugh.
You are part of me now; you are the meaning of my life.
I cannot even imagine my life without you.
I keep asking the same question repeatedly:
How could I exist all these years without knowing you?

BECKY (CONT'D)
Thank you for your being!

Thank you for your existence in this world!
I enjoy every second of my life now.
Before, there were times when life did not make
any sense to me,
when I did not really want to continue my life
because it was so dull, boring, and depressing.
You brought the light into my dark life.
I could never imagine that this dating website
would give me such a present.
I still cannot believe that I met you on the website.
I feel so bad now that I did not trust you at first.
I am so sorry for not trusting you!
Aaron, you are a gift from God!
You are the best! You are indeed number one.
You are my number one!
I thank God every day for your existence and
for meeting you.

BECKY (CONT'D)
Aaron, I do not want to lose you.
I do not know what I will do if I lose you.
I cannot live without you.
You are part of me now.
I have become so attached to you...
I will do anything and everything in order not to lose you.

A. THOREAU
Becky, my dear, you are shocking me
with your messages.
This website gave me a wonderful present too.
To be honest, no one has ever felt me and
understood me like you do.
Thank you for being in this world, and
thank you for being in my life!

A. THOREAU (CONT'D)
Becky, you will never lose me.
I will always be with you, and
I will always be there for you.
Please do not worry about anything.

BECKY
Aaron, I want to tell you something.
Sometimes the bad memories from the past bother me,
and I am afraid that those evil people will ruin my happiness.

A. THOREAU
Well, this is not good.
You should start forgetting all your bad memories.
You should live and be happy that you are alive.
As I said before many times,
You should enjoy every second of your life
because you never know what will happen tomorrow.
There is too much uncertainty in life.
Try to take everything you can from life and
please be yourself.
I told you this many times too.
Nobody will hurt you now,
you have me in your life.

A. THOREAU (CONT'D)
As you know, bad things happen in life,
but eventually all bad things come to an end.
Maybe your bad experience was just a life test
which you had to pass before finding your
true happiness.
Please think about it.

Next Day

Rebecca and Aaron meet online.

A. THOREAU
Hello, how are you?
How did you sleep last night?

BECKY
Hi, I am wonderful. I slept great!
How can I be not wonderful
after meeting you?

BECKY (CONT'D)
Oh my God, what happened to your profile picture?
Why did you post H. D. Thoreau instead of you?

A. THOREAU
Please tell me whom you think
I should have posted.
I think H. D. Thoreau fits my profile very well.
He was a very intelligent, fearless, and free-spirited man.
He fought against injustice, and he had strong beliefs.
He was not even afraid to resist the government.
He emphasized simple living in natural surroundings,
and he always stayed true to himself and his ideas,
in every situation that he encountered in life.
By the way, I have H. D. Thoreau's picture in my home office.

Rebecca smiles.

BECKY
Now I understand why you decided to live in New Hampshire.
H. D. Thoreau was a famous tax-resister in addition to his talents.
He was even jailed for not paying his taxes.
By the way, Sergey Mavrodi was arrested for tax evasion too.

I know that New Hampshire does not
have taxes. It is a tax-free state.

A. THOREAU
I decided to live in New Hampshire because it is a very beautiful,
quiet, and peaceful state.
I love the nature in NH and wilderness.
My dream is to build a small house in the
mountains, in the White Mountains in NH,
and live there surrounded by the beautiful
NH nature and with wild animals.
I would love to feed those wild animals.
As H. D. Thoreau says, "In wilderness is
the preservation of the world."
I also absolutely agree with Charles Lindbergh, an American
author and inventor, "In wilderness I sense the miracle of life,
and behind it our scientific accomplishments fade to trivia."

BECKY
Would you not be afraid to live there?

A. THOREAU
No, I am not afraid of animals.
By the way, one of my favorite places
in the US is the park in Colorado,
where you can drive and see the
different animals around you.

BECKY
Wow! You are very brave and fearless.
I wish I were like you...

A. THOREAU
Well, you should not be afraid
of anything too.
You have me now. That is all
that you need in your life.

I will protect you; I promise.

BECKY
Aaron, thank you so much for everything!
I really like all your worldviews and life principles.
You are a very interesting and extraordinary person.
I know I told you this before; you are not like everybody else.
I think people like you are very rare these days.
I have never heard anyone speak like you.
I have never seen anyone write like you.

Aaron smiles.

A. THOREAU
Well, as H. D. Thoreau says, "if you can speak
what you will never hear, if you can write what you
will never read, you have done rare things."

Rebecca smiles too.

BECKY
I absolutely agree with that statement.

A. THOREAU
I am sorry; I need to go now.
I hope to talk to you this evening.
Please call me whenever you want.

Next Day

Rebecca and Aaron meet online.

BECKY
Hi. How are you?

A. THOREAU
I am good. How are you?
How did you sleep last night?

BECKY
Everything is great, thank you!
Did you see that the website moderators had blocked
your picture of H. D. Thoreau?

A. THOREAU
They did not allow the photo to stay there
for a long time.
The website moderators aggravated me.
Oh well, what can you do?
Next time, it will be better if they block
their limited minds which cannot think freely.

Rebecca laughs.

BECKY
Please do not be upset because of that.
They blocked the photo of H. D. Thoreau because
It is a requirement of the website not to post
pictures of famous people.
If you post H. D. Thoreau's picture again, they will block it again.

A. THOREAU
Well, they can block H. D. Thoreau's picture
as many times as they want.
When the Russian government tried to
block Mavrodi's website, and when
some people wrote offensive comments about him on his website,
Mavrodi said, "They can write whatever they want.
They can comfort their fears and insecurities."
You know, many people insult Mavrodi because
they are jealous of his intelligence.
They all know that they will never be like him.

Sergey Mavrodi is a very smart and talented
person, and he is famous all over the world!
The level of his intelligence is very high, and
he proved it with real life actions.
So many people are jealous of him.
However, a lot of people like him and support him.
By the way, when a man wrote an insulting statement about
a girl who supported Mavrodi, he did not like that at all.
This is how Mavrodi responded to that man: "Please do not
offend ladies on my website. You can write whatever you
want about me, but do not insult females. If you want your
comments to be published on this website in the future, do
not offend females. I hope we understood each other."
Another person who insulted a different girl also received
a wonderful response. This is what Mavrodi said: "If you
cannot use appropriate language, then you cannot write
comments on my website. This will be our last meeting
here. We will never meet on this website again. I am
sorry, but you must not write your comments here."

BECKY
Wow! That was very nice of him!

A. THOREAU
Yes, Mavrodi always defends females on his website.
I think that he has a beautiful soul and a kind heart.
By the way, I believe that a person should prove
everything with actions, not words.
In addition, a person should always take responsibility
for the decisions that he or she makes.
As Mavrodi says, "Making decisions is
taking responsibility for them."

A. THOREAU (CONT'D)
Regarding what they did to H. D. Thoreau's picture,
this reminds me a dictatorship.

This reminds me the country where I had lived before
I moved to the United States.
There is no democracy on this website too.

BECKY
Did you live in a dictatorship?
Was it really bad in your country?

A. THOREAU
You know, there is a very interesting interview of Sergey
Mavrodi that appears in his book *Prison Diaries, or Letters
to My Wife.* This is what he said about government in
1994 when he was arrested by the Russian police:

"The government has been stealing money for centuries, and they
were never punished for that. However, when they unexpectedly
met with resistance, they did not like it. They were very angry
and upset. Unfortunately, such concepts as honor, honesty,
dignity, integrity, conscience, and responsibility do not exist for
the government. These concepts died a long time ago. It is very
difficult for the government officials to even imagine that someone
could go to jail for his beliefs and life principles. That is why,
they always try to find some evil intentions in my actions. I just
cannot stay indifferent when the government is stealing the money
of poor, defenseless, and unprotected people. The government
officials do not understand that I am fighting not for my money
but for the money of my investors. I am trying to protect the
interests of my investors. That is why, I am in jail now. However,
I will not give in, and I will not break. I do not regret anything
I have done, and I have no remorse over my decisions. If I could
start everything from the beginning, I would do the same thing."

A. THOREAU (CONT'D)
Mavrodi also said, "There was a time
when I believed in democracy.

My only fault is that I believed that nothing bad
could happen to me since I did not violate the law. I
did not violate even one paragraph of the law."
In addition, he said, "In this country, I am an outlaw.
I am a person who is excluded from the protection
of the law. The government can do to me whatever
they want, and the law does not protect me."

BECKY
What happened to Mavrodi?
Why was he arrested?

A. THOREAU
Sergey Mavrodi was the president of MMM
company, a financial pyramid.
By the way, "MMM" stands for "We Can Do A Lot."
In 1994, the Russian government closed the
offices of MMM for tax evasion.
Later the government officials accused
Mavrodi of deceiving his investors.
However, I do not believe that it was his fault.
Mavrodi did not violate the law.
Financial pyramids are not prohibited by law in Russia.
In addition, why should a person pay taxes to the
government if it is a financial pyramid?
I do not think that Mavrodi was supposed
to pay taxes to the government!
In the case of MMM, I believe that the government
destroyed the pyramid because they did not like the
fact that Mavrodi was very popular and powerful.
Mavrodi could even become the president of
Russia because a lot of people really liked him.
However, he was arrested and put in jail.
This is what Mavrodi said about his arrest: "The government
officials thought that in a couple of months, there would
be nothing, no government and no president. Only Sergey

Panteleevich Mavrodi would stay. These are not my words; these are the words of the police interrogators."

This is what he said about the Russian Government: "The government officials are omnipotent and omnipresent. If they do not like you, they can destroy you in seconds. If you disagree with the government, and if you do not like them, you will end up in jail. Power is temptation. A human being is weak. The government officials have so much, but they always want more. They have an enormous amount of power and money, but they always want more." "To be honest, I would not want to be the president. However, If I became the president of Russia, I would find replacement for all government officials. I would do that the very first second of my presidency. The government officials are all corrupt. After replacing the corrupt government, I would go home and drink my tea."

BECKY
Wow! That is a very interesting story.
I do not understand how the police can arrest
someone if he/she never violated the law.

A. THOREAU
Well, sometimes the police does not need
reasons for someone's arrest,
if the government is corrupt, and when there is no democracy.
In countries where democracy does not
exist, governments are corrupt, and
they are always right.
Those who oppose the government, those who disagree with
the government officials go to jail.

A. THOREAU (CONT'D)
By the way, Mavrodi did not steal the investors' money.
The Russian government destroyed MMM,
and I think that they stole the money.
As Mavrodi says, "Do I know who stole the investors' money?

Please ask me an easier question. What happens to money in this country? It disappears somewhere. The money goes into nothingness. It is a big mystery in Russia."

BECKY
I always thought that Russia is a democratic state.

A. THOREAU
There is no democracy in Russia. The political regime there is like a dictatorship. They just want the West to think that there is democracy there. This is what Mavrodi says about the so-called democracy in Russia: "Western countries always improve their democratic system, and our country appoints the "best" people. As a result, we have what we have. Thus, the Western model of democracy can never exist in Russia. Our government leaders think that they are Messiahs, that they know everything. Our political leaders think that the people are stupid, and they are geniuses. The government officials think that they know what is best for the people. They do not understand that the most prosperous societies are democratic societies, were true democracy exists. In our country, it is not a battle between good and evil, it is a battle between opposition and government leaders." Mavrodi also says, "I would like to live in a free country. Freedom is the most important thing for me. Everything else is not that important. I just want to have the rights and freedoms guaranteed by the Constitution. I want these rights and freedoms in reality not on paper." "The most important and fundamental rule of democracy is free elections. Unfortunately, we do not have free elections in this country. That is why, we have eternal present and no future. Nothing will change in our country until we have this political regime. Corrupt government officials fight corruption, and everyone knows that. Even the judges in this country are corrupt. There is no justice in courts since justice can be bought with money. Sometimes I feel that I live in a mental hospital because there are so many crazy people around me."

A. THOREAU (CONT'D)
Anyway, I need to go to a shoe store now.
I have to buy shoes again.
The shoes that I recently bought are not good.
Please call me whenever you want.

BECKY
Okay, good luck with the shoes.

Several Hours Later

Rebecca and Aaron talk online again.

BECKY
Did you have any luck with the shoes?

A. THOREAU
Yes, I did. How are you?

BECKY
I am good, thanks.
I want to talk to you on the phone.
I missed you so much when you were away.

A. THOREAU
Well, it is so nice to hear that from you.
Right now, I need to make an important phone call.
I will tell you about it when we talk.
I should be online a little later.

Several Hours Later

Aaron sends a message to Rebecca.

A. THOREAU
Hi Becky.
I am free now.
Please call me whenever you are ready,
or I can call you if you want.
As always, I really want to talk to you on the phone.

Next Day

Rebecca and Aaron talk online.

BECKY
Aaron, I could not sleep last night.
I was thinking about you.
You are such a wonderful person.
I want you to be happy,
you deserve happiness so much.
I would do anything to make you happy.
I have never felt as good as I feel now
because I have you in my life.

A. THOREAU
Becky, you know,
I have never felt so good too.
I have never felt so good with anybody else.
I can talk to you 24/7,
and it will still be not enough.
I feel so relaxed and incredibly wonderful
when I talk to you.

A. THOREAU (CONT'D)
As I said before,

Do not be afraid of anything.
You have me now.
I will always be there for you.
Our enemies should be afraid of us now.
Together we will win.

BECKY
I know I keep telling you this repeatedly.
I am sorry, but I cannot stop.
I am so happy that I have you in my life.
I am so grateful to this website, and
I am grateful to God.
Although I had some bad experience here,
this website has changed my life so dramatically!
It has changed my life forever.
It has improved my life so much!
Aaron, you have changed my life forever.
You are my fearless hero, and you are so intelligent!
You cam always provide an educated opinion and a helpful advice.

A. THOREAU
Thank you, Becky.
You see, we should be grateful to this site
for something good.
This site has improved my life too.

Aaron smiles.

A. THOREAU (CONT'D)
Thus, because of you,
I forgive the site moderators for
blocking H. D. Thoreau's picture.

Next Day

Rebecca and Aaron meet online.

A. THOREAU
Hi Becky,
You know, I was thinking about posting
a comment on this website
regarding evil and ignorant people.
I want to write something negative about those who
enjoy playing with other people's feelings, and who enjoy
hurting honest, good, and kind-hearted individuals.
I just cannot tolerate dishonest and not decent people.

BECKY
Hi Aaron.
I know how you feel…
I have zero tolerance for indecent and dishonest people.
I wish there was no evil and injustice in this world!

A. THOREAU
Well, our union will make our enemies afraid of us.
They will fear us because together we can do a lot.
Together we can overcome all the difficulties of life.
Our union will have a very negative effect on them.
What can we do?
They will get what they deserve.

A. THOREAU (CONT'D)
If they do not like us, it is not our problem.
We live in a truly democratic country, and
we have the right to tell the truth about them out loud.
Since I cannot say anything good about those people,
let them read the truth about themselves on this site.

A. THOREAU (CONT'D)
There may be some people on this site who will

absolutely agree with us, but they will be too afraid
to admit that this world is full of evil, injustice,
ignorance, indifference, and inhumanity.
They will be too afraid to accept that our thought
processes are going in the right direction.
Unfortunately, the majority of people have
incorrect understanding of life and happiness.

A. THOREAU (CONT'D)
Some people are afraid to accept that this
world is not a wonderful place to live in.
They like to live a life full of illusions and
misleading concepts about reality.
They have a false understanding about everything,
but they are happy, and
they do not want to know the truth since
the truth will destroy their "wonderful" life,
and it will make them unhappy.
They do not want to think about all the evil in the world.
These people like to live a life full of beautiful lies.
A lot of people do not want to hear the truth.
However, we are not like them...
R. W. Emerson once said, "What is the hardest
thing to do in the world? To think."
"Truth is beautiful, without doubt; but so are lies."
Unfortunately, very few people now understand his great
statement, "it is not length of life, but depth of life."

BECKY
A very famous French philosopher Rene
Descartes says, "I think, therefore I am."
Who are all those evil people who hurt others
without thinking about anything?
Why can't they think? What is wrong
with their thought processes?

Can they even be considered human beings
if they have no humanity at all?
I just do not understand why there are so
many indecent and dishonest people in
this world, who hurt decent and honest people.
Unfortunately, a lot of human beings lost
their humanity; they are not humane.
Such is our contemporary world; such is our contemporary life.
I think I told you this, even my best friend betrayed me.
It makes me so upset.

A. THOREAU
I am not surprised.
Our life is very different now.
The new generation will never live according
to the principles of the old generation, and
there is almost no one left from the old generation.
We live in a different time now. Our life was not always like this…
Mavrodi once said, "There are moments in life when such concepts
as honor, dignity, integrity, honesty, decency, and responsibility
seem to be ridiculous, old-fashioned, nonexistent, and dead."
Unfortunately, there are a lot of moments like this in life…

A. THOREAU (CONT'D)
You know, our life is full of evil and injustice.
Certain things are the same everywhere – evil,
injustice, jealousy, hatred, deception, etc.
Evil and injustice have always existed in the world.
Unfortunately, they are an essential part of life.
Mavrodi also said that "The laws of the universe are
the same everywhere. The fundamental constants
of life do not change over time." This statement can
definitely be applied to evil and injustice.

BECKY
I absolutely agree with that!

A. THOREAU

Please remember, our instincts, our inherent and acquired qualities, and the decisions that we make constitute humankind. We are the sum total of our instincts, qualities, decisions, choices, and personal experiences, whether good or bad. As one of the greatest American actors and film directors Woody Allen says, "We are all faced throughout our lives with agonizing decisions, moral choices. Some are on a grand scale, most of these choices are on lesser points. But we define ourselves by the choices we have made. We are, in fact, the sum total of our choices." Mavrodi says, "I always make my own decisions. Nobody can help me decide, and no one can influence me. I am my destiny" and "The destiny needed me to do great deeds." Mavrodi also says that "Your decisions and choices should be based on your free will. You should not choose anything out of the fear of punishment." Unfortunately, too many people make the wrong decisions these days. Unfortunately, too many people make morally unacceptable choices. Unfortunately, too many people choose to be evil by hurting others and being dishonest. We should try to avoid such people. Honest and decent people should keep together. We should be together... We can be happy together.

BECKY

I definitely agree that honest and decent people should be together. I believe that true love and true happiness exist in this world; we just need to find it. I think human beings can be happy if they make the correct decisions, if they go in the right direction. I think we should be responsible for our lives and for our happiness. We should be responsible for our actions and for our thoughts. We should take risks and enjoy our life.

We must not rely on what others think about
us, or what they want us to do or not do.
We should always think for ourselves and
make morally acceptable choices.
As one of the greatest American singers Madonna says, "Poor is
the man whose pleasures depend upon the permission of another."

A. THOREAU
I absolutely agree with you.
We should not follow the crowd. Some of the worst crimes
against humanity were committed because people blindly
obeyed their leaders and followed the obedient crowd.
As H. D. Thoreau says, "The mass of men lead lives of quiet
desperation. It is never too late to give up your prejudices."
As I said before, many people just do not want to think
about all the evil and injustice that is around them.
They just want to pretend that they are happy, and that
everything is okay. However, some of these people could
understand life if they accepted the true reality of their
everyday life, the harsh reality of their everyday life.

A. THOREAU (CONT'D)
I think that every person should understand
himself/herself before judging others.
Every person should understand his/her own
mind before trying to understand others.
Every person should learn before teaching others.
It is impossible to understand others without first
understanding yourself, your own mind.
As R. W. Emerson says, "He then learns that in
going down into the secrets of his own mind he
has descended into the secrets of all minds."
Unfortunately, too many people do not understand
life and their own minds, but they try to teach
others about what is right and what is wrong.

BECKY
Aaron, that is so true.
Nietzsche once said, "When a hundred men stand together, each of them loses his mind and gets another one. Insanity in individuals is something rare – but in groups, parties, nations, and epochs, it is the rule."
Many people are afraid to ask the most important questions because they do not want to know the truth; they are afraid to discover an answer, which will destroy their comfortable lives of ignorance. They think that they are happy, but in reality, they are not, and some of them are afraid to lose their imaginary comforts.
Some people are simply afraid not to find an answer to their question, since there are some important questions, which do not have answers.
Many people do not even bother to think about some of the most important life issues.
As Nietzsche says, "We hear only those questions for which we are in a position to find answers."

Aaron continues to talk about the majority of people.

A. THOREAU
You know how our life works...
If the majority of people think that something is right, then it is right. However, it can be so wrong to follow the majority. Majorities can be so evil. As you know, the majority of people in Nazi Germany thought that Jewish people did not deserve life... Every person should have his or her own opinion and should never blindly obey the majority. Even the Bible should not be blindly followed. As Mavrodi once said: "I do not care about what the Bible says. I have my own moral values, and I live and act according to them. Nothing and no one can make me do the things that I do not want to do. Nothing and no one can make me do the things that I do not consider necessary to do." I think everyone should think like that.

A. THOREAU (CONT'D)

If the majority of people think that something
is beautiful, then it is beautiful.
In addition, it may not always be beneficial to listen to experts.
Experts can be wrong too.
For example, think about works of art.
When experts say that something is beautiful, the majority
of people tend to think that it is indeed beautiful.
This is what Mavrodi said regarding art and experts: "Does
a person get aesthetic pleasure from looking at paintings?
Maybe that pleasure is their habit to listen to experts,
the fear to appear ignorant. It is difficult not to admire
something when everyone else around you admires it. In such
situations, a person usually thinks that maybe he/she does
not understand something since he/she is not an expert."
Mavrodi also says, "Do not listen to anybody's advice,
especially the advice of experts. Do not rely on anybody
when you are doing something serious. It is an illusion
that somebody else can do something instead of you."

A. THOREAU (CONT'D)

As you know, the majority can be very wrong.
This is probably the most important lesson that history teaches us.
Unfortunately, many people choose to follow the majority
of people because it is much easier to follow others and not
think than to stand out from the crowd and be yourself.
However, we should always think for ourselves and not
allows others to makes decisions instead of us. We should
always choose our own way in life and be morally good.
It may not be easy to stand out from the
crowd; however, we must do it!
Every person should think for himself/herself!
As H. D. Thoreau says, "Pursue some path, however
narrow and crooked, in which you can walk with love and
reverence. Whenever a man separates from the multitude
and goes his own way, there is a fork in the road."

I absolutely agree with H. D. Thoreau when he says,
"It is important to preserve the mind's chastity."
Mavrodi also makes an excellent statement regarding
the majority when he says, "Great deeds are done by
individual persons. Collective actions are not effective."

BECKY
I absolutely agree...
Unfortunately, very few people understand this.
I wish there were more people in the world who understood this.
I wish more people understood that it is wrong to accept
or do something without thinking whether it is good or
bad, and whether it will have detrimental consequences.
As H. D. Thoreau says, "What is called
resignation is confirmed desperation."
One must not do something just because
the majority of people do it!

Several Days Later

Aaron and Rebecca meet online.

BECKY
Hi Aaron, where have you been the whole day?
I miss you so much when I do not talk to you!
I want you to know that
I almost forgot all my bad memories.

A. THOREAU
Wow! It is very nice to hear that.
I miss you a lot too.

A. THOREAU (CONT'D)
If you started to forget your bad memories,
it should not take you a long time to
forget everything.

You will probably forget everything bad
that happened to you very soon.
Remember that all the wonderful events
are waiting for you in the future.
You just have to go in the direction of
those events, as H. D. Thoreau says,
you should go in the direction of your dreams.

BECKY
How are you today, Aaron?
Where have you been the whole day?

A. THOREAU
I am good.
I was in the hospital with my mom.
Right now, I am at home.
Everything is okay. How are you?

BECKY
Why were you in the hospital?
Did anything happen?
Is your mom okay?

A. THOREAU
Yes, everything is okay.
It was a regular check-up.
Everything is fine, thank God.

A. THOREAU (CONT'D)
How are you?
How do you feel today?

BECKY
Everything is great! I live like in a fairy tale now.
It is all because of you, Aaron.

A. THOREAU
That is just wonderful!
I will do everything I can
to make your life like a real fairy tale.

BECKY
God Bless You, Aaron!

A. THOREAU
Thank you very much, Becky.
All the wonderful things are awaiting us
in the future.
We will be very happy, and
we will have an equal amount of happiness.
We both deserve to be very happy and
to have it all.
I promise, your life will be like the best fairy tale.
It will not be any other way!
I will make you forget fear, disappointment,
sadness and dishonesty forever.

A. THOREAU (CONT'D)
I need to go now...
Please call me after 9:00 PM as usual.
I will be waiting for your call.

December 31, 2009 – New Year Day

Rebecca and Aaron talk online.

BECKY
Hi Aaron. Can I call you now?

A. THOREAU
Yes, you can call me.
Please call me in 30 minutes,

after I finish my dinner.
I am having a dinner with my mom.
She did not eat anything today.
Please give me 30 minutes.

30 Minutes Later

Aaron sends a message to Rebecca.

A. THOREAU
Hi Becky.
Please call me now.

BECKY
Hi Aaron.
I will call you now.

Several Hours Later

Rebecca and Aaron are talking on the phone.

BECKY
Happy New Year to you, Aaron.
Thank you very much for everything!
As always, I wish you all the best!
Most of all in my life, I want you to be happy.

A. THOREAU
Happy New Year to you too!
Thank you very much!
I am really happy because
you exist in this world and in my life.

BECKY
Oh my God! We met the New Year together on the phone.

This was definitely the most extraordinary
New Year Day in my life.

Aaron smiles.

A. THOREAU
This was definitely the most extra-ordinary
New Year Day in my life.

January 1, 2009 – Aaron's Birthday (Aaron turns 36)

Rebecca and Aaron meet online again.

BECKY
Aaron, Happy birthday to you!
I wish you all the best!
May all your dreams come true!
May the New Year bring you only happiness and joy!
Thank you so much for being my friend!
As always, I wish you all the best!
You deserve the best life!

A. THOREAU
Thank you very much, Becky!
May the New Year bring you only happiness and joy too!

Rebecca smiles.

BECKY
Of course, the New Year will bring me
only joy and happiness because
I have you in my life.
By the way, your birthday is a wonderful date!
You were born on a very good day – the
first day of the first month.

A. THOREAU
I agree that January 1 is a special day.
My mom used to tell me that I was born on the first day of
the first month of the year in order to be number one.
She told me that I should always be number one.
I must be number one in everything I do and everywhere I go.
As Mavrodi says, "There is only the first place and all other places."
I absolutely agree! I am either number one or no number at all.
Either I do something well, or I do not do it at all.
Mavrodi also says, "The best is an enemy of the good. Please
remember this well and always follow this life principle."
I absolutely agree. A person must always strive to be the best.

BECKY
I understand you. I am a perfectionist too.
If I do something, I do it well. I always try to do my best.
I could never understand the students who went to college
in order to waste their time.
So many of them did not want to get education.
They just wasted their time and money.

Rebecca smiles.

BECKY (CONT'D)
You want to be number one. That is why, you always try to win.

Aaron smiles.

A. THOREAU
I always try to win because I cannot lose.
If I lose, then injustice and evil will win.
I just cannot allow evil people to win.
We should always fight against evil and injustice.
We must never give up; we must never
lose hope in a better existence.
We will prevail over our enemies; it will not be otherwise.

Good will prevail over evil in the end!

Several Days Later

Rebecca and Aaron meet online.

A. THOREAU
Hi, how are you?

BECKY
Hi, I am fine.
What about you?

A. THOREAU
I am good. Why don't you call me?
When will you call me?

BECKY
I will call you tonight.
How are you today?

A. THOREAU
I did not sleep almost the whole night
yesterday.
I could not fall asleep until 5:00 AM
I feel better today.

BECKY
Why? What happened to you?

A. THOREAU
I do not really know...
Maybe it is because of those candies with liquor
that were given to me as a New Year present.
They were too strong.
After I ate a couple, I started to feel bad.

You know that I do not drink alcohol at all.
Liquor, even a little, has a very negative effect on me.
Now I know that I cannot eat candies with liquor.
I am not used to alcohol, even in very small amounts.

BECKY
Please do not eat those candies any more.

A. THOREAU
I will not eat them again.

BECKY
You must love sweets a lot.

A. THOREAU
Yes, that is one of my weaknesses.
I really like sweets. I especially like
dark chocolate; it gives me a lot of energy.
Sometimes when I had to drive at night,
dark chocolate helped me stay awake.

BECKY
Do you like cakes?

A. THOREAU
Yes, I do.
My favorite cake is a Russian
cake called "Margarita."
It is so good that I could eat
half of that cake by myself.
Now I try to stay away from it
because the more you eat it,
the more you want to eat it.
The cake is very delicious.

BECKY
Wow! That cake must be really good.

As you know, I do not really like sweets,
although it is good to eat chocolate.

A. THOREAU
Have you ever tried Lithuanian bread?
It is the most delicious bread in the world.

BECKY
I do not really eat bread, but
I will be happy to try the Lithuanian bread,
if it is so good.
I am sure it is very good if you say so.

A. THOREAU
It is very delicious.
You should definitely try it.
I am sure you will like it.

BECKY
Well, if you like it, then
it must be very delicious.
I am sure I will like it too.
Now I really want to try it.

A. THOREAU
I am sorry; I have to go now...
I have to finish some work related matters.
I am waiting for your call as usual.

A. THOREAU (CONT'D)
How is everything with you?

BECKY
I will try to call you tonight.
I am so tired today...

A. THOREAU
If you are very tired,
it will be better for you to rest.
We can talk tomorrow.

BECKY
OK, thank you for your understanding.

Several Days Later

Rebecca and Aaron talk online.

BECKY
Hi, Aaron. Are you at home now?

A. THOREAU
Yes. Why are you asking?

BECKY
I want to call you tonight.

A. THOREAU
Okay, please call me.
As always, I will be very happy to talk to you.

BECKY
How are you today?

A. THOREAU
I am good, thank you.
How are you?

BECKY
Everything is good.
I was very tired yesterday.
I had a lot of work to do.

I feel much better today.

A. THOREAU
That is very good.
What are you doing now?

BECKY
I am watching a movie now.
What about you?

A. THOREAU
I think I will be watching a movie too.

BECKY
I think there will be a snowstorm today in NH.
Please do not go out, stay inside.

A. THOREAU
Thank you. I have heard about the snowstorm.
We should not do anything today.
We should stay at home.
Maybe I will go somewhere later today.
I just do not want to be at home the whole day.

BECKY
I have heard that something terrible will happen
today in NH because of the snowstorm.

Aaron smiles.

A. THOREAU
Well, some people say that something terrible
will happen in 2012.
I just think they talk too much…

Rebecca smiles too.

BECKY

I think I know what they are talking about –
the end of the world predictions.
I do not really believe that the end of the world
will be in 2012.

BECKY (CONT'D)

By the way, it is getting very cold in my
apartment again.
I know I told you this before,
I have a very bad condominium management.
Sometimes it is 60 degrees in my apartment in
wintertime.
I pay a lot for a condo fee; however,
the services that we get…
It has been several years that I am having a problem
with the heat;
the property manager and the condominium manager
do not even want to listen to me.
They think everything is okay.
However, it is very cold in my apartment, and
I do not know what to do anymore.
I cannot prove my point to them.
I am so tired of complaining to the condominium
manager; he is not helpful at all.

A. THOREAU

Becky, I think I told you this many times.
You should find an appropriate agency
and file a complaint with that agency.
It looks like your condominium management
does illegal things, and you should report them.
This agency should have some specialists,
who will come and measure the temperature
inside your apartment.

If the temperature is below the acceptable minimum,
your condo management will be held accountable.
You should not accept what they do to you.
What they do to you is very unfair.

A. THOREAU (CONT'D)
In NY, we have a housing hot line,
where people call with their housing
complaints, issues, and concerns.
There must be a similar service in MA.
I will find out for you.
I worked as a property manager for many years,
I know how all this works.

BECKY
Thank you very much in advance!

BECKY (CONT'D)
By the way, how many degrees it is
now in your townhouse?

A. THOREAU
It is 75 degrees.
I have climate control inside, and
I control the temperature myself.

BECKY
That is very good to have control over
your temperature inside.
Unfortunately, I do not have climate control.

A. THOREAU
Please do not worry. We will fix your heating problem.
Now you have me, and I am here to always
help you and protect you.
Your condominium manager will be very sorry
for mistreating you and other tenants.

BECKY
Thank you very much, Aaron!
I am so happy that I have you now.

Rebecca smiles.

BECKY
Now everyone who mistreated us
will be very sorry because together
we will definitely win.

A. THOREAU
Please do not even doubt.
We will never lose if we stay together.
It is us against them, and their
power is nothing in comparison to ours.

BECKY
By the way, do you like Boston?

A. THOREAU
Yes, I like Boston.
There are a lot of educated people in Boston.

BECKY
One day I will definitely show you
the most beautiful places in Boston.

A. THOREAU
Thank you, Becky!

Several Days Later

Rebecca and Aaron meet online.

BECKY

Hi Aaron,

Thank you very much for helping me
resolve my problem with the heat.
I really appreciate everything that you did for me.

BECKY (CONT'D)

I want to meet you in real life.
I want to go somewhere with you.
I will go with you wherever you want.
I am ready to meet you, and my parents
do not have a problem with that.
We have been talking to each other online
and on the phone for a long time,
and it is time for us to meet in real life.
I trust every word you say, and I think that
you are indeed a wonderful person.
I really want to meet you in real life.
Maybe we could meet tomorrow.

A. THOREAU

We can go anywhere you want,
today or tomorrow...

Rebecca smiles.

BECKY

Okay, we can definitely decide where to go.

Several Days Later

Rebecca and Aaron meet online.

A. THOREAU

Hi Becky,
I am sorry we could not meet.

One of my friends had a problem, and
I had to go to NY for several days.

BECKY
Hi Aaron.
It is okay; please do not worry.
We will definitely meet...
By the way, when you called me yesterday,
why did you block your name and phone number?
Was that a joke?
I know your name and phone number.

A. THOREAU
No, I did not block my name and number.
I just have a private number.
My cell phone number was always private
because of my work as a property manager.
I had to call my tenants sometimes,
and I did not want them to know my
cell phone number.
I did not want them to call me all the time.
By the way, I already unblocked
your phone number.
Now when I will be calling you,
it will show up on your phone display.

BECKY
Do you like Sprint, your current cell phone provider?

A. THOREAU
I like Sprint; it has a good service.
I used to have two cell phones – one
from Sprint, and the other one was from Verizon.
Verizon cell phones have a very good service.
Verizon has the best reception.
When I was a truck driver, I needed my cell
phone to work in all states.

There are certain states where only
Verizon can have reception; other cell
phones do not work in those states.
When I stopped working as a truck driver,
there was no need to have two cell phones.
That is why I gave you my Sprint number
and asked you to call that number.
I already disconnected my Verizon cell phone.

A. THOREAU (CONT'D)
By the way, I do not like to send text messages, and
I do not like when my friends send me text messages.
I prefer that my friends call me rather than text me.
It so much easier to call someone instead of
typing a text message on the phone.

BECKY
I agree with you. I also like when my friends call me.

BECKY (CONT'D)
By the way, why do you have a NY area code on your
Sprint cell phone?
You live in NH…
The Verizon cell phone number had
the NH area code.

A. THOREAU
I have had that number for almost 15 years.
When I moved to NH, I just did not want
to change my phone number.
There are a lot of people who know me
all over the world, and
they have my NY number.

A. THOREAU (CONT'D)
By the way, I have an unlimited plan for
my Sprint cell phone.

BECKY
It is good to have an unlimited plan.
I have a family plan, and my
service provider is T-Mobile.
A couple of years ago, I had Sprint,
and to be honest, I was not happy
with their service because it always
had service interruptions.

A. THOREAU
I cannot complain about Sprint.
I do not really have service interruptions.

BECKY
I know, and I am very surprised.
Sometimes we talk to each other for many hours,
and your phone does not disconnect.

A. THOREAU
I also have a good battery, which can
last up to seven hours.
I think I told you this before…

Rebecca smiles.

BECKY
I remember, once we talked for
almost seven hours on the phone.
I like talking to you so much,
that it is very hard for me to say
good-bye to you on the phone.
You are such an interesting person.

A. THOREAU
I have a hard time saying good-bye
to you too.
You are a very interesting person as well.

BECKY
By the way, who is your
land line provider in NH?

A. THOREAU
It used to be Verizon.
Now it is a company called FairPoint.
They have a very bad service.
The people in NH are very unhappy.

BECKY
I Think I remember… FairPoint bought
New Hampshire, Maine, and Vermont.
We are lucky; we have Verizon.

Next Day

Rebecca and Aaron meet online.

BECKY
Oh my God! You have uploaded your
real pictures online.
Why did you do that?

A. THOREAU
Yes, I uploaded my pictures online.
I did it because one of the girls on this site
said that I was afraid to post my real pictures.
She said that I was afraid to show my real face.
Let them all see me now.

A. THOREAU (CONT'D)
Now she will get a response from me...

BECKY
Why don't you want to have your real pictures on

this website?

A. THOREAU
I will explain now...
I used to have my pictures here, and
hundreds of girls would write me every day.
I did not even have time to read all their messages.
I do not have time or desire to talk to them.
To be honest, I do not really talk to anybody on this site,
except for you. You are the only person that I talk to
because you are not like them.

A. THOREAU (CONT'D)
I do not want to have too many girls in my friends list.
I do not really want to read all their senseless messages.
I do not need any girlfriends from this site.
I think you know what I mean...

BECKY
Yes, I understand you very well.

A. THOREAU
It is just wonderful that you understand.
I do not really need anything on this site,
except for talking to different people.
I am not looking for a girlfriend on this site.
I just want to better understand the different minds
of people here, if we can say that they have minds...

BECKY
As always, I absolutely agree with you!
There are not any normal people on this website.

A. THOREAU
That is the thing that there are not any
normal people on this site.
However, in the case that we have,

we should spend our time somehow, and
this site is a good way to kill time.
That is why, despite everything,
we talk to these people sometimes.
When we talk to different people here,
we start appreciating ourselves even more
because we are not like them.
We are different.

A. THOREAU (CONT'D)
Also, sometimes it is good to talk to them
because we can have a lot of fun.
These online conversations can be like
"free nights of humor."
It is like a free humor show. Sometimes I cannot be serious.
As Mavrodi once said, "Our life is funny. It is hard to be
serious." These online conversations can be so funny.

Rebecca laughs

BECKY
I definitely agree with that.

Several Days Later

Rebecca and Aaron meet online.

A. THOREAU
Hi. How did you sleep last night?

BECKY
I could not sleep last night at all.
I do not know what is happening,
I do not understand...
This has never happened to me before.

A. THOREAU
You know, I could not sleep last night as well.
I think I slept no more than two hours last night.
This has never happened to me too.

BECKY
How are you today?

A. THOREAU
I was busy the whole day today.
I just finished my work.
I like your mood today...

BECKY
I miss you so much,
I want to be with you 24/7.
I want to see and hear you 24/7.

A. THOREAU
Well, of course, I am very happy to hear that.
I feel the same way.
I miss you a lot too, and I want to be with you
all the time.
I can talk to you 24/7, and it is not enough.
I feel so relaxed when I talk to you. However,
it is not enough to just talk to you on the phone.
What should we do now?

BECKY
Aaron, I feel so attached to you.
I cannot imagine my life without you.
I just want to be with you so badly.
I want to hug you so tight,
I want to see you in real life.
I want to touch your golden brown hair.
I want to hear your beautiful voice 24/7.
We should definitely meet as soon as possible.

BECKY (CONT'D)
Aaron, I am so sorry for telling you all this.
I feel so uncomfortable now.
You know I am a decent girl...
I just like you so much!
I did not think that something like this would
ever happen to me.
I told you that I never really liked anybody.

A. THOREAU
Do not be sorry, it is okay.
I feel the same way...
I have become very attached to you too.
We will definitely meet.

A. THOREAU (CONT'D)
Becky, do I attract you as a man?
Please answer...

BECKY
Yes, you do...

A. THOREAU
Becky, did you fall in love with me
on the phone?

Rebecca shivers inside as if she is freezing, but she does not respond
to this question.

Aaron continues.

A. THOREAU (CONT'D)
It is okay, Becky.
Do not be shy and do not feel uncomfortable.
You can tell me whatever you want.
You can tell me how you feel about me.
Please say it the way it is.

Do not hide anything from me.
I promise; everything will be okay.

Several Days Later

Rebecca and Aaron meet online.

A. THOREAU
Hi, how are you?
how did you sleep?

BECKY
I called you five minutes ago...
Why didn't you answer?
What happened?

A. THOREAU
I am sorry; I did not hear my phone ring.
Let me check my phone...

Aaron goes upstairs.

A. THOREAU (CONT'D)
Sorry, I missed two calls; I forgot my cell phone
on the second floor.
You know I live in a townhouse.
You can call me now.

Several More Days Later

Rebecca and Aaron talk online.

A. THOREAU
Hello. How are you?

BECKY
I am good, what about you?

A. THOREAU
I am not so good...

BECKY
Why? What happened?

A. THOREAU
One of my new trucks broke.
It was a brand new truck.
Now I have to pay $870.00 to repair the truck.
My driver had to wait several hours for help.
The truck broke in the middle of a highway.

BECKY
Wow! That is a lot!

A. THOREAU
This is actually not so bad.
It can be much worse...

A. THOREAU (CONT'D)
I just feel very bad for the driver.
He had to wait for help in this very cold weather.
He is a good guy, but very unfortunate.
Not long ago, his wife died.
He is all alone now...

BECKY
Aaron, you are so kind-hearted and compassionate.

BECKY (CONT'D)
Do you know how to drive a very big truck?

A. THOREAU
Yes, I know how to drive these trucks.
I have a special, commercial license.
Before opening my own trucking company,
I was a truck driver here for some time.
I think I told you this… That is when
I had my Verizon cell phone.

BECKY
You know, I always wanted to sit
in a very big truck and see how it feels
inside when someone is driving.
I would never be able to drive such a truck.
I do not even understand how people
drive these trucks.
I think it is impossible to make a left or right turn.

A. THOREAU
Yes, it is not easy to drive these trucks.
When I was a truck driver, I saw a lot of
terrible accidents involving trucks.
It is especially dangerous to drive in
southern states because of the weather.

A. THOREAU (CONT'D)
Also the police officers who check these
trucks at check points can be extremely
rude and unprofessional.
Sometimes police officers stopped
me without a reason and mistreated me.

A. THOREAU (CONT'D)
Once a police officer mistreated me,
and when I tried to defend myself,
he decided to punish me.
As a punishment, he made me stop for the
entire night, and he did not allow me to drive

until the next morning.
I was late for my destination
because of him.
It is very important to reach the
destination on time.

BECKY

Wow! I cannot believe police people
can be so unprofessional.
I really like police officers in MA.
They are always very nice and very fair.
They do not mistreat people here.

A. THOREAU

Well, in some states they are not as
nice and professional as in the other states.
You must remember what I said about NY police.
Once a police officer almost arrested two women
on the street because he thought they were
talking too loud.
They were friends, and they were just talking
to each other.
I had to interfere in their conversation in order
not to let the police officer arrest those women.

BECKY

Well, that is definitely not fair.
Now I am very happy that I live in MA.
Although I always wanted to live in a
southern state since I do not like the cold.

A. THOREAU

Believe me, it is not so good in the South.
The weather is not always nice there.
They have hurricanes, tornadoes, earthquakes, etc.
In addition, there is still a lot of racism in the South.
Life is still terrible for some people in the South.

BECKY

Wow! I did not know that there is still racism
in the South.
It is so terrible and unacceptable!
I have zero tolerance for injustice and discrimination!
I love how an American Civil Rights activist and the greatest
fighter for justice Martin Luther King says in his speech "I have a
Dream" that a person should not be judged by the color of his/her
skin; a person should be judged by the content of his/her character.
I think this is one of the best statements in the world!

A. THOREAU

Of course, discrimination is terrible and unacceptable!
I absolutely agree with what Martin Luther King says.
I also have zero tolerance for injustice and discrimination!
We should always fight for justice; we should always
try to win in this world full of injustice.

Aaron continues to talk about NY.

A. THOREAU (CONT'D)

You know, even some bus drivers in NY
are very rude and unprofessional.
One bus driver mistreated my ex-girlfriend,
who was from Colombia.
You should remember, I told you about her.
The bus driver insulted my Colombian ex-girlfriend.
Oh my God!
At that moment, I just wanted to take out
my knife and…
I almost lost control over myself.
You know, I just have zero tolerance for injustice.

BECKY

Wow! The bus drivers are not like that in MA.

A. THOREAU
In addition, the hospitals in NY are very bad.
A patient can wait for many hours in an
emergency room.
There are many cases of patients, who die
in the emergency rooms waiting for help.
It is terrible!
Moreover, the doctors are not as nice as in
New England.
That was one of the reasons why I moved to NH.
The hospital and the doctors that treat my mom
are wonderful.
Everyone is so nice, and my mom is very happy with
the hospital and the hospital staff.

BECKY
Wow! That is indeed terrible!
I am very happy that you moved here.

BECKY (CONT'D)
I see you really like helping people, and
you always fight for justice.

A. THOREAU
That is true. I always fight for justice.
Once one of my friends was mistreated
in a car dealership when she leased a car.
She called me from the car dealership.
I had to go and talk to the car dealer
in order to resolve their issue.

BECKY
Tonight is a snowstorm again in NH.
Do you have enough food at home?
The weather is very bad now.
I remember when there was no power
in NH for two weeks.

Also, the weather is colder in NH than in MA.

A. THOREAU
Yes, I have everything I need at home.
I remember when there was no power very well.
I slept in the living room with my fireplace.
It was so cold inside; it was about 40 degrees.
I was sleeping on the floor near my fireplace.

BECKY
Oh my God! That must have been so terrible.
I cannot even understand how you
survived that horrible night…
What about your mom?

A. THOREAU
My mom's friend from CT offered a room
in her house.
When the power went out,
I drove my mom to CT.
She stayed there for several days.
I had to come back to NH for one night.
The next day I went to NY to live with my friends.

BECKY
It is very important to have good friends that
you can count on in any situation.
People in NH had a bad luck with their power
during that storm.
Nothing like that happened in Boston.

Rebecca jokes.

BECKY (CONT'D)
You should hate NH after the power outage.

A. THOREAU

Becky, honey, I can never hate New Hampshire.
The beautiful state of New Hampshire has
a very special meaning for me.

BECKY

Do you like New Hampshire?

A. THOREAU

I love New Hampshire.

CHAPTER 9

NATURE IN NEW HAMPSHIRE

Aaron and Rebecca meet online, and Aaron decides to talk about nature in New Hampshire.

A. THOREAU

I love New Hampshire very much!

When I am in NY, I really miss NH.

NH is a very beautiful state.

I like the nature in NH a lot, especially the mountains and trees.

I love to look at the White Mountains. When I am around the mountains, I have peace of mind. As one of the greatest English poets William Blake says, "Great things are done when men and mountains meet."

I also absolutely agree with what George Wherry, a writer who loved the mountains, says about his experience, "Truly it may be said that the outside of a mountain is good for the inside of a man."

I live very close to the White Mountains. I can see the White Mountains from the windows of my townhouse.

New Hampshire and the White Mountains area is the perfect vacation destination.

The White Mountains is my favorite vacation place in the US.

My spirit belongs to New Hampshire; this is where my soul calms down and finds its true happiness.

My spirit lives in the White Mountains of New Hampshire.

I have been in almost all the states in the US, but NH is definitely the best state.

A. THOREAU (CONT'D)
The amazing nature in NH will always
attract me. I will always admire it.
As H. D. Thoreau says, "I believe that there is a subtle magnetism
in nature, which, if we unconsciously yield to it, will direct
us aright. Nature is full of genius, full of the divinity."
H. D. Thoreau also says, "All nature is your
congratulation, and you have cause to bless yourself."
I absolutely agree with him that we should
honor nature's gifts, joys, and beauties.
Even the greatest German physicist Albert Einstein
once said, "Look deep into nature, and then
you will understand everything better."
New Hampshire is the most beautiful state in the United States.
I will never be as happy in any other state
as I am here in New Hampshire.
The fantastic nature in New Hampshire with
its mountains and forests teaches me to do great
things; it inspires me to do great things.
Sam Walter Foss, a great American poet who
was born in New Hampshire, once said,
"The woods were made for the hunters of dreams."

BECKY
Wow! You love the state of New Hampshire so much.

A. THOREAU
Yes, I admire the nature in New Hampshire.

BECKY
Can you ski?

A. THOREAU
Of course, I can ski.
I ski very well.

BECKY
What about Vermont (VT)?
Have you been in Vermont?
One of my friends says that
VT is more beautiful than NH.

A. THOREAU
Of course, I have been in VT.
VT is not more beautiful than NH.
NH is definitely the most beautiful state.
NH is the best for me.
You know, different people have a different taste.
Some people like Alabama too.

BECKY
What is wrong with Alabama?
Is it a bad state?

A. THOREAU
According to the statistics,
Alabama is not a good place for living.

BECKY
Don't you like NY?
You lived so many years there…

A. THOREAU
Of course, I like NY as well.
I lived there for so many years.
I have many good friends in NY.
I know everything in NY, and I
know a lot of people there.
When I go to a store in some areas of NY,
sometimes, people recognize me there.

A. THOREAU (CONT'D)
I feel very comfortable in NY.

however, NH has a very different meaning for me.
NY is very crowded, and the streets are dirty.
There are always a lot of people on the streets,
who are very busy running around.
There are a lot of rude people in NY, who
do not have any manners.
NY is also a very criminal city.
NH is the complete opposite.
It is a very clean, quiet, and safe place.
One year Nashua was voted the safest city in the US.
I think NH is the most beautiful state in the country.
I love NH, and I am very happy to live there.

BECKY
What is your favorite place in NH?

A. THOREAU
I love the White Mountains.
I live very close to the White Mountains.
I really enjoy the mountain views of NH.
I can see the White Mountains from my
window. I can look at them for hours.
The beauty of the White Mountains cannot
be compared to anything else in the world.
As I told you before, this is where I dream
to build a little house and live there.

A. THOREAU (CONT'D)
I have been in the White Mountains many times.
Once I even climbed to the top of the mountains.
You know, it was very cold in the mountains.
I also have many pictures next to the White Mountains,
I can send them to you.

BECKY
Wow! I have never been in the White Mountains,
but I would love to see that wonderful place.

A. THOREAU
I can definitely show you the White Mountains.
I will be happy to show you these mountains.
Only be sure to bring a sweater with you
if you want to climb to the top.
It is very cold at the top.

BECKY
Thank you very much, Aaron!
I would love to go there with you.

BECKY (CONT'D)
What is your favorite season of the year?

A. THOREAU
I like summer and fall.
New Hampshire is especially beautiful in the summer and fall.
To be honest, I like all seasons. I think
NH is beautiful in all seasons.
The White Mountains are always very beautiful,
regardless of the season of the year.
There is something unique and very beautiful
in every season of the year.
Charles Dickens, one of the most popular English
novelists, once said, "Nature gives to every time
and season some beauties of its own."

A. THOREAU (CONT'D)
I think I told you this before...
I have a crazy dream to build a small house
in the mountains in NH, and
to live there alone surrounded by wild animals.
I would like to feed those animals every day.
As H. D. Thoreau says, "In wilderness is
the preservation of the world."
As Charles Lindbergh says, "In wilderness
I sense the miracle of life."

I love the beautiful nature of NH with its
incredible mountains and forests.
Sometimes I think that my spirit belongs to the
White Mountains of New Hampshire.
I feel so calm when I am around the White Mountains.
I want to be part of that fantastic nature.
According to H. D. Thoreau, "There are moments when all
anxiety and stated toil are becalmed in the infinite leisure and
repose of nature. Nature is full of genius, full of the divinity;
so that not a snowflake escapes its fashioning hand."
He also says, "As you simplify your life, the laws of the
universe will be simpler; solitude will not be solitude, poverty
will not be poverty, weakness will not be weakness."

I believe that "a man is related to all nature." These are not
my words; this is what Emerson once said. I would like
to become one with nature; I want to have a simple life in
natural surroundings. For me, the ideal and most desirable
state of mind is to be one with nature, to feel that I am an
essential element of the natural world, as mountains, trees,
animals, or rivers. I just want to feel what H. D. Thoreau
felt when he lived in the woods alone. I want to live in a
little house that I build in the White Mountains in NH.
I would like to learn more about myself and about
life in general by living in the mountains.
As an English naturalist John Lubbock says, "Earth and
sky, woods and fields, lakes and rivers, the mountain
and the sea are excellent schoolmasters, and they teach
some of us more than we can ever learn from books."

Rebecca smiles thinking that she will
live in that house with Aaron.

BECKY
I remember…
You also said that you would not be afraid

of wild animals.

A. THOREAU
No, I am not afraid of wild animals. I like them.
As you know, one of my favorite places is a park
in Colorado which has wild animals.
You must remember my picture with some
of those animals.
My Colombian ex-girlfriend thought I was crazy
when I came out of the car and came up to those animals.
She was so afraid...

BECKY
Will you feel comfortable all alone in that house
surrounded by the woods and wild animals?

A. THOREAU
I will respond with what H. D. Thoreau once said, "I have never
found a companion that was as companionable as solitude. We
are for the most part more lonely when we go abroad among
men than when we stay in our chambers. I went to the woods
because I wished to live deliberately, to front only the essential
facts of life, and see if I could not learn what it had to teach,
and not, when I came to die, discover that I had not lived."

A. THOREAU (CONT'D)
I think all human beings need silence sometimes
in order to better think about their life.
Silence may be very beneficial to the soul of the person.
As H. D. Thoreau says, "Silence is the communing of
a conscious soul with itself. If the soul attends for a
moment to its own infinity, then and there is silence. She
is audible to all men, at all times, and in all places."

A. THOREAU (CONT'D)
Also, please remember that to be alone does not mean to be
lonely. Sometimes one can be alone; however, he or she does

not feel lonely because he or she is surrounded by the beautiful nature. I agree with what an American writer Rachel Carson says about nature, "Those who dwell among the beauties and mysteries of the earth are never alone or weary of life."

Rebecca smiles.

BECKY
These are definitely wonderful quotes; however,
I would like to live with you in the house that
you build in the White Mountains.
Do you think I could be your guest?

Aaron smiles too.

A. THOREAU
Well, I will respond with H. D. Thoreau's quote again,
"I have three chairs in my house: one for solitude,
two for friendship, and three for society."

CHAPTER 10

AARON AND FIRE

Aaron and Rebecca continue talking online. Rebecca changes the subject of their conversation.

BECKY
Are you afraid of fire?

A. THOREAU
Of course, I am not.
I really like the fire.
It has a very special meaning for me.
I will tell you one day.
I have a beautiful fireplace in my living room.
I enjoy looking at the fire very much.
I can look at the fire for hours.
It has a very calming effect on me.

A. THOREAU (CONT'D)
I feel very good when I am sitting in my
massage chair, looking at the fire in my
fireplace and talking to you on the phone.
I feel so calm and so relaxed.
As H. D. Thoreau says, "The fire is the main comfort
of the camp, whether in summer or winter, and it is
about as ample at one season as at another. It is as well
for cheerfulness as for warmth and dryness."
When I talk to you and look at the fire, I am very relaxed.
This is one of the best feelings that I can ever have.

Rebecca smiles.

BECKY

I feel incredibly good too when I am talking to you.
When we talk on the phone, there are three of us – you, fire, and I.

Aaron smiles too.

A. THOREAU

As H. D. Thoreau says, "Fire is the most tolerable third party."

A. THOREAU (CONT'D)

You know, fire is indeed amazing; it is very powerful. It can
be very destructive and very creative. Fire can do a lot for us
– it can destroy our lives, and it can help retaliate against our
enemies. Human beings can use the fire to their advantage. I
agree with what a Scottish writer Thomas Carlyle says about
fire, "Fire is the best of servants; but what a master!"
One day you will definitely know the special
meaning that fire has for me.

BECKY

Aaron, is there anything in this life
that you are afraid of?

A. THOREAU

I would say the only thing that I am afraid of
is to lose my mother.
Nothing else in this world scares me.

BECKY

Are you really not afraid of fire?
I could never think that there is a person who is not afraid of fire.

A. THOREAU

No, I am not afraid of fire. I actually love the fire.
As I said, fire has a very special meaning for me.
When I look at the fire in my fireplace,
it calms me down, it makes me so relaxed.

One day I will tell you what meaning
the fire has for me.

BECKY
Okay, I am very interested to know what
special meaning fire has for you.
Please tell me when you think it is the right time for me to know.

A. THOREAU
One day I will definitely tell you everything…
You know, fire is one source of comfort and relaxation for me.
Without fire, there would be no life.
H. D. Thoreau once said, "The animal merely makes a bed,
which he warms with his body in a sheltered place. But
men, having discovered fire, boxes up some air in a spacious
apartment, and he warms that… Thus, he goes a step or two
beyond instinct, and he saves a little time for the fine arts."

A. THOREAU (CONT'D)
By the way, when I talk to you, I feel very relaxed.
When I hear your voice, it is like hearing a beautiful song.
I love sitting in my massage chair,
looking at the fire in the fireplace and talking to you.
I can fall asleep with a headphone in my ear.
It is the best feeling to fall asleep while talking
to you on the phone.

A. THOREAU (CONT'D)
You know, fire can have a very destructive power, but
it can help us in our vengeance against our enemies.
If you want, we could scare your enemy from NY.
We can take him somewhere in the woods,
tie him to the tree, and pour gasoline on him.
Then we will light up a lighter in front of his face and
pretend that we want to burn him alive.
We can mentally break him; he will experience
mental and emotional death.

I do not even want to tell you what else we could do to him...

A. THOREAU (CONT'D)
Becky, please forget what I said.
Please do not pay any attention to what I just said.
Please let us talk about something else.

BECKY
Aaron, everything is okay.
Please, do not worry.
It is always very interesting to talk to you.
I always learn something new.

BECKY (CONT'D)
Do you know the worst torture methods?
How do you know them?

A. THOREAU
One day you will know...
One day I will tell you everything.
I do not want to lie to you,
but I cannot tell you everything at this time.
I am sorry; I cannot tell you everything now.

A. THOREAU (CONT'D)
You know, I have been through a lot in this life.
I have seen many terrible things in life.
You do not know me.
You do not even know what I am capable of doing.
You cannot even imagine what I can do to our enemies.
I can do a lot. I should do a lot in 2009.
The year of 2009 will be very important for me.
I need to accomplish so much in 2009.

BECKY
I want to know you.
I want to know everything about you.

A. THOREAU
You will, Becky.
One day you will know everything.

Rebecca smiles.

BECKY
I have never met anyone like you.
You are so mysterious, extraordinary, and interesting.

Aaron smiles too.

A. THOREAU
Does that attract you even more?

Rebecca smiles again.

BECKY
Yes, it does…

BECKY (CONT'D)
Aaron, I know that I asked about this before, but
I want to ask you again.
Are you afraid of anything?

A. THOREAU
Becky, there is a person who answered this question so well,
when the journalists asked him if he was afraid of anything.
This is how Sergey Mavrodi, a Russian businessman and
financier, answered this question: "Am I afraid of anything?
You must never be afraid of anything, not in this life and
not in the next life. Fear humiliates you; it makes you
lost in life. I do not have any fear, and nothing will stop
me in this life. I am not afraid of the government and
their threats. I will do whatever I think I should do."

A. THOREAU (CONT'D)

I absolutely agree with that wonderful statement.
You should not be afraid of anybody or anything.
To be afraid is to be degraded and humiliated.
Mavrodi was not afraid to stand up against the government,
and he even went to jail for his beliefs. This is amazing!
Sergey Mavrodi is not afraid of anyone or anything.
So many people are jealous of him because
they will never be like him!
He had been through so much injustice, but he
stayed true to himself and his beliefs.
He did not break, and he did not change
his beliefs and life principles.
Mavrodi is a very intelligent, interesting, and talented person!
I think that he is indeed a Genius; he is the only one!

A. THOREAU (CONT'D)

I am not afraid of anyone or anything too!

BECKY

What about death?
Are you not afraid of death?

A. THOREAU

Mavrodi once provided a wonderful response to this question:
"Regarding the questions about life and death, I always take
these questions in a calm manner. I think that we live eternally.
One person made a wonderful statement when he said that
a human being can never meet with death. When there is a
human being, there is no death. When there is death, there is no
human being. In addition, I think that our life is meaningless in
all its forms." He also said, "I never think about my age. Why
should I think about age? We all will die; we all will be there."

Rebecca smiles.

BECKY
Wow, Aaron!
That is a very interesting response.
By the way, you are so courageous and fearless.
I think that you have become my hero.
Given all your courage, intelligence, and kind-heartedness,
I think you will always win.

Aaron smiles.

A. THOREAU
Thank you, Becky.
As Mavrodi once said, "Heroes must never lose."

BECKY
I would like to call you now.
Let us talk on the phone.

A. THOREAU
OK, please call me. Let us talk.
As always, I will be happy to talk to you on the phone.

CHAPTER 11

AARON AND BOXING

Several Days Later

Aaron and Rebecca meet online. Aaron decides to
talk about boxing.

BECKY
Hi, how are you?
How did you sleep last night?

A. THOREAU
I slept well. How are you?
When will you call me?

BECKY
I will call you tonight after 9:00 PM.
You can call me first if you want.

A. THOREAU
By the way, I lost yesterday.
My predictions regarding the boxing match
did not come true.
I thought Antonio Margarito would win...

A. THOREAU (CONT'D)
This is called "upset" in boxing.
Margarito was favorite 4-1 before the fighting began,
and I cannot understand what happened to him.
This was not the Margarito which I know, and who I
have seen in fighting,

although Shane Mosley is a legend.
According to all my counts, Margarito lost in almost all
the rounds.
I can agree that he won only in one round,
and that can be doubted too.

Mosley just destroyed him; this happens very rarely.
In boxing, every boxer may have a "not his night."
Yesterday was not Margarito's lucky night.
However, such defeats can ruin the careers of many boxers.
After such defeats, it is very difficult to find the moral
strength again.
However, I think, over time, he will find that strength.
This is all a matter of time now...

It is just a miracle what Mosley did yesterday.
This is also a very rare case in boxing.
Therefore, for me, it was a lucky night that I did not bet
on Margarito yesterday.

BECKY
Well, maybe Margarito had some personal issues
or some other problems, and
that is why he lost yesterday?

A. THOREAU
I do not know whether Margarito had personal problems,
but I know for sure that Mosley did have personal issues.
Two weeks before yesterday's fighting,
Mosley had to go to a training camp, where his wife was,
in order to sign divorce papers.
I am sure you know that this is not a pleasant experience...
Mosley, as a boxer, if we take his boxing titles,
is much better than Margarito.
He won twice in the fighting with Oscar De La Hoi.
I just think that his career in boxing has ended.

He is 37 years old, and in such boxing categories,
his age has a negative effect on his boxing speed.

A. THOREAU (CONT'D)
Margarito won his last fighting with Migel Cotto
by knockout.
Migel Cotto was considered a king in this
boxing category, and he even won a fighting with Mosley.
It was logical to think that Margarito would win the fighting
with Mosley since he was stronger physically
and bigger in size.
However, everything happened the other way around...
Mosley, who was weaker and smaller, destroyed Margarito.
I want to emphasize again that such things can happen in
boxing, but they happen very rarely.
Yesterday was that rare case.

BECKY
Aaron, it is just a miracle that I met you
on this website.
You are so knowledgeable about everything.
You know so much about boxing.
Too bad miracles do not happen more often...

A. THOREAU
Well, if miracles happened often, they would not
be called miracles.

A. THOREAU (CONT'D)
By the way, Mavrodi does not believe in miracles.
This is what he said regarding miracles: "As I
always said, I do not believe in miracles.
The belief in miracles comes from human weakness. There is
the world, and there are its rules. The rules are the same for
everyone. Why should there be miracles? In addition, the world
is a miracle in and of itself. There cannot be any other miracles."

Rebecca smiles.

BECKY
Well, that is definitely an interesting opinion.
However, I think that there are miracles in this world.
For example you, Aaron.
I think that you are a miracle in this world!

Aaron smiles too.

A. THOREAU
Thank you very much, Becky.
You are a miracle in this world too!

Aaron continues to talk about boxing.

A. THOREAU (CONT'D)
For example, Tyson vs. Holyfield.
In that fighting, no one could predict that
Holyfield would win in the 11th round.
Before the fighting, Tyson was favorite 24 to 1.

BECKY
Yes, that is amazing.

A. THOREAU
It is true. No one could even imagine,
but it happened.

BECKY
Who is your favorite boxer?

A. THOREAU
Both Mike Tyson and Evander Holyfield
are excellent boxers; however, Tyson
is my favorite boxer; I think he is the best.
Tyson is a true legend.

I watched all his boxing matches, no one
can be compared to Mike Tyson.
I remember reading a very interesting book about Tyson.
He was a difficult teenager; he was even sent to a reform school.
In that school, Tyson's great boxing potential was noticed, and
he was directed to a famous boxing manager
and trainer, Cus D'Amato.
D'Amato became Tyson's legal guardian, and
he helped him become a legend.
Despite being a difficult teen, Tyson achieved so much.
I enjoyed reading that book a lot.

BECKY
Wow! That is really amazing!
I did not know that Tyson was in a reform school.

A. THOREAU
I know, Tyson's story is amazing.
Unfortunately, Tyson's mother died before he became a legend.
It was an emotionally shattering experience for him.
Tyson wanted his mother to be proud of her son.

BECKY
It is very sad that Tyson's mother died so young.
You know, life is very unfair.

A. THOREAU
I agree...

BECKY
By the way, do you like Muhammad Ali?
I know that he is a legend in boxing too.

A. THOREAU
Of course, I like him too.
Ali is one of the greatest heavyweight boxers in the world.

A. THOREAU (CONT'D)
I think I told you this before; I always
wanted to open a boxing school.
Maybe one day I will open my own boxing school.
I want to teach young boys how to be strong and invincible.
I want to teach them the art of boxing.
If you see all my boxing awards, you will
understand how much I like boxing.

BECKY
I will be happy to see your boxing awards.
I am sure one day you will definitely
open your own boxing school.
You are a very talented person.

A. THOREAU
Thank you, Becky. I hope so...
I am sorry; I have to go now.
I will be online a little later.
Please do not miss me.

BECKY
Okay, Aaron. I will be waiting for you.

Several Days Later

Rebecca and Aaron meet online.

BECKY
Hi Aaron.
Where have you been yesterday?
I was waiting for you on the website.
You promised to call me back, but
you never called me back.

A. THOREAU
I am sorry, Becky.
Two Colombian friends came over.
They recently came to the United States from Colombia.
They wanted to see me.
We had to deal with some problems.
There were some issues that we had to resolve.
I was busy the whole day yesterday.

BECKY
What problems do you have?
Can I help you with anything?
Did anything happen?

A. THOREAU
Everything is okay now.
I will tell you one day who my Colombian
friends are.

A. THOREAU (CONT'D)
You know that I have very important
connections all over the world.
I think I told you this story.
One of my friends is a rabbi, and he lives in Europe.
Once his synagogue was vandalized.
He called me for help, and I used my
connections to help him.
I did everything to make sure my rabbi-friend
was safe.
After I interfered, no one ever vandalized his
synagogue again.

BECKY
That is so wonderful that you help everyone.
Are you done with your work?
Are you free now?
Can I please call you?

Please let me know.

A. THOREAU
Yes, I am free now.
You know that I am always free for you.
You can call me whenever you want.
I am always happy to talk to you.

CHAPTER 12

FRIENDSHIP FOREVER

Next Day

Rebecca and Aaron meet online.

BECKY
Hi Aaron. I am very sick.
I wanted to meet you in real life this weekend,
but I got so sick.
I did not go to work for several days. I do not feel well.
I was even taken to the emergency room.
The doctors thought that it was pneumonia, but it was bronchitis.
I am sorry. I feel so bad that I cannot
even talk to you on the phone.
I am so frustrated that my illness prevented us
from meeting in real life.
I really wanted to meet you this weekend.
I just cannot wait anymore…

A. THOREAU
Hello Rebecca.
Please get better soon. I miss you a lot.
I hope you feel better very soon.
Please do not worry about anything.
We will definitely meet when you get better.
Dear Becky, you need to get better.

A. THOREAU (CONT'D)
I want to continue talking to you on the phone.
I want to meet you in real life.

Have a wonderful day today!
Get better very soon.
Take care of yourself.

BECKY
Thank you very much, Aaron!
I miss you a lot too, and I want to
talk to you as soon as possible.
I am so sorry we cannot meet at this time.

A. THOREAU
It is okay, Becky.
Please do not worry about anything.
We will definitely meet when you feel better.

Several Days Later

Rebecca and Aaron talk online.

A. THOREAU
Hi honey. Today is a crazy day for me.
It is a big snowstorm in New England.
As always, there is a lot of snow in New Hampshire.
There is so much snow on the trees.
Snow-covered trees look amazing.
It is very beautiful, but I need to do so much work outside.
Everything is full of snow; I need to
shovel a lot.
I will be online a little later,
and I hope you will be here.
How do you feel? I miss you a lot.
I miss our telephone conversations.
Please, get well soon.
I will be online later and hope to talk to you
online.

BECKY

Aaron, thank you so much for your support!
You are helping me so much.
When I talk to you even online, I feel much better.
I do not need any medicine when I talk to you.
You are my best medicine!
You are the best in the world!
The day I met you online is the happiest day of my life.
You brought me back to life, and you
continue to do that every day.

A. THOREAU

You are shocking me.
Your message has shocked me yesterday.
To be honest, I even felt a little uncomfortable
when I read your message.
How is your health? Can you talk?

BECKY

I am still sick. I take different medications,
such as Tylenol, and then I want to sleep.
I cannot even concentrate at work because
I have a terrible headache, and I really want
to sleep from those cold medicines.

A. THOREAU

I can imagine...
How do you feel in general?

BECKY

Unfortunately, not so good.
I wish I could have a better answer.
How are you?

A. THOREAU

I am good, thank you.

BECKY
I will try to call you today after 9:00 PM.

A. THOREAU
OK. I need to resolve a few work related issues now.
I will be waiting for your call after 9:00 PM.

Next Day

Rebecca and Aaron meet online.

A. THOREAU
Hi Becky.
You know, nothing like this has ever
happened to me before.
I do not remember anything that I told you yesterday,
when we talked on the phone.
I hope I did not say anything that
I was not supposed to say...
I do not understand what is wrong with me.

BECKY
Hi Aaron, please do not worry.
You did not say anything bad yesterday.
However, I cannot understand this...
Why did you forget everything?

A. THOREAU
Sometimes strange things happen to me.
Now you know a different Aaron too...

BECKY
Please do not worry, Aaron.
Everything is okay.
I hope nothing like that happens again.

A. THOREAU
I hope so too...
This has never happened to me before.

A. THOREAU (CONT'D)
I need to go to a drug store now.
I think I got sick too.
I will be online a little later.

BECKY
Well, that is not good.
I hope you feel better.

A. THOREAU
Thank you, Becky.

Rebecca jokes.

BECKY
I hope I did not make you sick.
I hope I am not contagious on the phone.

Rebecca smiles.

BECKY (CONT'D)
I think that it is impossible to get sick over the phone.

A. THOREAU
Well, distance may not matter in our case.
We understand and feel each other so well that
we may make each other sick over the phone too.

Several Hours Later

Rebecca and Aaron talk online.

BECKY
Are you busy now?

A. THOREAU
Yes, a little. I will be free soon.

A. THOREAU (CONT'D)
How are you?

BECKY
I think I am a little better.
How are you? How is your mood?

A. THOREAU
My mood is good. I am just a little sick.
I got a cold. Everything else is great.

Two Days Later

Aaron and Rebecca talk online.

A. THOREAU
Hi Becky. I am still sick.

BECKY
You probably need to take antibiotics.
Regular cold medications may not be so effective.

A. THOREAU
I know, I already bought some antibiotics, and
I started taking them.
My friend-doctor from NY has prescribed
them to me.

BECKY
Do you know that you have to take antibiotics

for seven days?

A. THOREAU
Well, it depends...
Sometimes I take them for five days.

BECKY
Please, be careful. It may not be a good
idea to take antibiotics for five days.
Unfortunately, regular cold medications
do not help when you are sick; they just
make me very drowsy.

A. THOREAU
I know, regular cold medications do not help.
That is why, when I am sick, I take antibiotics.
I cannot even take Tylenol because it makes
me very drowsy.

A. THOREAU (CONT'D)
My throat started to hurt badly.
I need to go now...
I will be back online in 15 minutes.

Next Day

Rebecca and Aaron talk online.

BECKY
Hi Aaron. How are you?
I called you yesterday,
but you did not answer the phone.
I was worried about you...
Yesterday you said that you would be back
online in 15 minutes; however,
you never came back.

A. THOREAU
I am sorry about yesterday.
I fell asleep; I just woke up now.
How are you today?

BECKY
I am better, thank you.
How are you?
Are you sick?

A. THOREAU
Yes, a little. I have a sore throat.
I want to stay at home until tomorrow
and get better.
You were sick, now I am sick.
We take turns...

BECKY
Well, I hope you get better very soon.
I do not want you to be sick.
I want you to feel better.

Rebecca jokes again.

BECKY (CONT'D)
I hope I did not make you sick...

A. THOREAU
I probably got it from you because we feel
and understand each other very well.
Maybe the distance indeed does not matter for us.

BECKY
Do you have enough medicine at home?

A. THOREAU
Yes, I have all the necessary medications.

This is not the first time that I am sick.
I know how to deal with this.

BECKY
Aaron, my dear and wonderful friend,
I really hope that you get better very soon.

BECKY (CONT'D)
You know, now I completely think like you.
Almost all of the people are stupid and ignorant.
They have become disgusting to me.
I cannot talk to anyone anymore, except for you.
Before, I just did not like anybody.
Now all of them disgust me.

A. THOREAU
Well, that is wonderful.
At least you got something good from me.
Like you, everyone disgusts me these days.
They disgust me more and more every day.
You are the only person that I can talk to.

Rebecca changes the subject of their conversation.

BECKY
You know, I was offered to teach some Philosophy courses
at one of the high schools in Boston, and I accepted that
job offer.
I really like Philosophy, and I have always
wanted to teach Philosophy.
However, I am not happy with some of the
students that I have in my class.

BECKY (CONT'D)
Some of the students in my Philosophy class
make me very upset and frustrated.
Sometimes they mistreat me in front of other students.

It is so humiliating. I do not deserve that!
I always try to help my students.
However, when some of them disagree with their grade,
they start yelling at me.

BECKY (CONT'D)
I teach a couple of Philosophy courses,
and I have these two students in my class...
These two students mistreat me very badly.
One of them always laughs at me and makes fun of me
in front of other students.
She degrades, humiliates, and disrespects me all the time.
She just cannot talk to me normally.
She thinks that I am stupid, and
I cannot teach Philosophy.
The other student has been mistreating me
from day one.
The very first day I started working at the school,
she told me that she did not want me as a teacher.
I do not understand why she said...
I cried the whole night. I am so upset.
I cannot deal with them any more.
I do not know what to do...
You cannot imagine how I feel.
These two students make me cry all the time.
They do not take me seriously.

BECKY (CONT'D)
Some other students always yell at me.
I do not understand why they cannot
behave themselves.
These are High School students.
They are not little kids.
I always try to help them, and
I always do my best; however, very few
students appreciate that.

It is so sad. I just do not see a reason for them
to treat me like that.
I am always nice with them, and I always help them.

A. THOREAU
Well, I do not even know what to say here.
You can call me in about 10 minutes,
and we will talk about everything

A. THOREAU (CONT'D)
I can definitely say that I cannot stand
when people raise their voice at me.
I cannot stand when someone yells at me!
Everybody deserves to be treated with respect.
No one should be mistreated.
No one should behave like those two students.

BECKY
I completely agree with you, Aaron.
Sometimes I feel so sad and upset that I want to quit my job.
The work related stress is just unbearable.

A. THOREAU
You know, Mavrodi actually quit his job because
he did not like the work environment too.
Once he said that "I quit my job in order to be free and open my
own business. Freedom for me is like the ability to breathe."

BECKY
Mavrodi definitely made the right decision.
I wish I could quit my job. I wish I did
not have so many student loans.
In addition to being mistreated and disrespected
by those two students, my salary is very low.
I am paid very little for teaching Philosophy, but the school
promised to give me a salary raise after several months.
My salary is $35,000 per year.

A. THOREAU

Oh my God! That is unbelievable!
You should start looking for a different job.
With your level of education and intelligence,
you should be getting at least $70,000 per year.
It was not worthwhile to study so many years and
to take so many loans in order to be paid your current salary.
Also, it makes no sense to wait for a promotion
since the salary raise will be no more than $1.00 or $2.00 an hour.
Trust me, I know how a salary raise works...
My advice to you is to start looking for a different job,
and to apply to a Philosophy PhD program as soon as possible.

A. THOREAU (CONT'D)

Furthermore, please do not pay attention to
those students who mistreat you.
They do not take you seriously because they are jealous of you.
You are young, beautiful, smart, successful, and educated.
They are jealous because they want to be like you.
If you want, we can definitely revenge against those two
students who make you upset. These two students are idiots.
I really like what Mavrodi said about idiots: "Regarding
idiots, they will never change. You will never change them.
Do not even try to do that. It makes no sense to spend
your precious time on trying to change the idiots. They
are human garbage. You just need to disregard them."
I absolutely agree with Mavrodi. Idiots and those who betray
others are not human beings; they are human garbage. Becky, you
should disregard these two students. They are just jealous of you,
and as Mavrodi says, "Jealousy is a sin." These two students will
never change, and they will always be jealous of other people who
are better than they are. Please do not let them ruin your life.
You should always try to be free, regardless of life circumstances.
As Mavrodi once said, "I was always free, even when I was in jail."

BECKY

Aaron, as always, thank you very much for the wonderful advice!
Thank you for always supporting me and helping me.
I will try to find a different job, and I will
try to ignore those two students.

BECKY (CONT'D)

You know, people always mistreat me.
Others always insult and humiliate me.
I do not understand why they do that to me!
I have never done anything bad to anybody!
I have always helped people and never mistreated anyone.
It is such an emotionally shattering
experience to be unfairly treated.
Sometimes I feel that injustice follows me everywhere I go.
I always try to help those two students; however,
they do not like me for some reason.
They always mistreat me. Sometimes I
just want to cry because of that.

A. THOREAU

Becky, please do not be upset because of those two students.
Trust me, they do not even deserve your attention.
They are just jealous of you.
They will never be like you, and they know that.
That is why, they mistreat you.
As I said before, if you want, we can
definitely teach them a lesson…

BECKY

You know, even when I was a child, I was mistreated.
Some students in schools are so cruel…
When I was a child, other kids bullied me.
It may be stupid, but I still remember
everything they did to me. It was so horrible!
The things they did to me…

When I remember, I may even get upset because of that.
I had a very painful experience in my childhood.

BECKY (CONT'D)
Unfortunately, those who bully others do not
realize what a terrible thing they are doing.
Bullying is indeed terrible; some kids even
commit suicide because of that.
No one should be bullied; nobody deserves that!
I believe school teachers should interfere and prevent bullying.
They should not stay indifferent to the injustice
that is happening in their classrooms.
It is so terrible to be indifferent to the suffering of others!
I think indifference is the most terrible thing in this cruel world!
I still remember how one boy was beating me up
in the classroom, and everyone was standing there
and watching, even my teacher was watching.
The teacher did not help me. It is so sad and unfair!

BECKY (CONT'D)
When I was a little girl, sometimes I just wanted to run away
from this cold and very cruel world. I just wanted to run
away from the unbearable pain and intolerable reality.
I wanted to hide somewhere, where it would be nice and warm.
My grandparents were always worried about me,
especially my wonderful grandmother.
I lived with my grandparents when I was bullied in school.

A. THOREAU
Becky, trust me, it is not stupid to remember
painful childhood experience.
I know very well how painful some of our
childhood memories can be.
For example, the number 11 has a very special meaning for me.
When I was 11 years old, I almost killed another boy.
That boy with other boys beat me up,

and then he made a very insulting statement
in regards to my mother.
He should have never done that...

A. THOREAU (CONT'D)
The next day, I came to his place.
I knocked on the door of his apartment.
When he opened, I asked him to apologize
for what he said about my dear mom.
However, instead, he said the same
thing again.
Oh my God! You should have seen me.
This is when I lost control over myself.
I took out a knife, and I stabbed him with a knife
I almost killed him because he insulted my mom.
The knife passed through his body.
Can you imagine that?
I could see the knife in his body.
I wanted to revenge for my mom so badly that
I completely lost control over myself.

BECKY
Wow! You could have ruined your life!
That stupid kid could have ruined your life.

A. THOREAU
I know, my parents made a lot of
arrangements with the government.
I never went to a corrections facility
for what I did.
No one ever punished me for that. By the way, the number
11 has a special meaning for Sergey Mavrodi too. He was
born on August 11. In addition, all very important events
in his life happened on the eleventh day of the month.

A. THOREAU (CONT'D)
You must remember, I told you the story

about my mentor who lived in Europe.
He taught me many important lessons.
He taught me how to stand up for myself and
fight for justice.
He was an excellent boxer, and he inspired me
to become a boxer too.
I started practicing boxing when I was eight years old.
When I was thirteen, I had my first tournament, and I won.
My mentor loved me as if I was his son.
Once a man on the street beat me,
my mentor almost killed that man.
He was a very brave and wonderful man.

BECKY
Where is your mentor now?

A. THOREAU
Unfortunately, he and his girlfriend were killed.

BECKY
I am sorry; that is very sad.
Aaron, you are so strong.

A. THOREAU
Becky, honey, I will teach you how to be strong.
I can teach you a lot.
By the way, if you want, we can find that boy
who beat you up when you were a little girl.
We can revenge against him too.
Trust me, I have all the necessary connections around the
world in order to revenge against everyone who hurt us.

BECKY
Aaron, you are so brave and fearless!
You are also so kind-hearted.
Thank you very much for everything!
As always, I wish you all the best!

Please take all the necessary cold medications.
I hope you get better.

A. THOREAU
Thank you very much!
I wish you all the best too!
I do not want to sleep now.
Rest well, and if you feel better,
please call me.

BECKY
Okay, Aaron. Thank you!

Several Days Later

Rebecca and Aaron meet online again.

BECKY
Hi, how are you?

A. THOREAU
I am fine. How are you?

BECKY
I do not know what is going on with me.
I have never felt so bad.
I was okay for several days; however,
something happened, and
I feel worse and worse every day.
Nothing helps me.
I have seen doctors, but they are unable to help me.
I am sorry I cannot talk to you now, and
I am sorry that I did not call you for the past several days.
I wanted to meet with you this weekend, but...
I do not know when I will get better.

Please do not think that I do not want to talk to you
any more, or I do not want to meet you in real life.
I am just really very sick. I can barely go to work.
Aaron, I do not want to lose you.
I do not know what I am going to do without you.

A. THOREAU
Your sickness is shocking me....
I do not feel that well too.
It may be because of the weather.

A. THOREAU (CONT'D)
I miss you a lot. I am so used to you
and our telephone conversations.
I am sorry if I ever said or did something
you did not like.
I am sorry if I did something wrong.
Please remember that I will always be waiting for you.
I will always be with you,
and you will never lose me.
You are the most intelligent person I have ever met.
I miss our telephone conversations a lot.
Please get better soon. I need you so much.

Several Days Later

Rebecca and Aaron meet online again.

BECKY
Hi. How are you?
What is new?

A. THOREAU
Hi. Everything is the same.
How do you feel?

What happened to you?
Where did you disappear?

BECKY
I have been very sick.
I was in bed all these days.
I do not feel well.
I miss you so much.
Aaron, I want to spend every second
of my life with you.
I am so upset because of this illness...
I am so afraid to lose you.
I do not know what to do.

A. THOREAU
It is very nice to hear that.
I do not even know what to say.
It is so nice to know that you want to spend
all your time with me.
I even thought that maybe you do not
want to talk to me anymore.
and it was a nice way to say "good-bye."
I am sorry that I thought so...

BECKY
Oh my God!
How could you think that I disappeared
because I did not want to talk to you?
I felt so bad all these days!
I almost died in the emergency room.
Yesterday I spent the whole night in the
emergency room.
I even wanted to call you and say "good-bye."
I want to talk to you more than anything else in this life!
You are part of my life!
I am so afraid that I will lose you.

I am so afraid that you will find
some other interesting person to talk to.
I am so sick now, and I do not have any control over this.

A. THOREAU
Becky, you are the only person who interests me.
You are the only person that I can talk to.
You are the only person that I talk to.
You will always be the only one in my life.
You will always be the only special person in my life.
Believe me, you are a very special person in my life.
You and my mom are very special people in my life.
I do not have anybody else in my life.

A. THOREAU (CONT'D)
Thank you for all your words!
Thank you for everything!
I am so sorry for thinking that you
wanted to say "good-bye" to me.
I will never think so again.
You know, let us not talk about this ever again.
Please do not worry about anything.
I will be waiting for you
as long as you need me to wait.
I will wait until you feel better,
and then we will talk.
The most important thing is that you do
everything that is necessary to get better.

A. THOREAU (CONT'D)
Your health is the most important thing for me.
Please make sure that your health
always comes first.
If you need to go to the hospital, please do so.
Do not worry about work or anything else.
Health is the most important thing in life.

You should take a good care of yourself.
Please forgive me for my crazy thoughts.
Please get better as soon as possible.

Next Day

BECKY

Hi Aaron. Something terrible happened to me yesterday.
I had a hard time sleeping because I was coughing all night.
Also, I had a hard time breathing because of that coughing.
I could not even breathe for a few seconds.
I was so scared. I was taken to the emergency room the third time.

A. THOREAU

Hello. You are shocking me more and more.
Do not rush to go back to work now.
The most important thing is that you get better.
Please remember health is the most important thing.

A. THOREAU (CONT'D)

The fact that you had a hard time breathing normally can
be because of your nervous system too.
Please remember, stress affects us very negatively.
Stress can have a very negative effect on everything.
17 years ago, I had experienced the same thing, and
I also thought that it was just a cold.
I do not want to scare you...
Please do not think about anything bad.
The most important thing now is that you take care of
yourself and your health.
I know it is easy to say, but please do not pay attention
to conflicts at work; do not take them seriously.
Please do not pay any attention to those two students.

A. THOREAU (CONT'D)

God forbid, but if this is related to stress,

not a single doctor will be able to properly
diagnose this disease.
When it is hard to breathe,
and when it is tight inside your chest...
Do you feel anything like that?

BECKY
No, Aaron. I have not experienced that.
I do not think that I have that disease.

A. THOREAU
Becky, I do not want to scare you, but
the name of that disease is Panic Attack.
A panic attack is an episode of intense, sudden fear.
Sometimes I was not able to breathe normally at night.
I remember one of those nights when I was sweating all
night long, and I had to change several T-Shirts.
This was one of the long episodes of a panic attack.
When that happens, I not only cannot breathe normally,
I also have a very uncomfortable, burning sensation in my chest.
However, over the years, I have learned how to manage
these symptoms, and I do not get them so often.
I know how to deal with this terrible disease.
Sometimes I take antidepressants,
but I do it with caution because I do not want to get used to them.
Sometimes antidepressants help me with my panic attacks.
However, a person must be very careful
when taking antidepressants
because he or she can easily get addicted to them.
It is very important not to take a lot of those medications.

Aaron continues to talk about panic attacks.

A. THOREAU (CONT'D)
Many doctors misdiagnosed me.

At first, they thought that it was pneumonia
because I was coughing and could not speak.
They did all sorts of Ex-Rays and prescribed different
cold medications, but nothing was helping me.
Finally, one doctor explained to me the disease that I have.

A. THOREAU (CONT'D)
You know, all great people suffer from panic attacks
because people like that are not ordinary people.
It is normal for them to have panic attacks because
they go through a lot of extraordinary events in their life.
I can give you some of my medications if you have a panic attack.
You only need to tell me, and I will come over immediately.

BECKY
Thank you, Aaron.
I will definitely let you know…

Next Day

Rebecca and Aaron talk online.

BECKY
Hi Aaron.
I am not getting better. I still feel very bad.
I do not want to go to work, but I have to return to work.
I have no more sick days left, and it is
just the beginning of the year.
By the way, I started taking Vitamin C.
I do not think that I suffer from panic attacks.

A. THOREAU
Well, Vitamin C is always good.
I just wish you got better sooner.
You did not go outside in the cold.
Please think why you got sick the second time.

You did not even get better from the first
cold, and now you are sick again.
Maybe this is a side effect of the first cold.
I know that things like that happen...
I do not even know what to do now.
How will you go back to work?
How can you work with all these symptoms?

A. THOREAU (CONT'D)
I do not even know what to say here.
I do not feel that well myself because of
the cold that I had.
What if something happens while you are at work?
Then what? I do not know what to say...
I can say many things, but my words will not help you
get better. Just hang in there...
I am sorry; I need to go now for a little while.
I will be back later.
Please do not be sad and do not be bored.

Later Today

Rebecca and Aaron talk online again.

BECKY
Aaron, I know I am going to lose you.
You do not need a friend like me.
I have been sick forever...
I think it will be better for you to try to
find someone else to talk to.
I know that I am losing you because of my sickness.
It just ruined everything for you and me.
I cannot even talk to you on the phone
because I always feel very bad.
I can barely go to work.

I cannot sleep at night because I am coughing all night long.
Medications do not help me at all.
You must be so bored without our phone conversations.

A. THOREAU
Rebecca, honey, what are you talking about?
What do you mean you are losing me?
I told you this many times…
You are a very special person in my life,
and you will always be very special for me!
Nothing will ever change that!
I will be waiting for you as long as you need.
Trust me, I know how to wait.
If necessary, I will wait for you the whole life.
I have a lot of issues to care about now, so
I am not bored. I have other things to do until we
start our telephone conversations again.

A. THOREAU (CONT'D)
Please do not think that I will disappear somewhere.
It is impossible to run away from yourself.
You have become a very special person in my life,
and that will never change.

How could you even think so?
Didn't you understand my attitude towards you?
The most important thing for me right now is that
you get better, and
please do not think about anything bad.
Everything will be okay.
I will wait for many years if necessary.
Please be sure in that!

A. THOREAU (CONT'D)
I would be very happy to do something for you
in order to help you.

If I can do anything for you, please let me know.
Please do not be shy.
I will do anything and everything that is
necessary.
Do not even doubt that.
Trust me, I can do that too.
So get better and do not worry about anything.
We will definitely meet in real life when you get better.
I am waiting for you, and
I will always be waiting for you...

I am a man of honor and dignity, and when
I say something, I definitely do it.
It cannot be otherwise.

Please remember, words for me have more value than my life.
I never lie, and if I promise something, I do it.
You are a very special person in my life;
nothing and no one will change that!
You and my mom are two very special people
in my life; I do not have anybody else.
Please remember I will always be there
for you. I will always help you.
No one will ever hurt you, my dear Rebecca.

Next Day

Aaron and Rebecca talk online.

A. THOREAU
Hi. How do you feel today?

BECKY
Hi. I am still not doing well.
Thank you very much for all your support.

I will never forget all your wonderful words
and all your moral support.
Your support gives me strength to continue.
You are the only thing that helps me fight
this illness.

A. THOREAU
Please listen to me; maybe it will be better for you
if you stay at home for several days and
get enough sleep and rest?
Maybe it will be better for you not to go to
work tomorrow?
What if you start feeling very bad while driving?
Please think about that...

BECKY
Thank you again for trying to help me!
I really appreciate everything you do for me.
However, I cannot really miss work.
I need to be at work tomorrow.
I will be fine; do not worry about me.

A. THOREAU
Oh well, but please take a good care of yourself.
Try to think about all this according to the principle
of one of my former neighbors...
One of my former neighbors in NY,
I told you once about her –
she gave me the tickets to a hockey game;
she always used to tell me these things, and now
I want to tell them to you.
This will be good in your case.
She used to say, "I am number one, I am number two,
I am number three."
Do you understand?

BECKY
Yes, Aaron, I understand... Thank you!
I will try to say these things to myself.
Maybe they will help me get better...

A. THOREAU
I am sorry, honey.
I need to go to sleep now.
I have to wake up early tomorrow morning and
resolve some work related issues.
I hope you feel better...
If you need anything, please call me.

Several Days Later

February 14, 2009: Valentine's Day

Rebecca and Aaron meet online.

BECKY
Hi Aaron.
Happy Valentine's Day to you!
I hope you find your true happiness!
I hope you find the person of your dreams.
I wish you to meet the girl of your dreams,
who will make you truly happy!

A. THOREAU
Happy Valentine's Day to you too!
I wish you all the best too regarding
meeting the person of your dreams!
I wish you the greatest happiness of life!
I think I already met the person of my dreams...

BECKY
Thank you, Aaron.

I am very happy to hear that.

A. THOREAU

I was in NY yesterday,
when I came back to NH,
It was already too late...
How do you feel today?

BECKY

I think I am getting a little better.
However, I still do not feel well.
Aaron, thank you very much for everything
you did for me!
Moreover, thank you for everything
you are doing for me!
I will never forget all your help and support!
Thank you so much!

A. THOREAU

Becky, you always say, "thank you for
everything you did for me."
I am sorry, but I did not do anything special
for you.

A. THOREAU (CONT'D)

It is very nice that you really understand
me so well, but please remember, all the best things
are waiting for us in the future.
The most important thing is that you get better.
Please do not worry about anything.
I told you this many times.
Health is the most important thing.
I am sure you will get better soon.
Everything will be okay.
Please keep away the unnecessary thoughts.
Get better soon.
Everything will be okay.

BECKY

Aaron, I cannot wait to meet you.
I want to meet you so much!
Sometimes I think that we will never meet.
Sometimes I think that we will never see each other in real life.

BECKY (CONT'D)

I am even thinking about meeting a psychic or
a fortune-teller.
I just want to know what will happen to me.
What if something terrible will happen to me?

A. THOREAU

Becky, please do not even think about that!
Everything will be okay!
Please do not go to psychics or fortune-tellers.
Those people can be very dangerous.
I know that based on my personal experience.
Once my Colombian ex-girlfriend made me
go and see a psychic.
That psychic predicted a terrible thing, and
that thing came true.
Please never go to those people.

A. THOREAU (CONT'D)

Please do not think negatively.
Do not be negative all the time.
As I said before, positive thinking helps.

BECKY

I am trying to think positively,
I am just still very sick, and medications do not help.
I still have a hard time sleeping at night because
of my coughing,
and my cough medications are not helpful at all.
A doctor prescribed one medicine with codeine, but
it is not helpful at all as well.

A. THOREAU
Oh my God!
Did they prescribe you a medicine with codeine?

A. THOREAU (CONT'D)
I remember I was taking some medications
with codeine after my surgery.
Codeine is a very good painkiller.
You probably feel so good and calm now
because of the codeine?

BECKY
I do not really feel the effect of codeine.
Wow! You were at the hospital, and
a surgery was performed on you.
Why? What happened to you?

A. THOREAU
I was in an accident, and I was very injured.
My left side was so damaged that I could barely walk.
I had terrible scars all over my face.
I was afraid to look at myself in the mirror.
I was so afraid that I would stay ugly and gruesome
for the rest of my life.
I did not want to be a "scar face" for the rest of my life.
I did not want to scare people with my appearance.
You know, your face is very important...
I could not even look at myself in the mirror.

A. THOREAU (CONT'D)
However, one doctor saved my life.
He completely restored my outer appearance and
corrected all my skin defects.
The plastic surgery that he performed was a miracle!
I do not have any scars on my face.
You saw my pictures...

BECKY

Wow, Aaron! I would never think that you had
a plastic surgery performed on you.
I could never tell by looking at the pictures that you sent me.
You look so handsome in those pictures.

A. THOREAU

Well, that plastic surgeon was a genius!
I did not think that I had a chance to get my
normal face back.
I was so afraid to look at myself after the surgery,
but when I looked in the mirror, I could not
believe my eyes.
All the terrible scars were gone.
I had a normal outer appearance again.

BECKY

Wow! Incredible things indeed happened to you!

A. THOREAU

Yes, my life is such.
I almost died several times, and I was
brought back to life.
I even saw the light at the end of the tunnel.
One day, I will tell you everything...
One day I will tell you everything that
happened to me.

One Month Later

Rebecca and Aaron meet online.

BECKY

Hi Aaron, I finally got better with your support.
Now I am finally ready to meet you in real life.
I was sick for a long time...

BECKY (CONT'D)
I really want to talk to you in real life.
The test of time has been over for you a long time ago.
I trust you; I do not have any more doubt.
I could not meet you sooner because I was very sick.
I am sorry about that.

A. THOREAU
Becky, my dear, no problem.
We will definitely meet one of the weekends.

A. THOREAU (CONT'D)
How is your health?
Are you sure everything is okay?

BECKY
Thank God, I am better now.
I was so sick for such a long time.
This has never happened to me before.
I heard one doctor was saying that
stress can really prolong an illness, and
I have a lot of stress at work, and
I had a lot of stress at home too.
You know, I had a lot of conflicts
with my mom because at first, she did not
want me to talk to you since you are 12 years older
than me, and
you were married and had other relationships.
However, now she is okay with that.
My mom finally understood
that you are the only person that I need.
My dad helped me with that; he supported me.

BECKY (CONT'D)
How are you today?

A. THOREAU

I am good. I am just trying to improve my future.
I need to improve my life.
You must remember, I told you that the year of 2009 is
very important for me.
I need to do a lot of things this year.
I must resolve a lot of issues...

BECKY

Aaron, I hope you achieve everything you want.
You deserve to be happy and successful.

A. THOREAU

Well, thank you. You deserve that too.
I just need to fight until the end, and that is
what I am doing right now.
I will definitely win; it is just a matter of time.

BECKY

Aaron, I am sure you will win.

A. THOREAU

Well, I just cannot lose in any situation.
Failure is not an option for me.

A. THOREAU (CONT'D)

How do you feel today?

BECKY

I feel good, thank you.
I am just coughing a little, but I
feel much better.
I miss you a lot.
Can I call you now?

A. THOREAU

Of course, you can call me.

I miss you so much, and I miss
our long telephone conversations.
I just do not want to bother you when you
do not feel well.

A. THOREAU (CONT'D)
Do you remember the website that you gave me,
where I can listen to music?
Could you please write that website again?

BECKY
Yes, of course.
Please let me know if you need anything else.

Rebecca writes the website and changes
the subject of their conversation.

BECKY (CONT'D)
How is it going with your businesses?

A. THOREAU
Unfortunately, I do not have any good news.
The economic situation in the country destroyed my businesses.
My businesses are going bankrupt.
I think I am going to sell my trucking company.
Currently, I am looking for a job as a property manager.
I cannot even make my mortgage payments anymore.
You know, I could not afford the very high interest rate,
and I decided to modify my mortgage loan.

BECKY
How is it going with your mortgage modification?

A. THOREAU
It is not going very well.
I stopped paying my mortgage
because I was advised to do so by my lawyer

from Florida.

BECKY

I have a very good lawyer. You should talk to him.
Since we have the same bank for our loan,
you may get mortgage modification as well because
you cannot pay.
I do not think it is a good idea not to pay the mortgage.
It can result in a foreclosure for you.
You should definitely talk to my lawyer.

A. THOREAU

I do not know his phone number...

Rebecca writes the phone number of her lawyer.

A. THOREAU

OK, thank you. I will call him tomorrow.

Several Hours Later

Rebecca and Aaron talk online again.

BECKY

Hi Aaron. where is your cell phone?
I called you, but you did not pick up.

A. THOREAU

Hello. My cell phone is with me.
When I connected, you disconnected.
Please, call me again.

BECKY

Are you at home now?
Can I call you now?

A. THOREAU
Yes, I am at home.
You can call me any time.

Several Days Later

Aaron and Rebecca meet online.

A. THOREAU
Hi Becky.
Where did you disappear?

BECKY
Are you back in New Hampshire?
I do not want to bother you when you are in NY.

A. THOREAU
I am still in NY.
You know, one of my friends promised to help me with the job.
I worked here as a property manager for so many years.
Many people know me in NY; I have
better chances to find a job here.

BECKY
I understand…
I just feel so sad every time you go to NY.
I really do not want you to move to NY.
I want you to stay in NH.

A. THOREAU
Becky, trust me, it was not my choice.
If the economic situation in the country was better,
I would never consider moving back to NY and working
as a property manager again.
You know, I was so tired of this job, and
I was very tired of living in NY.

BECKY
Can I call you?

Fifteen Minutes Later

Aaron sends a message to Rebecca.

A. THOREAU
I am sorry; I did not see your message.
Of course, you can call me.
As always, you can call me any time.
You do not need to ask.
Please call me any time you want.
I am always very happy when you call me.

BECKY
Are you sure that you are not busy?

A. THOREAU
I am never busy when you call.
I am always free for you.
Please do not be shy.
You can never interrupt me.
Please call me any time you want.

Several Days Later

Rebecca and Aaron meet online. They have not
talked to each other for several days.

BECKY
Hi Aaron, where are you?
Where did you disappear?
You did not call me for several days.
I did not see you online.

I was so worried about you.
Are you still in NY?
Is everything okay?
I have been waiting for you online...

A. THOREAU
Hello Rebecca. I am still in NY.
I am resolving very important issues right now.
Please call me whenever you can.
Please do not be shy. I miss you.
I want to talk to you.

BECKY
Are you sure that you still want to talk to me?

A. THOREAU
What kind of a question is that?
Do you think I have another person to talk to?

A. THOREAU (CONT'D)
Becky, I miss you a lot, and I
I miss our telephone conversations.
I just need to do a lot of things.
I told you that the year of 2009 is my year.
The year of 2009 is very important for me.
I need to resolve a lot of complex issues, and
I need to deal with many important problems.
You can call me any time.
I hope to be back at the end of this week.

BECKY
I am sorry; I just thought that maybe you
found a more interesting person in NY.
I even thought that maybe you found a girlfriend in NY.

A. THOREAU
Oh my God!

That will never happen! I have you in my
life, and I do not need anybody else.
Trust me, nothing has changed between us, and
nothing will ever change between us.
You are the only special person in my life, and
you will always be the only special person in my life.
Nothing will ever change that!

Several Weeks Later

Aaron sends a message to Rebecca.

A. THOREAU
Hi dear Becky.
I need to tell you something.
My life has changed a little.
With the help of my friend, I finally
found a job in Manhattan, NY.
I have to work as a property manager again; I have
no other choice.
My friend, who was my partner, lost his car dealership.
He was a very wealthy man, but he lost everything.
I am in the process of selling my trucking company.
I had to go back to my previous occupation.
I need to move to NY temporarily.
I know you will be upset, but I have no other choice.

BECKY
I am very sorry to hear about your friend and your business.
Why didn't you try to find a job in Boston?
I wish you found a job in Boston or in Nashua.
To be honest, I do not want you to move to NY.

A. THOREAU
Becky, honey, I have a lot of opportunities in NY.

I have a lot of connections; many people know me here.
It is much easier for me to find a well-
paying job with good benefits in NY.
I need to have a good health insurance, and my
new job has excellent health benefits.

BECKY
I am happy for you; I am happy that you found a
well-paying job with excellent health benefits.
However, I am so sad that you have to move to NY.
I know how much you love NH.
When can I see you?
Can we meet this weekend?
It is just so frustrating that every time we want
to meet in real life, something comes up.
Something prevents us from meeting in real life.
First, I was afraid, and my mother was against our meeting.
Then I got very sick and could not meet you.
Now you found a job in NY, and you are going to move there.
It is just very frustrating!

A. THOREAU
Becky, my dear, I want to meet you in real life too.
Trust me, I would never move back to NY if I had another choice.
I really love the state of New Hampshire.
This is where I am very happy.
I will definitely move back to NH.
I will not stay in NY for a long time.

A. THOREAU (CONT'D)
We will definitely meet one of the weekends.
Unfortunately, my mom is very sick, and she is not getting better.
She has a lot of doctor appointments every week.
You know, I work Sunday through Thursday.
Every Thursday evening I come back to NH, and

Every Saturday evening I have to go to NY because
my work starts on Sunday morning.
On the weekends, I have to take my mom to different doctors.
The chemotherapy is not working well. My
mom's condition is getting worse.
I do not know what to do now. I am so afraid now...
You know, I love my mom very much. I
just cannot see her suffering.
I hired a personal nurse for my mom, so that she
can take care of her while I am in NY.

BECKY
Aaron, I am so sorry to hear about your mom.
I wish I could help...
Please let me know if there is something I
could do for her while you are away.
I will be more than happy to go to NH and help your mom.
Please do not worry about anything.
We will meet when things get better for you.
I have been waiting for our meeting for so long...
Trust me, I can wait more.
I am sure everything will be okay.
As I said before, the doctors in the United
States are the best in the world.
We have the best laws and the best doctors!
Everything will be okay.
Please let me know if your mom needs anything.

A. THOREAU
Becky, thank you very much for your understanding and support!
I really appreciate everything!
I do not know what I would do without you.

Several More Weeks Later

Rebecca and Aaron meet online.

BECKY
It must be very hard for you to drive
so much from NY to NH and from NH to NY.
every week.

A. THOREAU
To be honest, I like driving.
I just do not want to fall asleep.
When I drive from NY to NH on Thursday
night after work, I really want to sleep
after a couple of hours of driving.
I am afraid to fall asleep while driving
so I listen to music.
When I do not listen to music, I talk to you.
It definitely helps me stay awake.

BECKY
It is very dangerous to drive
when you want to sleep.
Maybe it is better for you
to stop somewhere and sleep.

A. THOREAU
Even my mom says that when you
want to sleep, it is better to stop somewhere
for the night and sleep,
and then continue driving the next morning.
Once I had only 20 minutes left to reach NH,
but I just could not drive anymore because
I really wanted to sleep, so I stopped and slept
until the next morning.

BECKY
You must get very tired at work.
I know how hard it can be to work as
a property manager and always deal
with unhappy and rude tenants.
I hope the tenants do not mistreat you.

A. THOREAU
Please do not worry about me.
Over the years, I have learned how to
deal with them;
I am used to this work.

BECKY
It is very good that you do not work 24/7 now.
I am very happy for you.

A. THOREAU
To work 24/7 is impossible for me now.
My manager had to make certain
arrangements for me. As you know,
I have two days off,
on Fridays and on Saturdays.
Every Thursday evening, I go back to NH,
and every Saturday evening
I come back to NY because my work starts
on Sunday morning.

BECKY
It must be very lonely for your mom to be
in NH without you.
I can imagine how much she misses you.

A. THOREAU
Well, my mom understands me, and she
says that I must do whatever I need to do.
I hired a very good nurse for my mom,

She takes a good care of her.
Now I need to do everything possible to
survive.

Suddenly, Aaron starts talking about his failed businesses.

A. THOREAU (CONT'D)
I would love to stay in NH and continue
working in my trucking company, but
as you know, I had to sell it.
I had plans for my company to grow, but…
I wanted to buy more trucks and hire more people.
My mom knows that I had no other choice
but to come back to my previous work.
I never thought that I would be working
as a property manager again.
I was so tired of that job and of that city.
I worked as a property manager in NY for 16 years.
I was very tired of that life, and
I decided to move to NH and to be
far away from NY.
I just could not work
as a property manager anymore.

A. THOREAU (CONT'D)
You know, I had a good trucking business here.
I actually had two businesses here.
I think I told you about my second business.
In addition to having my own trucking company,
I also worked with my friend in NY, who had a big
car dealership. It was a BMW car dealership.
We were selling expensive BMW's in Europe.
We were shipping those cars to Europe
and selling them there.
Oh my God, we used to have so many customers.
I even thought about opening such a business

in Boston and working with you since you are
a very intelligent girl. .
You must remember the pictures which I sent you.

BECKY
Yes, it was a very beautiful BMW.
I really liked it, and I really liked
your idea about opening a branch in Boston.
I would be the happiest person in the
world if I could work in your company.

Aaron continues talking about BMW cars.

A. THOREAU
Those BMW cars are considered luxury cars.
That business was doing really well
before the economic crisis.
The economic crisis ruined everything
for me and my friend.
I know it ruined the lives of many people…
My friend in NY has lost everything.
He was very wealthy; he had a house
like a mansion and multiple very expensive cars.
He used to go on a vacation with his wife
and kids several times a year.
Now he does not have anything.
That car business is doing very badly, and
He has a lot of debt. He started drinking,
and I do not know what will happen to him
and his family.
I feel very bad for them.

BECKY
I am so sorry to hear that.
Aaron, please do not be sad or upset
about anything.

I am sure everything will be okay.
You moved to NY temporarily,
and your work there is temporary too.
Very soon, everything will change for you.
I heard the economy is going to get better,
and all your work related dreams
will definitely come true.
You will move back to NH permanently,
and you will open another business,
a better one than you had before.
I know that you will be very successful.
I will definitely help you and support you.
You know, I will always support you.
I will always be there for you
like you are there for me.
I will never leave you alone.
The most important thing for me is
your happiness.
It does not matter where you live
and where you work.
The most important thing for me is
your happiness and health.
I want you and your mom to be happy and healthy.
Please let me know if you need anything.
I will be more than happy to help you with
whatever I can.
I will do for you anything you need.
Please let me know if you or your mom needs anything.
I will do everything I can to help you be happy.

A. THOREAU
Rebecca, honey, thank you very much!
I really appreciate everything!
Thank you for offering to help me.
You are helping me a lot because you exist in my life.
There are only two people in my life

who completely understand me and support me —
it is you and my mom.
You and my mom are very special people in my life.
You help me go through all my difficulties.
It is a very difficult time now, but I have you,
and that helps me a lot.
I do not know what I would do without you.

BECKY
Do you have any news about
your mortgage modification?

Aaron replies sadly.

A. THOREAU
As you know, I took the advice of my lawyer
and stopped paying my mortgage.
Now I am very afraid to lose my home in NH.
I am very afraid that there will be a foreclosure on my
townhouse.
Oh my God! I think I am losing my townhouse.
I do not even know what to do.
I think I am losing everything and everyone.
My mom is in NH… She likes our townhouse a lot.
I rent a room in NY now for $700.00 a month,
and if something happens to my home in NH,..
I am so afraid to lose everything.
I am very short on money now.
There was a time when I paid a monthly bill of
almost $10,000. I could afford everything I wanted.
I could not even think that I will lose my businesses.

A. THOREAU (CONT'D)
To be honest, I am very tired of everything.
I just hope everything will be okay.

BECKY

Aaron, please do not worry.
I am sure everything will be okay.

A. THOREAU

Thank you for your support, Becky.

BECKY

It must be very uncomfortable for you to live in that room.
I know that you do not like noisy places.
By the way, who was that little girl who was crying yesterday,
when we were talking on the phone?

A. THOREAU

It is okay; I must survive everywhere.
That little girl was my neighbor's daughter.

A. THOREAU (CONT'D)

How is your mortgage modification going?

BECKY

I am sorry to hear that there is no luck
with your mortgage modification process.
I am sure everything will be okay.
I will definitely help you.
My mortgage modification is going well.
I will be more than happy to talk to
my lawyer about your townhouse.
Since we have the same bank for a loan,
you may have success with my lawyer as well.
I think my mortgage will be modified soon.
By the way, I never stopped paying my mortgage.
I know I told you this before,
but it was not a good idea to stop
paying the mortgage.
Your lawyer from Florida is not a good lawyer.

A. THOREAU
Thank you very much, Becky!
I am very unhappy with my lawyer.
I think I am going to change him.

BECKY
Aaron, you know that life is very unfair.
Some people have it all, and
others have nothing at all.
But we should always try to live our
life to the fullest. Please remember, you were
the one who told me that.
For me, the most important thing is you.
I do not care about anything else.
I want to be with you always,
You know that I really want to meet you
in real life.
Once again, I am so sorry that I did
not trust you at first.
Also, I am very sorry that it took me so long
to get ready to meet you in real life.

A. THOREAU
Becky, please do not apologize.
Everything is okay. I understand
that you had to have some time after that
terrible experience in your life.
I told you that you could have as much time as was
necessary before you could trust someone again.
We will definitely meet; I want that too.
I just need to resolve a few issues
at this time.
Unfortunately, I do not come to NH
every weekend.
Sometimes I need to stay in NY.
I have a lot of issues, which

I need to resolve in NY.
One day I will tell you about everything…
If I am in NH and if my mom does not
need to go to a doctor or to have her
chemotherapy,
we will definitely meet that weekend.

BECKY
Aaron, please do not worry about that.
You waited for me for so long, and
I will definitely wait for you for
as long as necessary.
We will meet when you resolve all your personal
and work related issues.
You are such a wonderful person, and as you
know, bad things always happen to good people.
Unfortunately, our life is very unfair.

A. THOREAU
Becky, thank you very much for
understanding me so well.
I agree; good people always suffer.

BECKY
Aaron, you are so wonderful.
You helped me so much.
No matter what issue, problem, or concern
I have, you always have a very helpful advice for me.
You always know how to help me.
You are the only person who understands me
very well and who helps me with everything.
I know that I can tell you everything, and you
will always find a way to help me.

BECKY (CONT'D)
I know I told you this so many times.
I still cannot believe that I found someone

like you on this dating website.
Before meeting you on this website,
I felt so lonely and so empty inside.
Sometimes I felt like going against the world
because I could not find anyone who would
completely understand me.
I was very depressed after that incident with Jeff.
however, you helped me overcome all my difficulties
and forget all my bad experience.
The day I met you here is definitely the
greatest day in my life.
The day when I meet you in real life will
be the happiest day of my life!
I just want you to know that you can
always count on me.
Now I definitely know that miracles happen.
You are my miracle!

A. THOREAU

Becky, honey, I think it is a miracle
that people like you still exist in this world.
I am also very grateful to this dating website
for finding you.
We are so different from the rest of the world,
and we are so similar to each other.
I think we are meant to be together.
As I said before, people like us should
definitely keep together.
My friend Nathan, who is a doctor in NY,
lives according to our life principles too.
I will definitely introduce you to him.
We should definitely meet the next year together.

BECKY

I would love to meet the next year with you
and your friend-doctor.

Rebecca smiles.

BECKY (CONT'D)
I want to meet the next year with you in
real life, not on the phone.
Although there was something
interesting about that too...
Nobody probably met the New Year
on the phone except for us.
That was very unusual.
Whenever it is a good time for you,
I would love to meet you in real life.
I can wait for you all my life.

A. THOREAU
Becky, thank you so much!
You are so supportive and understanding.
I do not know what I would do without you.
You are my miracle too.
We will definitely meet in real life,
and everything will be wonderful.
Our life will be like the best fairy tale.
I will turn your life into the best fairy tale.
We will definitely meet the next year
together in real life, although I liked
how we met the year of 2009...
We will meet all the upcoming years together.
I know that you need a serious and long-term
relationship in your life, I do too.
I feel we can have a wonderful relationship.
Let us give each other what we need.
Let us give each other what we want.
We just need to see each other in real life, and
everything will be wonderful.

BECKY

Aaron, I wish you were near me now.
I wish we were closer to each other.
I want to be with you 24/7; I want to hear
your very beautiful voice 24/7.
Now I cannot even imagine my life without
you; I cannot live without you.
My emotional attachment to you is so strong; it is
much stronger than everything else in the world.
My emotional attachment to you is bigger than
the universe and longer than eternity.
My emotional attachment to you is more valuable than my life.
My emotional attachment to you is beyond the
physical world, and it is above good and evil.
You made my life so much better; I cannot
live a day without talking to you.
I could never think that something like
this would ever happen to me.
You know, I never really liked anybody.
I never had a serious relationship with anybody
because I never really liked anybody.
However, I really like you. I have never met anybody like you.
I have never felt anything like this before.
You indeed brought so much light into my very dark life.
You made the clouds that covered the sun above me
go away; you made the clouds go away forever.
You made my life full of joy and happiness;
you made my life like in a fairy tale.
Because of you, I forgot all the terrible experiences of my life.
I forgot about all my emotional pain and sadness.
Thank you so much for everything you did for me!
I am so happy now; I was never as happy as I am now.
You were so right when you said that miracles do not happen
often, if they did, they would not be called miracles.

BECKY (CONT'D)
I have lived 23 years in this world, and I met
someone like you for the first time in my life.
I met a very intelligent, interesting, kind-hearted, compassionate,
understanding, and polite person for the first time in my life.
You are so smart. I have never met anyone who
knows philosophy and politics so well.
I have never met anyone who has such a
beautiful soul and kind heart.
I have never met anyone who has such wonderful life principles.
To be honest, I do not even think that there
is someone else like you in this world.
I think you are the only one; you are so
different from everybody else.
You are indeed a miracle in this world! You are a miracle in my life!
I am willing to do anything and everything
for you. I will go wherever you go.
I really like you a lot, and I really want to
spend the rest of my life only with you.
I want to spend every second of my life with you.
You are the first person in my life that I like so much.
I have never liked anyone as much as I like you.
I want to be as much part of your life as you are part of my life.
I am sorry for telling you all this. I am sorry
for being so honest about my feelings.

A. THOREAU
Honey, please do not be shy, and please do not feel uncomfortable.
You should never be sorry for being honest.
Please never say, "I am sorry."
You can tell me everything the way it is.
You can tell me everything you want. I understand everything.
It makes me feel so special to hear all this from you.
I am also very happy that I met you, and
that I have you in my life now.

You are the miracle of my life too, and I want
to spend the rest of my life with you!
As I said before, you are a very special person in my life,
and you will always be very special. I will make your life
much better than it is now. You can be sure in that.
I want to be with you 24/7, and I want to be
with you every second of my life too.
You are also not like everybody else, and I think it is
a miracle that we met on this dating website.
We will definitely be together, I promise.
We just need to see each other in real life, and then our life will be
wonderful. Our life will be a real miracle after we meet in real life.
I am sure it will work out between us in
real life. I have no doubt in that.
When two people love each other, that
is the most important thing.
I promise, our life will be like a fairy tale
after we see each other in real life.
You know, I never say things for the sake of saying them.
If I say something, I mean it.
If I promise something, I do it.
I live according to a great statement by H. D. Thoreau,
"Be true to your word, be true to your friend."
I think a person should always prove his words
and beliefs with real life actions.
As Mavrodi says, "I do not believe; I act. I will
show you my beliefs through my actions."

BECKY
Aaron, I just cannot wait until the day when we meet in real life.
I have been waiting for this day for so long.
However, I understand that you have a lot of problems now.

A. THOREAU
Becky, honey, we will definitely meet very soon, and
we will be much happier than now.

Trust me, we will be much happier when we meet in real life.
Thank you for your understanding and patience!

BECKY

Please do not be sad.
You were the one who told me that one should always
think positively, and one should never give up.
You used to be so positive when we first met online.
I just do not want you to be sad.

A. THOREAU

Becky my dear, thank you very much for your support.
You know, when we met, I was a successful businessman, and
I did not have any issues.
However, I lost my businesses, and I am
losing my townhouse in NH.
I had to move back to NY and work as a property manager again.
I could never imagine that I would end up where I started.
However, the saddest thing is that I think
that I am losing everyone I love.
My poor mom is not getting better. Nothing helps her.
I just do not know what to do.

BECKY

Aaron, I will always be with you.
No matter what happens, I will be with you.
I will always support you. You will never lose me.
I thank God every day for meeting you
and for having you in my life.
I have never liked anybody as much as I like you.
Your problems are my problems now.
Together, we will resolve all your issues and problems.

A. THOREAU

Honey, thank you very much for everything!
I thank God every day for having you in my life too.
You are the light in my dark life!

I have never met such a wonderful and kind-hearted person.
You are such a beautiful person inside and outside.
Thank you for being in my life!

BECKY

Aaron, I have never met anyone like you too!
Thank you for being in my life!

Several Days Later

Rebecca changes her profile picture on the
dating website and talks to Aaron.

BECKY
Hi. How are you?

A. THOREAU
Hello. Do we know each other?

BECKY
No, we do not.
However, I would like to know you.

A. THOREAU
Why are you so interested in me?

Rebecca laughs.

BECKY
Oh my God, Aaron! This is Becky.
You did not recognize me! It was a joke.
I wanted to make you laugh.

A. THOREAU
I am sorry; I did not recognize you.

Aaron smiles.

A. THOREAU (CONT'D)
That was an interesting joke.

Rebecca changes the subject of their conversation.

BECKY
I cannot believe I will finally meet you in real life.
I just cannot believe we will finally see each other in real life.

Aaron jokes.

A. THOREAU
Trust me, you will meet me; you will not
meet an alien from a different planet.

Rebecca laughs.

BECKY
I am sure you are a human being, probably
the best person in the world.
You know, we have the same moral values and life principles.
I have never even dreamed about meeting someone like you.
I have become so attached to you. I cannot
live a day without talking to you.
I cannot live a day without hearing your beautiful voice.

BECKY (CONT'D)
Aaron, you have become the meaning of my life.
I do not know how I lived my life when I did not know you.
I cannot wait to see you in real life.
I want to talk to you in real life.
I want to hear your beautiful voice in real life.

Aaron smiles.

A. THOREAU

Thank you very much, Becky.
I feel the same way.
You have become the meaning of my life too.
I do not know how I lived my life without you.
I cannot wait to see you in real life too.

CHAPTER 13

REBECCA AND AARON

Rebecca and Aaron talk online and on the phone every day. They usually talk every evening after 9:00 PM. Aaron calls their 9:00 PM conversations "dates" on the phone. During their telephone and online conversations, Aaron tells Rebecca about himself. He tells her that Henry David Thoreau is indeed his relative. He likes and admires Thoreau because he was a very intelligent person, who had a free spirit, and who was not afraid to fight against injustice. Aaron says that he is a man of honor, who would rather die than lie. Aaron always criticizes dishonest and indecent people. He especially does not like the majority of people on dating websites. Aaron associates himself with the idea of simple living in natural surroundings. Aaron's dream is to build a little house with a fireplace in the mountains in New Hampshire and live there alone surrounded by wild animals. Aaron is not afraid of wild animals, and he would like to live with them. Aaron loves the state of New Hampshire, and his favorite place is the White Mountains.

Aaron likes fire; fire has a special meaning for him. He promises to tell Rebecca some day what meaning fire has for him. He loves to sit in his massage chair, look at the fire in his fireplace, and talk to Rebecca on the phone. He tells Rebecca that when he talks to her, he feels so relaxed and incredibly good. Aaron tells Rebecca that he enjoys talking to her a lot, and that she can call him any time. Aaron says that he can talk to Rebecca 24/7, and it would still be not enough for him. At first, Rebecca feels uncomfortable to call Aaron because she is afraid to bother him, to interrupt him. However, Aaron says that she never bothers or interrupts him, and that he is always free for her. Aaron says that he always has time to talk to Rebecca. He can never be busy when she calls.

Aaron has very good manners; he is extremely polite, and he never makes any inappropriate statements or suggestions. He never uses improper words or expressions. Unlike many other people on dating websites, Aaron never offers anything inappropriate to Rebecca since that is immoral and against Aaron's life principles. He definitely knows how to talk to a woman and how to treat a woman well. Aaron treats Rebecca very well, and he is always extremely polite. Aaron is very generous and kind-hearted. He enjoys helping his friends and his loved ones. He even helps the people on the streets who ask for money; he always gives them at least one dollar.

Aaron offers to retaliate against Rebecca's enemies; he especially wants to revenge against Jeff for what he did to her. Aaron tells Rebecca that he will always help her, and he will always be there for her. Aaron says that Rebecca should not be afraid of anything or anyone since she has Aaron in her life now. Rebecca has never talked to such a nice and polite person.

Aaron's townhouse is located not far from the renowned White Mountains in New Hampshire. It is surrounded by the incredible nature and unforgettable mountain views. The living room is warm, inviting, and comfortable with a beautiful fireplace. Aaron lives there with his sick mother. Aaron's mother has leukemia, and she has to go through chemotherapy a couple of times a year. Aaron loves his mother a lot, and he cannot even imagine his life without her. He would never agree to take his mother to a nursing home. In one of their telephone conversations, Aaron says that he is very afraid to lose his mother, and he cannot understand how some people allow their old parents to live in nursing homes. He would never do anything like that to his mother.

In another telephone conversation, Aaron tells Rebecca a truly shocking story. He says that the number 11 is his lucky number because it has a special meaning for him. When Aaron was 11 years old, he almost killed another boy who insulted his mother. It was a miracle that the boy survived after being seriously injured. Aaron will do anything and everything possible to make his mother feel better, and he will never allow anyone to mistreat her. Once Aaron tells Rebecca that he got very upset at the hospital one day when his mother felt worse after her chemotherapy. He got so mad at the doctors that the hospital staff had to call security. The doctors did something wrong, and his mother almost died. Aaron was very upset, and he even called his doctor-friend in NY for an advice. Fortunately, the doctors understood their mistake on time, and nothing happened to Aaron's mother.

Aaron's mother is a History teacher, and she used to teach History in schools all her life. Aaron's father is a pilot, who knows how to fly civil and military airplanes. Aaron's father wanted him to become a pilot too; however, Aaron did not live up to his father's expectations. Aaron does not talk much about his father, who lives in Europe. Aaron's birthday is January 1. This date has a special meaning for him too. Aaron tells Rebecca that his mother used to say that he was born on the first day of the first month (January) in order to be number one in life. He should be number one in everything he does and everywhere he goes. Aaron should always be number one in life because he was born on January 1.

Aaron tells Rebecca that he had four long-term relationships with women; one of them was a marriage. However, all of the relationships were a big disappointment and failure for him. All those women disappointed and mistreated Aaron, and he cannot trust anybody anymore. He tells Rebecca that everyone wanted to take advantage of him, and nobody wanted to understand him. He says that he does not have any children; however, all the women wanted children by him.

Aaron talks a lot about his ex-girlfriend from Colombia, who lived with him in NY and his last ex-girlfriend from Russia, who lived with him in NH for some time. He had a terrible experience with the Russian ex-girlfriend, who had a mood disorder. Aaron does not like candles at home; he does not like when someone lights up candles at home because it is too dangerous. His Russian girlfriend liked candles very much, and she put candles everywhere. In addition, she had a borderline personality disorder, and it was almost impossible to live with her due to her constant mood changes. Aaron also accepted her 12-year old son, but the boy did not treat him well too. Aaron wanted to break up with his Russian ex-girlfriend for a long time. However, his mother felt sorry for that woman and her child because they had no place to live, and she did not want them to break up. Aaron tells Rebecca that his mother is a wonderful and very kind-hearted woman, and she wants everybody to be happy.

Aaron says that a lot of women fall in love with him, but they are not for him. He cannot find the right person. He tells Rebecca interesting stories about all the woman that fell in love with him.

Aaron worked as a property manager in NY for many years before he moved to NH. When he worked as a property manager in NY, some of his female tenants would fall in love with him. Some of them were married and had children. Once a female tenant hugged and kissed Aaron so unexpectedly that Aaron felt very uncomfortable. He came to the girl's apartment in order to fix her problem with the heat; he never provoked that girl.

One of his mother's nurses fell in love with Aaron, The nurse was married and had two kids, but she was ready to leave her husband because of Aaron. Even Aaron's mortgage broker, who lived in Colorado (CO), and who helped Aaron buy his townhouse in NH, fell in love with him and wanted him to move to Colorado and live with her. Another girl would not leave Aaron alone for five years. That girl loved Aaron very much, and she even tried to commit suicide a couple of times because she wanted Aaron to marry her. Even that girl's relatives called Aaron and asked him to marry her since the girl loved him so much. However, Aaron was not in love with that girl, and he could not marry her.

Aaron admires two very interesting men – Henry David Thoreau, an American philosopher and Sergey Mavrodi, a Russian businessman.

Aaron associates himself with the ideas of H. D. Thoreau and Mavrodi. He always mentions their famous quotes. In addition, Aaron likes Mike Tyson. He watched almost all of his tournaments and championships. Aaron admires Tyson because he achieved everything in his life due to his hard work and determination. Unfortunately, Tyson's mother died when he was a young boy, and she did not see her son's boxing matches. Aaron says that he has a picture with Tyson, and he sends that picture to Rebecca. Aaron tells her that he has many awards for boxing; he is a boxer too. He promises to show Rebecca all of his awards when she is in his townhouse. Boxing is one of his hobbies, and it is an important part of his life. His passion is not only airplanes but boxing too. He wants to open a school for boxing and teach young boys.

In his free time, Aaron likes to fly an airplane with his flight instructor, to run in the mornings, to practice boxing, to play hockey and football, to ski in the mountains, and to listen to his favorite music. Aaron says that he does not drink or smoke at all, and people do not understand him because of that. Aaron has one very good friend in NY who understands him; he is a doctor. Aaron's friend always tries to help Aaron when he catches a cold, and he always helps Aaron's sick mother with his recommendations. Aaron likes sports a lot, especially boxing and running in the morning. He runs every morning. On the weekends, he enjoys flying an airplane with his flight instructor. Aaron is tall (6'2") and handsome. He says that he looks like his mother. Aaron tells Rebecca that he does not want to upload his real pictures to the dating website because more people will be writing him. Once, when he had his pictures on the website, he received about one hundred messages in one day.

Aaron tells Rebecca that when he lived in NY, he worked as a property manager. He worked as a property manager for almost 16 years. His last manager was a very good man, and Aaron did a lot for him. Some of the tasks he performed were not related to his job responsibilities. He always went above and beyond his job responsibilities. Aaron's manager was a very wealthy man, and

Aaron acted as his personal bodyguard sometimes. Aaron also tells Rebecca how difficult it was for him to get a license for repairing air conditioners and refrigerators since he did not speak English well when he came to the United States 20 years ago. He tells Rebecca that it was the hardest test he ever took.

Aaron always gives helpful suggestions on how Becky can improve her life. He even says that she should find a new job because, given her education and the amount of loans she has, she should be paid at least $70,000 a year. Rebecca is not making a lot of money in the school where she teaches Philosophy. At first, Aaron even offers a job opportunity to Becky at his trucking company. He says that he has been looking for a smart and educated person for a long time. Then he thinks about investing in real estate, and tells Becky that they should think about that together.

However, in one of their telephone conversations, Aaron confesses that he has a very serious problem. He suffers from panic attacks. He has panic attacks because of everything that he has been through. He has had panic attacks for a long time, and he is able to manage his panic attacks now, but they still bother him. He feels very uncomfortable when he tells Rebecca about his panic disorder. However, he says that it is not unusual for people like him to have anxiety disorders. He thinks that all great people have anxiety disorders.

Once Aaron tells Rebecca that he almost stabbed a little boy with a knife because that boy insulted his mother. Rebecca does not tell this story to her mother. Elizabeth, Rebecca's mother, does not think that Aaron is the right person for her daughter. He is 12 years older than Rebecca, and he had four long-term relationships, which were unsuccessful. Aaron causes tension between Elizabeth and Rebecca. The relationship between a mother and a daughter becomes very tense. Elizabeth even tries to prevent Rebecca from calling Aaron. However, she is not able to do that, and finally, she accepts Aaron as Rebecca's friend.

CHAPTER 14

DREAMS COME TRUE

September 22, 2010: Boston, Massachusetts (MA) – Boston University

Elizabeth continues her speech at Boston University...

ELIZABETH
Rebecca and Aaron finally agreed to meet
one of the weekends. Their meeting day
was supposed to be on Saturday, 05/09/2009.
They chose that special date accidentally.

May 9 is a special day in the whole world.
It is a Victory Day. It marks the capitulation
of Nazi Germany in the Second World War.
The whole world became free again on that day.
For me and for my daughter, this day has become
special on so many different levels.
The best day in the history of humanity has become
the worst day in the history of my family...

ELIZABETH (CONT'D)
Aaron is not sure if he can be in NH on Saturday, 05/09/2009,
and he says that he will call Rebecca.
He calls her on Thursday evening, and says that he will be in NH,
but he is not sure if he is free on Saturday.
He needs to take his mom to a hospital for chemotherapy.
He says that he will call on Saturday morning and let her know.

Rebecca feels that Aaron is a little reluctant
to meet her for some reason.

At first, he always invited my daughter to different places.
However, now when she is ready to meet him, and
she dreams to talk to him in real life,
Aaron does not seem so enthusiastic about their meeting.
Rebecca is afraid to think that this may be because of all
the time that it took her to have full trust in him and
then recover from her illness.
Rebecca wants to think that Aaron has changed a little
because he is going through a very difficult time in his life.
Aaron lost his businesses. He is losing his townhouse in NH,
and his mom is very sick and feels worse and worse every day.

ELIZABETH (CONT'D)
Aaron calls Becky at about 11:00 AM on Saturday, 05/09/2009,
and he says that he can meet her that day.
He tells Becky that he needs to be back in NY in the evening
since he should be at work on Sunday morning.
Aaron works on Sundays, and his days off
are on Fridays and Saturdays.

My daughter and Aaron decide to meet in a park in Lynn, MA
next to North Shore Community College.
We live not far from that park.
Becky provides the address to Aaron, and
he says that he will not have trouble finding that park
since he has a good GPS in his car.

Becky is very happy and excited.
I have never seen my daughter as happy as she was that day.
For Becky, this is the happiest and the most special day in her life.
The mere thought of meeting Aaron in real life gives
my daughter hot flashes.
She thinks that she will faint when she sees Aaron in real life.
Becky is a little afraid that Aaron may not like her in real life...
Rebecca wants to look very beautiful.
I even thought that my daughter would not be able to say anything

because she was too happy.

ELIZABETH (CONT'D)
Becky wants to hear Aaron's beautiful voice in real life.
She has been talking to him only on the phone.
She wants to hear the sound of his amazing voice in real life.
My daughter is so happy and delighted that
her eyes shine with happiness.
Becky puts on beautiful make-up.
She puts up her gorgeous, long, black hair.
She wears a long, black skirt, a black blouse with silver flowers,
a beautiful white jacket, golden shoes with
high hills, and black stockings.
My poor daughter completely forgets
about her terrible skin allergy.

Becky was not supposed to dye her hair because
she has an allergy to hair dye.
However, she colored her hair in order to be more beautiful.
She wanted to have black hair color because
it looks very good on her.
In addition, my daughter was afraid that Aaron would not like her.
Now she has a terrible burning and itching sensation on her scalp.
She could not sleep for the past several nights.
Rebecca almost lost her life because of that hair dye.
She dyed her hair in order to be more beautiful for Aaron.
There are no medications to treat that kind of allergy, and
my daughter's medicated shampoos do not help.
She knows that there is no treatment from that kind of allergy.
Becky already had that allergy once, and
she felt a little better only after several years.
However, she risked her life for Aaron again.
Now her health is almost ruined.
She can barely survive with those terrible symptoms.

However, Rebecca does not care about her skin problems today

because it is her happiest day in life.
She has been waiting for this day for such a long time
that she cannot even believe that the day
of their meeting has finally come.
She does not believe that she will finally meet Aaron in real life.
First, Rebecca was afraid to trust Aaron.
Then I did not want them to meet because I was afraid
that something bad will happen to my daughter.
Then Becky was sick for a long time, and when she recovered from
the illness, Aaron moved back to NY temporarily.

My daughter is so beautiful today.
I have never seen Becky as beautiful and happy as she was that day.

Saturday, May 9, 2009: Lynn, MA – Rebecca's Apartment

It is 12:10 PM. Rebecca is brushing her long, black hair.

BECKY
Mom, I am so happy.
I have never been as happy as I am today.
I think Aaron is the best person in the world,
No one can be compared to Aaron.
He is incomparable on so many levels.
I know I told you this many times before,
but he is unlike anybody else I have ever met.
It is such a great pleasure
just to talk to him on the phone.
By the way, I think he has the most beautiful
voice in the world.
He helped me forget everything bad
that ever happened to me.
I thought I would never forget Jeff; however,
I can barely remember him now.
What he did to me does not bother me anymore.

Mom, I am not afraid to admit that
he is the love of my life, the meaning of my existence.
Aaron is the most wonderful and the most
polite person in the world!

ELIZABETH
Becky, dear, I am very happy that
you are so happy.
I am very happy that Aaron treats
you so well.
I just hope that everything you
say about him is true.
You know, I did not trust him at all at first.
I also did not think that he is
the best match for you.
However, if you like each other so much,
I will not interfere in your relationship.
Nevertheless, please do not idealize him.
Please remember that no one is perfect.
Please remember that there is something
negative about everyone.

BECKY
Mom, thank you so much for finally
understanding me.
Believe me, Aaron is indeed wonderful.
He is very different from everybody else.
He is just incapable of doing something bad.
I think he does not have any negative qualities.
I understand that we all have weaknesses,
and I know that nobody is perfect,
but I like everything about Aaron.
I am sure that he will never hurt me or
disappoint me.
I have full trust and full confidence in him.

ELIZABETH
Well, Rebecca, if you like each other
in real life too and decide to have a relationship,
I will not interfere.
However, our families will need to meet.
Our families will have to be introduced to each other.

BECKY
Of course, mom!
Aaron's mother is a wonderful person.
You and dad will be happy to meet her.
I am sure you will like Aaron a lot too.
It is just impossible not to like him.
He is my fearless hero – the mysterious friend
from New Hampshire.
Aaron is a very special person in my life!
I think he is the best person in the world!
I have been waiting for him all my life!
I just cannot wait to see him in real life.

*Saturday, May 09, 2009: Lynn, MA – North Shore Community
College Park*

It is a sunny and beautiful day. It is a little windy
outside, but it is almost 70 degrees.
The nature is amazing in the park, where Rebecca and
Aaron decided to meet. The tree are in blossom, and they
are surrounded by blooming flowers. The white clouds
cover the dark blue sky. The birds are singing. The sun
is smiling. It appears that the summer is coming.

Rebecca is waiting for Aaron in the park. It is
already 1:00 PM, but he is not there yet.

Rebecca calls Aaron.

BECKY
Hi Aaron.
I am just a little worried…
Where are you?
Is everything okay?

A. THOREAU
Hi Becky.
Everything is fine.
I am sorry for running late.
I did not realize that there is so much traffic in Lynn
because the streets are very narrow.

BECKY
No problem, Aaron.
I am in the park next to North Shore Community College.
I am standing next to the college entrance, and
I am waiting for you.

A. THOREAU
I am very close to the park.

Aaron drives closer to the destination.

A. THOREAU (CONT'D)
I think I see you…

Rebecca sees a black SUV driving by the college.

BECKY
I think I see you too…

A. THOREAU
Okay, let me park my car somewhere.
I will park my car, and I will be in the park very soon.

Rebecca comes up to a bench, which is not far from the college entrance and stands there. She puts a blue bag on the bench. Inside the bag, there is a present that she prepared for Aaron. She bought his favorite CDs and a DVD.

Finally, at about 1:20 PM, Rebecca sees a man approaching her. As the man comes closer and closer, her heart starts beating faster and faster. Rebecca cannot imagine that in a couple of seconds, she will meet the person of her dreams, her mysterious and fearless hero that she loves so much. In a couple of seconds, Rebecca will meet her mysterious friend from New Hampshire. The approaching man sees Rebecca and waves his hand, and Rebecca waves her hand too, but she cannot see Aaron well since he is still too far from her. Finally, after talking to each other online and on the phone for about seven months, they meet in real life. Aaron comes up to Rebecca, and she sees him.

Rebecca does not believe what she sees. She does not believe her eyes. Rebecca is speechless and motionless. She does not know what to say or what to do. It is like being hit by lightning or being electrocuted. She does not understand anything. Rebecca's world turned upside down the second that she saw Aaron. The first thing that she notices is that Aaron is not as tall as he said he is. He said that he is very tall (6'2"), but he is not much taller than Rebecca, and she is 5'7". Rebecca looks taller because of her high hills. Aaron is a little taller than Rebecca; he is about 5'10".

Then Rebecca notices that Aaron has big scars all over his face; they are especially visible when he smiles. The scars are very big around his eyes. Aaron's scars that are all over his face look very scary. Moreover, his face has a very unhealthy color. Rebecca remembers that Aaron told her that he had been in some accident, but he said that the plastic surgery completely restored his outer appearance and corrected all his skin defects. The pictures that Aaron sent Rebecca did not have any scars and did not show any skin problems. However, the reality is very different. The scars on Aaron's face shock

Rebecca and make her feel very uncomfortable. For a moment, she even feels sorry for Aaron. Rebecca does not understand why the plastic surgery did not help him at all.

Then Rebecca notices Aaron's unusually big eyes, and that one of the eyes looks much smaller than the other. His eyes are very big, dark brown, and very shiny. She cannot even look in his eyes; they seem to be so unreal. She has never seen anyone with such huge and shiny eyes. In addition, Aaron has very deep wrinkles around his mouth. He looks much older than 36 years old. Rebecca sees that almost all of his hair is gray, but in the pictures that Aaron sent her, he has a very beautiful, golden brown hair color. In those pictures, he has very beautiful eyes, and he does not have any scars on his face. He even looks a little younger than 36 years old in some of those pictures. However, in real life, Aaron does not look like 36 years old at all.

On one of his arms, Aaron has bright red spots, which look very visible in real life. In the pictures that he sent Rebecca, those red spots were almost invisible. Rebecca did not even pay much attention to them. She could never imagine how bad those red spots look in real life. It appears that these bright red spots on his arm are scars from being burned by fire. Then Rebecca looks down at his hands; they look so rough and big. His fingers are unusually large, and they look as if they were burned by the fire too. Rebecca does not even understand how he could type on the computer or work as a property manager with such hands. It must be extremely uncomfortable. It appears that Aaron's skin has been terribly disfigured by the fire. Maybe Aaron was indeed burned by the fire; that is why, he said that the fire has a special meaning for him. Maybe the fire destroyed his outer appearance and his life.

Then Rebecca looks down at Aaron's neck and chest. The skin on Aaron's neck looks old; she sees some of his black chest hair sticking out of his red T-Shirt. Rebecca cannot understand why Aaron's skin looks so old and so disfigured, and why the color of his skin is very unhealthy. Aaron, Rebecca's fearless hero, was supposed to be an honest, decent, trustworthy, polite, compassionate, young, handsome, attractive, and athletic person. Rebecca cannot even recognize the person standing in front of her; she cannot believe that this is the person that she talked to for almost seven months.

As Rebecca looks at Aaron, she wonders if he is really a boxer, and if he can fly airplanes.

She also remembers all the stories that he told her about the women who fell in love with Aaron because he has inner beauty and outer beauty. Rebecca used to think about their first date a lot, and how Aaron brings her flowers, and she hugs him so tight that she feels his heart beat. She wanted to hug him and kiss him when they met in real life. She wanted to touch his beautiful golden brown hair. She wanted to talk to him and hear his beautiful voice in real life. However, Rebecca does not know the person standing in front of her; she has never seen that person before. For a moment, Rebecca even doubts that this is the person that she has been talking to on the phone and online for so many months. Rebecca is so shocked that she cannot move or speak.

When Aaron comes up to Becky, they greet each other. Aaron does not have any flowers for her.

The fact that Aaron did not bring any flowers surprises Rebecca. She expected that he would bring her flowers on their first date. Aaron wears blue jeans, black sneakers, a red T-Shirt with something written on it, and a light brown jacket. His blue jeans look a little dirty. Aaron does not look like a boxer at all. His body type is not athletic. He is too thin to be a boxer. It does not seem that he likes sports.

It was Rebecca's dream to hug Aaron so tight, to touch and feel him. However, she is paralyzed by what she sees. In real life, Aaron is a completely different person; he is a severely disfigured person. At first, Rebecca does not even know what to do and what to say. She has never been in a situation like this before. She has never seen a person like that before. Rebecca decides to act as if nothing happened, and everything is okay. Rebecca decides to act as if the person in front of her is the man that she expected to meet.

As Rebecca looks at Aaron, she remembers a story that he told her once, a story that she never told her mother.

BECKY
Aaron, after what Jeff did to me, I am so scared.
Sometimes I feel that I am afraid of everybody.

A. THOREAU
Becky, honey, please do not be afraid of anybody or anything.
Sometimes I think that you are afraid of me too.
Please do not be afraid of me; I will never hurt you.
I just need to tell you something...
There are two things that can scare you when we meet in real life.
However, please do not be afraid of me.

Saturday, May 09, 2009: Lynn, MA – North Shore Community College Park

After looking at each other for several seconds,
Rebecca and Aaron start talking.

BECKY
Hi Aaron.

A. THOREAU
Hi Rebecca.
I am sorry for being late.
There was a lot of traffic;
I did not realize that the streets in Lynn
are so narrow.

BECKY
It is okay; please do not worry.

Even my driving teacher, many years ago,
used to say that if a person knows how
to drive in Lynn,
that person can drive anywhere else.

BECKY (CONT'D)
By the way, this is for you.

Rebecca gives Aaron a blue bag, a little gift that she put together for him with so much love. Inside the bag, there are two music CDs with his favorite songs "House of the Rising Sun" by the Animals and "Losing my Religion" by R.E.M and one CD by *Blatnoy Udar* that he dreamed to have but could not get it anywhere. Rebecca found Aaron's favorite CD by *Blatnoy Udar* on one music website, and she bought it for him. Rebecca wanted to surprise Aaron. She also decided to give Aaron one of her favorite CDs, a CD by Amedeo Minghi with the song "The Memories of My Heart." Inside the bag, there is also one DVD. It is Aaron's most favorite movie *With Fire and Sword* – a Polish historical drama, which was very difficult to find online. Aaron loves historical films a lot since his mother is a history teacher. He had seen *With Fire and Sword* multiple times, and he dreams to watch it again. Rebecca paid almost $60.00 for that film because she wanted Aaron to have it.

Aaron is very surprised by the gift.

A. THOREAU
Oh my God! Is this for me?

BECKY
Yes, this is for you.
Please take it.

Aaron takes the little bag, but he does not look inside.

A. THOREAU
Thank you very much!

I did not expect this!
I am so shocked!
I do not have anything for you now.
However, I owe you a lot for this.
I will definitely do something in return.

Becky replies sadly.

BECKY
Thank you, I do not really need anything.

Rebecca offers Aaron to sit on one of the benches in the park.

BECKY (CONT'D)
Let us sit here.

Rebecca and Aaron sit down. Rebecca tries not to look
at Aaron too much, and she tries not to show that she
is shocked, astonished, and feels uncomfortable.

Rebecca stares at Aaron again. She has never
seen such a disfigured person in real life.

A. THOREAU
Why are you looking at me like this?
Maybe you are not used to seeing me in real life.

Rebecca tries to smile.

BECKY
Well, I am looking at you, and
you are looking at me.
We are just looking at each other and talking.

Aaron and Rebecca continue talking to each other...

A. THOREAU

Becky, let us change this bench and sit somewhere else.
The sun is too bright where we sit, and I feel uncomfortable
because of the bright sun.

BECKY

Okay, no problem.
Let us sit on a different bench.

Aaron and Rebecca choose a different bench in the park, and they sit
down. Aaron crosses his legs when he sits on the bench and stares at
Rebecca. They sit very close to each other, and Rebecca is able to see
very well everything that Aaron hid from her for such a long time.

A. THOREAU

It is a beautiful place here.

BECKY

Lynn is not considered a safe place.
There are a lot of criminals here.

A. THOREAU

Well, I think it is beautiful here.
You have the ocean view.

BECKY

Yes, the area by the ocean is very beautiful.

A. THOREAU

Were you able to remove the black hair color
from the wooden floor?

Rebecca accidentally spilled her hair dye on the
floor when she was coloring her hair.
She told Aaron about it on the phone, and he
advised her to buy a stain remover.

BECKY
No, I did not remove it.
The black stain is sill on the floor.
I did not have a chance to buy a stain remover.
Do not worry about that.
I am happy that my hair color is black now.
I like black hair color.

Aaron looks at Rebecca's hair.

BECKY (CONT'D)
My hardwood floors are not good any way.
They need to be renovated.

A. THOREAU
Do they need to be polished?

BECKY
Yes, probably...

Somebody calls Aaron, and he cannot find his
headphone. Finally, he finds the headphone.

A. THOREAU
Hello, I am at a business meeting now.
I will call you later.
I will call you in about two hours.

Aaron and Rebecca continue talking...

A. THOREAU (CONT'D)
You know, life breaks some people.
They become depressed and start drinking or
using drugs.
One of my very good friends was so successful.
Then something happened, and he
became a drug addict.

He lost his humanity because of that.
He lost everything and everyone because of drugs.
Now he does not have anything or anyone left.

Rebecca remembers one of their telephone conversations…

BECKY
Unfortunately, there are so many people who use drugs.
I wish they understood that drugs ruin human lives.

A. THOREAU
Becky, you are absolutely correct.
Drugs are terrible, and they can definitely ruin a person's life.
A person should never use drugs!
However, a lot of people ruin their lives in order to get
seconds of pleasure.

BECKY
Do you know what it feels like to take drugs?

A. THOREAU
When one takes drugs, he or she feels very relaxed.
The pleasure that one receives is unforgettable and incredible.
It cannot be compared to anything else in the world.
The pleasure from taking drugs is very similar to
the pleasure that one gets from having sex.
That pleasure lasts only a few seconds, but it is amazing.
It is like swimming in the cold ocean after being burned by fire.
It is like eating your favorite food after having starved for a week.
It is like drinking your favorite juice after being thirsty for a week.
Unfortunately, that pleasure lasts only several seconds…

A. THOREAU (CONT'D)
By the way, this is how Sergey Mavrodi describes
having sex in his book *Temptation*:
"They were experiencing the feelings of pleasure,
pain, passion, admiration, and awe.

They were flying high in the skies and
then falling down underground.
They were dying and being reborn together."

BECKY
Wow! You know so much about sex and drugs.
Have you ever tried drugs?
Have you ever wanted to try them?

A. THOREAU
Oh my God! Of course I have never tried drugs, and
I never wanted to try them.
I was smart enough not to ruin my life
because of seconds of pleasure.

BECKY
Then how do you know so much about drugs?

A. THOREAU
I have seen my friends take drugs...

*Saturday, May 09, 2009: Lynn, MA – North Shore Community
College Park*

Rebecca and Aaron continue talking. Rebecca
tries to show concern for Aaron's friend.

BECKY
How is your friend doing now?
Does he still use drugs?

A. THOREAU
He stopped using drugs now, but he cannot
get back his humanity.
He not only lost everything and everyone...
Unfortunately, he has some mental issues now.

Aaron talks very quietly, and at times, he seems to be very sad. He talks to Rebecca in a very calm manner. Aaron has a very beautiful voice in real life. However, his voice sounds a little different in real life than on the phone. Aaron's voice is very beautiful and extraordinary. In real life, his voice is a little softer than on the phone. It is very pleasant to hear his voice.

Aaron tries to look happy; Rebecca tries not to look at Aaron anymore. She looks down at his hands. Aaron tries to cover the bright, red spots on his arm with his gray jacket.

Aaron continues to talk about the harsh reality of everyday life.

> A. THOREAU (CONT'D)
> Our life is such that it can break anybody.
> Some people become alcoholics,
> others become drug addicts.
> Some people commit suicide...
> However, it is very important not to break.
> We must be strong in order to survive and win.
> We should never break regardless of circumstances.

Rebecca changes the subject of their conversation.

> BECKY
> How do you like your job
> as a property manager in NY?

Aaron replies sadly.

> A. THOREAU
> This is the only thing that I can do right now.
> I cannot do anything else.

Aaron looks at Rebecca, and his eyes shine even more.

A. THOREAU (CONT'D)
I mean there are a lot of things that I can do…
I just do not want to risk my life.

BECKY
No, you should not risk your life.
Please do not risk your life.

Rebecca changes the subject of their conversation again.

BECKY (CONT'D)
How is your mom?
Is it okay that you left her alone at home?

Aaron looks down and replies sadly.

A. THOREAU
It is okay. She has been watching movies
about World War Two and crying all morning.

BECKY
Do you know that now it is possible to
turn black and white films into colorful movies?

Aaron is surprised.

A. THOREAU
Really? I have never heard about that.

BECKY
Yes, that is true.
Now they have the technology to do that.

A. THOREAU
It is getting very cold here.
We can go to a coffee shop, sit inside,
and continue our conversation.

BECKY
No, thank you.
There are no good coffee shops around here.
You know, this is Lynn…

A. THOREAU
I have seen one when I was driving.
It is close to this park.

BECKY
I really do not think that there are good coffee places around here.
Please, let us stay in the park.

A. THOREAU
Okay, no problem.
If you want to stay here, we can stay here.

A woman passes by the bench where
Aaron and Rebecca are sitting.

BECKY
Look at that woman.
Why did she look at us like that?
What is her problem?

A. THOREAU
Do not pay attention to that woman.
Please forget about her.

A. THOREAU (CONT'D)
It is getting very cold here.
It is very windy where we sit.
I think I am freezing here.
Please let us change the bench again.

BECKY
Are you really that cold?

I think it is almost 70 degrees outside.

A. THOREAU
The wind here is just killing me.

BECKY
Okay, if you want, we can change the bench again.

A. THOREAU
Let us move to a bench that is at the end of the park.

A. THOREAU (CONT'D)
Please do not be afraid of me.
Do not be afraid of anyone.
Do not be afraid of anything.
You have me now, and you do not need anybody else…

Rebecca says sadly.

BECKY
I am not afraid…

Rebecca and Aaron start walking towards a different bench…

As they walk, Aaron starts talking about their online experience.

A. THOREAU
How long have we talked online?

BECKY
We have talked for about seven months.

Aaron smiles.

A. THOREAU
Oh, no. That cannot be just seven months.
I think it is much longer than that.

It is probably longer than one year.

A. THOREAU

BECKY
No, I am sure it is about seven months.

A. THOREAU
Can we find out exactly?
You are smart.
You know computers very well.
I do not know computers well.
You can probably find out that.

BECKY
No, I do not think so...
I do not know how to do that.

Rebecca and Aaron sit on one of the benches at
the end of the park. There is one more bench
on the opposite side of where they sit.

Rebecca sees a man. She thinks that the
man is approaching their bench.

BECKY
Look, I think that strange man
is approaching us.

Aaron looks in the direction of that man.

A. THOREAU
Please do not be afraid of that man.
Do not be afraid of anything or anyone.
Now you have me, and
that is all that you need in your life.

Rebecca sadly looks at Aaron and does not say anything.

Suddenly, somebody calls Aaron. He apologizes and answers the phone. Aaron stands up and talks to that person for about 20 minutes. As Aaron talks on the phone, he becomes very emotional and a little upset.

One sentence catches Rebecca's attention.

A. THOREAU
I wanted to kill them all.

As Aaron talks on the phone, Rebecca notices
that about 10 pigeons fly over their heads.
Later she will understand the meaning of these pigeons...

Aaron ends the telephone conversation and
continues to talk to Rebecca.

A. THOREAU (CONT'D)
My father from Europe called.
He wanted to wish me a Happy Holiday.
You know, today is a Victory Day.
It is a very important Holiday for my father
and for the whole world.
You know, my father is a pilot, who was trained
to fly military airplanes in addition to civil airplanes.

BECKY
Your father must miss you a lot...

A. THOREAU
My father has a lot of things for me in Europe.
He has everything in Europe, and
he has prepared a different life for me there.
However, I do not want to go there...
I cannot leave my mom here alone.

It is getting very cold; the temperature has dropped dramatically. The sun has been covered by the dark clouds, and the sky looks gray. It appears that it will rain soon.

Rebecca sees several teenagers in the park, who wear only T-Shirts and no jackets.

BECKY
Oh my God!
Aaron, look at those teenagers.
They only have T-Shirts on,
and take a look at me...
I look so ridiculous in this warm jacket.

A. THOREAU
Well, look at me too.
I look ridiculous too then.
Do not compare yourself to these teenagers.
They do not feel the cold; they are used to
this kind of weather.

BECKY
I am sorry that I invited you to this park
in this windy weather.
You must be very cold; you are shivering...

A. THOREAU
It is okay; please do not worry.
The wind is just very bad for me.
I can get sick easily when there is wind.

A. THOREAU (CONT'D)
I wish I knew that it would be so cold here,
I left my sweater and a cap in the car.
I could have brought them with me.

BECKY
I did not think that it would be so cold outside.
Do you know how many degrees it is now?

A. THOREAU
It was 67 degrees in Lynn when I came.
This was the temperature that the thermometer
in my car showed.

It is getting colder and colder in the park. The sun is completely covered by the dark clouds.

The cold wind is blowing. It does not feel like spring anymore; it feels like winter.

Aaron wants to go home.

A. THOREAU (CONT'D)
OK Becky, I see you are getting very cold now.
Let us go home.

Rebecca sadly looks at Aaron again. Aaron and
Becky stand up and start walking...

As they walk, Aaron looks at Becky and
smiles. He tries to look happy again.

A. THOREAU (CONT'D)
Once again, thank you very much for the gift.
I will definitely do something in return.

BECKY
You are very welcome, Aaron.
I do not need anything in return.

As they are getting ready to say good-bye to each other, Rebecca stares at Aaron again. She looks at the deep scars all over his face, the unrealistically big eyes with one eye smaller than the other, the deep wrinkles around his mouth and on his forehead, the large hands with burned fingers, the bright red spots on one of his arms, and the gray hair on his head.

Deep sadness fills Rebecca's heart and soul, but she tries to smile.

A. THOREAU
Do you want me to walk with you to your apartment?
I can walk with you if you do not want to walk alone.

BECKY
No, thank you.
I live very close to this park.

Aaron takes out his cell phone and shows
it to Rebecca. He smiles again.

A. THOREAU
Please call me if something happens.

BECKY
OK, I will call you if something happens.
However, I do not think that anything
will happen to me...

BECKY (CONT'D)
Once again, sorry that I did not choose a
better place for our first meeting.
I feel very bad because of that.

A. THOREAU
Please do not worry...
We will think about something interesting
for our next meeting.

Aaron smiles.

A. THOREAU (CONT'D)
We will definitely find a better place for our next meeting...

These are Aaron's last words in the park. Aaron says these words to Rebecca and walks away. Rebecca walks home in the opposite direction. Rebecca and Aaron were in the park for almost two hours.

As Rebecca walks home, completely lost and confused, she looks at passing cars and thinks about everything that Aaron used to tell her. She remembers all the beautiful words, the wonderful promises, and fascinating personal stories. Rebecca refuses to believe that the person she just saw in the park was her mysterious friend from New Hampshire.

Rebecca comes home and calls Aaron hoping to find answers to her many questions.

BECKY
Hi Aaron.
How are you?

A. THOREAU
Hi Becky, I am good.
I hope everything is fine with you.
You know, now I understand why you told me once
that you are afraid to walk the streets alone in Lynn.
You are a very beautiful girl.
Also, you are an amazing girl. Your gift shocked me.
I did not expect to receive a gift from you. I was so surprised.
I will definitely do something in return...
Thank you so much for the present!
You found all my favorite music. I just love that music.
Thank you very much for the movie too!

Aaron smiles.

A. THOREAU (CONT'D)
By the way, I was listening to *Blatnoy Udar* when you called.
I really like their song "You Are My First Love."

Rebecca is still too shocked to ask any questions. She hopes that Aaron will tell her the truth without asking. However, Aaron continues to behave as if nothing happened.

A. THOREAU (CONT'D)
You know, when I came home, I was so tired.
I went to sleep.
However, I had to wake up because I need to go to NY tonight.
Tomorrow morning I have to be at work.
I am so happy that I can listen to my
favorite music in the car when
I will be driving to New York and back to New Hampshire.

Later when Rebecca's parents come home, she tells them what happened. They are shocked by this story too. Rebecca's parents tell her to forget Aaron and not to call him again.

Rebecca also remembers that a couple of weeks before their meeting in real life, she had a very strange and upsetting dream. She did not tell anyone about that dream. In her dream, she saw Aaron who was a completely different person. He was not as nice and polite, and he was with some girl. Rebecca was standing next to them, but Aaron ignored her; he did not even look at her. He was hugging and kissing that girl. When Rebecca asked about that girl, Aaron replied that he was going to leave the United States forever and go to Italy with that girl. When Rebecca asked if she could call him, he said that she should not call him anymore, and he added that it was his revenge for everything she did to him. Rebecca did not understand his response.

As Rebecca washes her hair in the evening of that day (May 9, 2009), she cannot stop crying. She almost cannot breathe because of her tears. Rebecca goes into her bedroom and closes the door. She sits in front of a dresser; she cries so hard that she cannot see herself in the mirror. Rebecca cannot even brush her beautiful, long hair. The unbearable pain inside her is killing her; it is eating her alive. She cries the whole night. Rebecca understands that the wonderful fairy tale, in which she lived for seven months, is over now. The beautiful story of Aaron and Rebecca ended in the park. Rebecca will cry many more nights and days waiting for Aaron to call and remembering their unforgettable meeting in real life. Rebecca has so many unanswered questions, and she does not know if they will ever be answered. She understands that her dreams and hopes may have been shattered forever.

CHAPTER 15

SHATTERED DREAMS AND
BROKEN PROMISES

Aaron does not call Rebecca for the next several days. Rebecca cannot wait anymore, and she uses "Reverse Phone Search" on one of the websites in order to find out the truth about Aaron's identity. It is enough to have a person's cell phone number in order to find out their real name, age, address, relatives, marital status, etc. Background check can be done as well, and a criminal report can be generated. In addition, someone's death records and marriage records can be obtained via these websites. Rebecca pays only five dollars and finds out Aaron's real name, his real age, and where he lived.

Aaron Thoreau is Daniel Gorski, who is 44 years old, and who lives in Hudson, NH. (The word *Gorski* in Russian and Polish means from or pertaining to a mountain). Daniel's birth date is January 1, 1965. He was honest about his birthday, January 1. Aaron never lived in Nashua, NH; he lived in Hudson, NH. He also lived in several places in NY. It also appears that he lived in Allston, MA since that city was listed on one of the websites as his place of living.

Rebecca calls Aaron to hear the truth about him directly from him, however, Aaron does not respond to her phone call. Rebecca tries to call him many times, but Aaron ignores all her phone calls. Rebecca calls Aaron for the next three weeks; however, she is not successful.

Rebecca, completely hurt and lost, sends a message to Aaron over the Internet.

June 9, 2009 – Rebecca's Last Message for Aaron

Hi Daniel,

It has been one month since the day of our meeting in real life…

Aaron is a very beautiful name. You chose a beautiful name for your online profile and for your imaginary character, the character which unfortunately does not exist in real life.

Aaron Thoreau sounds very good, but Daniel Gorski does not sound that bad either.

To be honest, I like the name Daniel more than Aaron.

You have become a mystery to me, an unsolved mystery that nobody can probably solve.

I wanted to find a key to your mysterious soul, but your soul has been locked for me; I hope not forever.

It has been one month since our meeting in real life. The meeting that has changed my life forever. The meeting that I will never be able to forget. When you saw me in real life, you probably understood that I was always honest with you, and everything I told you was true and real. I never lied to you, and I trusted every word that you said. I took you and everything you told me very seriously. I treated you exceptionally well.

I have never treated anyone as well as I treated you. I have never respected and admired anyone like I did you. I even prepared a gift for you and did everything I could to make sure that you liked it. You saw my gift…

Unfortunately, it looks like it was just a game for you. It looks like you never took me seriously, and that you were just playing with my feelings all this time. It appears that everything you said was a terrible lie. I could never imagine that I would have to talk to you like this. I could never think that I would have to send you this message. I trusted you so much! You were everything for me! You were the meaning of my life! The pain that I feel now is above and beyond human comprehension. As I am writing this message to you, I am full of unbearable emotional pain and indelible memories, which will haunt me forever. I know I will never forget what happened… Sometimes I think that even after I die, I will remember this.

However, now I know a lot of true facts about you. I know that your real name is Daniel Gorski; you are 44 years old, and you live in Hudson, NH. You never lived in Nashua. I absolutely do not understand the point of not telling me the truth about your place of living. I know that you told me the truth about the trucking company. You had and maybe still have a trucking company, but I am not sure about your new job as a property manager in NY. I also know that you have a beautiful daughter, who is 20 years old, and who lives in Houston, Texas with your ex wife. This is probably the little girl from the pictures that you sent me and told me that it was your friend's daughter. Oh my God! You have a daughter who is almost my age, and you said that you do not have any children.

I also know that you were born in West Ukraine. I do not understand why you never told me the country of your birth. Was that part of your mysterious personality too?

There are a lot of other facts about you which I do not know at this time, but I can find out everything. Now I know that it is possible to find out everything on the Internet. It is possible to find out any information about anybody online. I did not know this before. How could I be so ignorant? I will never forgive myself for being so ignorant.

To be honest, I hoped that you would tell me all this at our meeting in real life or after the meeting. I wanted you to tell me the truth about yourself. I called you after the meeting to hear the truth. I do not understand why you did this to me and then chose to disappear. You were telling me that I was special for you, and that you would never hurt me or mistreat me. You also said that I could trust you 200%. I trusted you even more than that…You even wanted to revenge against my enemies… Did you consider me one of your enemies? Was this your revenge against me? Did you decide to revenge against me because I always treated you so well? Why did you do this to me? Please answer my questions...

You said that you will never disappear, and that you will always be there for me. Where are you now? Why did you never call me or write me anything after our meeting in real life? Do you remember how you said that everything would be wonderful in our life, that you only need to see me in real life, and we will live like in a fairy tale? Is this the fairy tale that you promised?

What happened to all those wonderful promises and beautiful words? Are you a real person or maybe you are just my imaginary friend who does not exist in reality? Maybe you only exist in my mind; maybe you never existed in reality. I wanted you to exist in reality, and it looks like I ruined everything. I insisted that we meet in real life. I asked you to come to that park in Lynn. I destroyed the wonderful world that I lived in for seven months. I do not know what to think now, and how to continue living my life. You said that I will never lose you; why do you ignore me now?

I do not understand anything anymore. It is like the beautiful fairy tale turned into the worst nightmare for me.

I do not understand why you did this to me. What did I do to deserve something like this? There has to be some logical explanation. I am sure there is a logical explanation for all this. Right now, I do not really understand anything. Please help me understand... Please help me; I need your help like never before. You are the only person who can help me now. You are the only person who can help alleviate my excruciating pain. Not to have any explanation from you is like the worst torture. I need to have an explanation. Please help me...

Please do not ignore my message; please respond to me.
I hope to hear from you soon.

Rebecca

Two Weeks Later

Aaron reads the message on the website and calls Rebecca.

Rebecca's Last Telephone Conversation with Aaron

Aaron sounds very upset.

> A. THOREAU
> Hello, how are you?

Rebecca is very surprised that Aaron called her.

> BECKY
> I am fine; what about you?

Aaron is very upset.

> A. THOREAU
> You know, my friend Neil,
> that I told you about, he died.
> He was only 65 years old.
> He was a wonderful person.
> He was my very close friend.
> He was a real friend.

> BECKY
> I am sorry for your friend.

Rebecca waits for Aaron to tell her something regarding the message that she sent him.

> A. THOREAU
> Well, I read your message online...

> BECKY
> And...

A. THOREAU
You know, to be honest,
I did not expect to get
such a message from you.
I thought that you understood me well.

Rebecca is very upset and confused by Aaron's response.

BECKY
Aaron, you deceived me!
You lied to me!
You were not honest with me!
You did not tell me the truth!
You told me all these beautiful lies...
All your beautiful words,
wonderful promises, even your identity...
Oh my God! Everything was a terrible lie!
You lied about everything!

BECKY (CONT'D)
You always criticized dishonest and indecent
people, but look what you have done to me.
Oh my God! You used to tell me that I should be very careful
when I meet someone online.
You used to criticize fake people on dating websites.
Look what you have done to me!
You lied about everything! Were you ever honest with me?

Rebecca is so upset that she is almost crying.

Aaron replies in a calm manner.

A. THOREAU
About what was I dishonest with you?
What was a lie?

BECKY
You lied about your first and last name
and about your age.
Your first name is not Aaron,
your last name is not Thoreau.
You are not 36 years old.
You lied about your age too!

BECKY (CONT'D)
You never lived in Nashua.
You lived in Hudson, NH, and
you have a daughter, who lives in TX
with your ex wife.
You said that you do not have any children.
Maybe you have other children too;
I do not know that...
You are such a mystery to me.

BECKY (CONT'D)
Oh my God!
I am so upset and so frustrated.
I am so disappointed now!
I am devastated by what you did to me.
I trusted every single word you said.

A. THOREAU
Yes, I did not tell you the truth about my age.

A. THOREAU (CONT'D)
Oh my God, Becky!
I do not understand why you are
so upset and frustrated.
I thought that you knew all this
from the very beginning,
given all your intelligence and abilities.

Rebecca gets very upset. She cannot hold her tears anymore.

BECKY
Oh my God!
I did not know anything!
You lied about everything!
You lied about your name too!

A. THOREAU
Nobody knows my real name...

Rebecca starts crying harder and harder.

BECKY
Oh my God, you used to tell me that I am the
only person that you talk to.
You used to tell me that I am a very special
person in your life.

A. THOREAU
I was honest with you.
You were the only person that I talked to.

BECKY
Do you remember that we used to talk for so
many hours on the phone?

A. THOREAU
Was that a bad thing?
Don't you think it was wonderful?
I think it was wonderful.
Both of us felt good when we talked to each other.

A. THOREAU (CONT'D)
There are very few good people left in this world.
If you were not a good person, I would never talk to you.

BECKY
I always treated you exceptionally well.

A. THOREAU
I think I treated you exceptionally well too.

Aaron gets a little aggravated by this phone conversation.

Rebecca continues to cry, but she tries to change the subject of their conversation.

BECKY
Are you in NY now?

A. THOREAU
Yes, I have moved to NY permanently.
It just happened so that I cannot be in NH now.

BECKY
Aaron, who are you?
Please tell me, please...

A. THOREAU
I do have some secrets.
Why do you want to know them?
You do not need to know about them now.

Rebecca is aggravated by the answer.

BECKY
I would like to know everything
about you, and
I would like to know now.
I am going to try to find out everything.
I need to know the truth.

A. THOREAU
Please do not try to find out my secrets.
It will be better for you if you do not know.
I know your abilities...

You will find out everything anyway.
You will read it in my book.

Rebecca is very surprised now. She even stops crying.

Aaron continues to talk about his book.

A. THOREAU (CONT'D)
One day, I will definitely tell you the truth.
One day, you will find out
everything about me.
The whole world will know everything.
I plan to write a book about my biography.
This book will be about my life.
Please be sure to read my book.

Rebecca tries to be sarcastic about Aaron's upcoming book, thinking
that it is just another lie.

BECKY
Will you please sign that book for me?
You should definitely sign that book for me.
I want your autograph.

Aaron smiles.

A. THOREAU
Yes, of course, I will sign it for you.
I will have a special autograph for you.
This is what I will write for you:
"Be Happy and Good Luck."

Rebecca does not understand if Aaron jokes about the book and the
autograph.

BECKY
What will the title of your book be?

A. THOREAU
I have four possible titles for my book.
I have not chosen one yet.
I will let you know when
I choose the title for my book.
You will definitely know.

Rebecca is completely lost now. She does not even know what to say.

BECKY
No one can solve your mystery.

Aaron jokes.

A. THOREAU
Yes, not a single robot in the world can
solve my mystery.

The tone of Rebecca's voice is not so angry and frustrated anymore.
Rebecca replies quietly.

BECKY
I am sure your secrets are fascinating.

A. THOREAU
Do not even doubt.
When you read about them in my book,
you cannot even imagine what will
happen to your head.

A. THOREAU (CONT'D)
I am writing about my life.
I do not have a lot left.
The book should be ready soon.
If I have enough time and patience,

it will be ready very soon.

Rebecca tries to be sarcastic again.

BECKY
Can I be the first person to read your book?

A. THOREAU
You are the most deserving person
to read my book first.

Rebecca says sadly.

BECKY
I am sure you will have many fans
when you write your book.

Aaron smiles.

A. THOREAU
I hope so...

BECKY
Aaron, why don't you trust anyone?
Sometimes you need to trust someone.
It is very important to trust
at least one person.

A. THOREAU
To trust someone...
It is good, but not in my case.

BECKY
What do you appreciate in people?
What do you appreciate in people in general
and in women in particular?

A. THOREAU
What do I appreciate in people?
Nobody has that now.
Regarding women, I am sorry,
but I do not trust women.

BECKY
Oh my God!
You never trusted me!
You do not trust me!

A. THOREAU
Did I say that?
You are a very different person.
People like you are very rare these days.
You are intelligent, and you write very well.
There are very few normal people left
in this world.

Rebecca starts crying again.

BECKY
Then why did you disappear
without any explanation?
Did I say anything wrong?
Did I do anything wrong to you?
What did I do to you?

A. THOREAU
Of course, you did not do anything wrong.
I had certain reasons for my disappearance.
You have nothing to do with those reasons.

Rebecca changes the subject of their conversation.

BECKY
You know, I do not care how a person looks.

A person's outer appearance is not important for me.
I only care about a person's inner world.
For me, a person should be beautiful inside.
The inner beauty is what is important for me.
That is the only thing that matters.

Aaron smiles.

A. THOREAU
I see your worldviews do not change.

BECKY
You know Aaron, although I know a lot
about you now,
Sometimes I have a feeling that
I do not know you at all.

A. THOREAU
Of course, you do not know me.
Unfortunately, I can never be honest with anybody.
Believe me, it is not my fault.
Isn't it enough for you the way I treat you?
Why do you need to know all my secrets now?
Why do you need to know all the details of my life?
You do not need to know these details now.
When I write my book, then
you will know all these details.
When my book comes out, you will know everything.

A. THOREAU (CONT'D)
By the way, I do not know you too.

BECKY
Oh my God!
What do you mean you do not know me too?
I never said a word of lie to you.

Rebecca says ironically.

BECKY (CONT'D)
At least, you know my real name.

A. THOREAU
I do not have any proof that it is your real name.
Maybe your name is not real.

BECKY
Oh my God, Aaron!
What are you saying? What do you mean?
Are you trying to say that I lied to you too?

A. THOREAU
Do you remember how you blocked your
phone number for several weeks?

BECKY
Aaron, I apologized so many times for doing that.
You know very well why I was afraid to trust you at first.

Rebecca remembers Jeff and gets very upset. However, she changes
the subject of their conversation.

BECKY (CONT'D)
Do you remember the gift that I gave you when we met?

A. THOREAU
Yes of course, those CDs are
the only music that I listen to.
I listen to these songs all the time.
I listen to them in the car and at home.

Rebecca changes the subject of their conversation again.

BECKY
Are you afraid of anything?

A. THOREAU
Everyone is afraid of something.
However, to speak about that is
to reveal your weaknesses.

BECKY
Do you miss NH?
Don't you feel sad that you must be in NY now?

A. THOREAU
When you miss something or someone,
it is a weakness; sadness is a weakness.
One must try to avoid his/her weaknesses.

BECKY
Do you know what my biggest weakness is?

A. THOREAU
I am your weakness.

Rebecca turns red and starts shivering inside because of Aaron's response.

BECKY
Yes, that is correct.

Rebecca starts crying again.

BECKY (CONT'D)
I am sorry; I feel so ashamed now.

A. THOREAU
Please do not be ashamed.
Forget all your insecurities and fears.

They should be left in your past life.

BECKY
Do you know how terrible it is to
experience emotional pain?
Emotional pain is much worse than
any physical pain.
Emotional pain is terrible!

A. THOREAU
Of course, emotional pain is the most painful.

Rebecca changes the subject of their conversation again.

BECKY
Since love can cause the worst emotional
suffering, should we even try to find it?
Does true love exist in this world?

A. THOREAU
You know, Sergey Mavrodi, the famous Russian
businessman, has a wonderful book.
The title of his book is *Temptation*. I think that he is a very
intelligent and talented person. In that book, he is trying to
show how easily a human being can be tempted to do
something, even if that something is very immoral and obscene.
The book *Temptation* is about the unlimited human capabilities
and fantastic imagination, especially when it comes to temptation.
This book is about human temptation and human nature.
Mavrodi once said, "I understood that I have a right to talk
about human temptation and human nature when I was
in prison, when I was at the very bottom. I wrote the book
Temptation in prison. You know, once I was at the very top. I
did not even have dreams because I could have everything I
wanted. However, I know very well what it means to fall down
from the top. When you can have everything, you do not want
anything. There, on the top of the world, there is nothing – there

is vacuum. However, to understand that, you must rise to the top. When I was falling down from the top, I understood that."
The book *Temptation* is a truly amazing book!
I have never read anything like that!
This is what Mavrodi said about his book: "The book *Temptation* is the greatest book in the world. There is no other book like that. If people do not understand that, it is very bad for them."
You know, it is very hard to resist human temptation, especially when there is no true love between two people.

A. THOREAU (CONT'D)
This is the dialogue between two characters
from the book *Temptation*:

CHARACTER 1: Is there true love in this world?
CHARACTER 2: Love alone cannot fill up your heart and soul. There is always jealousy, fear, and hatred in addition to love.
CHARACTER 1: He teaches people to love. What do you teach?
CHARACTER 2: You cannot teach someone to love. Love either exists or it does not exist.
CHARACTER 1: So what do you teach?
CHARACTER 2: I teach people to be free.
CHARACTER 2: It is said: "Do not tempt people." That is true! A human being cannot fight temptation. He or she is too weak.

Rebecca says sadly.

BECKY
Sometimes people are tempted to do evil things...
Sergey Mavrodi seems to be a very smart person.

Aaron smiles.

A. THOREAU
Yes, Mavrodi is very smart and talented.
He even once said that "My literary talent is not
less significant than my financial talent."
I think I told you before what Mavrodi says about
himself: "I am not a Genius, I am the only one."

A. THOREAU (CONT'D)
By the way, the word *Mavrodi* in Greek means black, dark.

BECKY
Have you ever liked anybody so much that
you thought that you could not exist without that
person?

Aaron smiles again.

A. THOREAU
No, I have never had such a person in my life.
As Mavrodi says, "Nobody in the whole world can tempt me or
seduce me. No one can influence me, not even God or Devil."

Rebecca continues to cry.

BECKY
Aaron, who are you in real life?

Aaron smiles again.

A. THOREAU
Becky, I cannot tell you this right now.
Maybe it is better for you not to know…
As Mavrodi says, "It is better not to know the answers to certain
questions. Poisonous questions have poisonous answers."

BECKY
Aaron, please tell me who you are in reality.

Please, tell me. I really want to know.
I will never tell your story to anybody else.
You can trust me; you can really trust me.

A. THOREAU
I told you, you will read about everything
in my book.
All my secrets will be there.
Please remember, I do not say anything for
the sake of saying it.
If I say something, I definitely do it.
By the way, I think I chose the title for my book...
I think the title of my book will be
A Dark Mystery in the White Mountains.

Aaron smiles

A. THOREAU (CONT'D)
I hope you like the title of my book.

Rebecca gets very upset again.

BECKY
Oh my God!
Do you remember how you promised
to show me the White Mountains in New Hampshire?

A. THOREAU
Do not worry, maybe you will see
the White Mountains of New Hampshire some day...

BECKY
Aaron, I am so shocked.
I could never expect that life would hurt me like this!

Aaron smiles.

A. THOREAU
Becky, I told you a long time ago that
life is the most unidentified science.

Rebecca understands that this may be her last telephone conversation
with Aaron, and she may never hear his beautiful voice again.

Rebecca continues to cry.

BECKY
Aaron, I will never forget you.
I will never forget your beautiful voice.

Aaron jokes.

A. THOREAU
Becky, of course you will never forget me.
Legends never die!

Rebecca decides to change the subject of their conversation again.

BECKY
You have a very interesting phone.
I have never seen such a phone.

Aaron smiles.

A. THOREAU
Of course, I have an interesting phone.
Everything is interesting about me.
I am a very interesting and mysterious person.

BECKY
Oh my God, Aaron!
I used to have these dreams…
I do not even know where my dreams are now.

A. THOREAU
Becky, do not be upset about your dreams.
As Mavrodi says, "Even if your dreams disappear forever,
never regret anything in this life."

Somebody calls Aaron.

A. THOREAU (CONT'D)
Can you please hold for a second?
I have someone on a second line calling me.

Rebecca is crying very hard now. She cannot even speak with Aaron
anymore.

Aaron switches back to the line on which Rebecca is holding.

A. THOREAU (CONT'D)
It is a work related phone call.
I have to talk to this person.
Can I please call you back later?

Rebecca replies sadly and very quietly.

BECKY
Yes, of course.
You can call me back.

Aaron hangs up. He does not call Rebecca back.

CHAPTER 16

HOPE LOST FOREVER

September 22, 2010: Boston, Massachusetts (MA) – Boston University

Elizabeth continues her speech…

ELIZABETH
Rebecca tries to call Aaron many times after their
last telephone conversation. She wants to talk to him again.
She wants to hear his beautiful voice again.
My daughter hopes to let Aaron know
how she feels about everything.
Deep inside she hopes to bring back the character of
Aaron Thoreau that she misses so much.
Becky just cannot live without that character.
She even regrets the fact that they met in real life because
their meeting destroyed everything.
Their meeting in real life turned a beautiful fairy tale
into a terrible nightmare. A sweet lie turned into a bitter truth.

Rebecca is too attached to Aaron, and
she cannot do anything with that attachment.
My daughter is unable to break it or forget about it.
Without Aaron, her life is so dull and empty.
Rebecca's emotional attachment to Aaron is much
stronger than everything else in the world, and that is why
she is ready to forgive him and forget everything.
Rebecca wants to accept Aaron the way he is.
For Becky, it is better to forgive Aaron for
what he did than lose him forever.

Rebecca tries to call Aaron for the next several weeks,
but he ignores all her phone calls.
He never answers the phone again.
The person who used to say that Rebecca could call him any day
and any time, and that he would love to talk to her 24/7,
and it would not be enough for him, completely ignores her now.
Aaron does not seem to understand how
badly he hurt my daughter,
and that he is hurting her even more by ignoring her phone calls.
He destroys Rebecca even more by ignoring her.
Aaron has ruined her life; he has destroyed her dreams
and hopes forever. Rebecca will never be the same again.
Aaron was the meaning of her life, the comforter and
caregiver of her depressed and deprived soul.
Aaron was my daughter's happiness, her only joy in life.
Becky wanted to continue living her life because
of Aaron and for Aaron.
Now Rebecca feels that Aaron has deprived her of life.

The person who used to ask Rebecca to call him
every day disappears.
The person who used to tell Rebecca how special she was,
and that she would always be a very special person for
him, and he would always be there for her is gone.
Aaron disappears as if he never even existed in Rebecca's life.
The perfect online character of A. Thoreau dies, and
he takes my dear daughter with him.
Rebecca cannot exist without her mysterious friend
from New Hampshire.
My daughter becomes deeply depressed because of what
happened to her.
Rebecca cannot even think that she will
never hear Aaron's beautiful
voice again. She is so used to talking to
him every day after 9:00 PM.
My daughter cannot imagine living a life without Aaron, her

fearless hero, her mysterious friend from New Hampshire.
Her heart is full of pain, the unbearable pain caused by betrayal
and disappointment. Rebecca's little world
has been destroyed forever.

ELIZABETH (CONT'D)
Dear students,
I would like to read you the
letter that Rebecca wrote Aaron.
She never sent this letter to him
because she was too afraid that he would
not respond to this letter as well.
However, my poor daughter really wanted to read
Aaron's response to this letter…

July 19, 2009 – Rebecca's Letter to Aaron

Hello Aaron/Daniel,

I have no other choice but write this letter. I am going to send it to
your home address in Hudson, NH. I called you so many times, but
you do not answer the phone. You ignore me.

Why did you fake everything about yourself and pretend to be the
best person in the world?

Why did you make me have full trust in you and fall in love with
you? Why are you hiding from me now? Why did you come to
that meeting in real life? Why did you decide to reveal your true
personality and outer appearance that way? What did I do to you to
deserve something like this? You know that I was able to discover a
lot of true facts about you. You probably could not imagine that I
would find out almost everything about your identity. As you can
see now, I am not as stupid as you thought I was.

The saddest thing for me is that my honesty, decency, and innocence
turned into stupidity and ignorance for you. You took all the positive
qualities in my personality as being negative. Was it a joke when you

were telling me how smart and wonderful I was? Did you also joke when you said that I was the only person that you talked to, and that I was a special person in your life? Do you treat all "special" people like this? How many more girls did you deceive before you met me? How many more helpless and hopeless victims do you have besides me now? How many more helpless and hopeless victims will you have after me?

What about all those stories regarding many women who fell in love with you because you are so handsome and exceptionally wonderful? Were all those love stories fake stories too? What about all your girlfriends? Were they also fake? Daniel, who gave you the right to ruin other people's lives just because your life may not be as wonderful as you wanted me to believe? Who gave you the right to destroy the lives of other women just because your ex wife or ex-girlfriend may have hurt you? Why do you think that it is the fault of other people who have never hurt you, and who have never done anything wrong to you? It is not my fault that you are not Aaron Thoreau, and that terrible things happened in your life. I have nothing to do with that!

Every day I have more and more questions and less and less answers. To be honest, I do not really understand anything. What happened to me is beyond understanding. You are the only person who can explain everything; you are the only one who can help me now. I know that for you everything was just a game, but I do not understand the meaning of that game. I trusted you, I respected and admired you, but it looks like everything was just a terrible lie. It looks like you just played a wicked game with me; you played with my sincere feelings.

You lied to me from the very beginning and until the very end. You were playing with my feelings even at our meeting. You continued your senseless game even when we met in real life. I just do not understand why you did that to me. Why did you say at our meeting, "Please do not be afraid of anyone or anything. You have me now, and that is all that you need in your life?" Were you making fun of me? Did you enjoy degrading and humiliating me? Did you really enjoy hurting me so much?

Was that a joke when you said that you wanted to be with me all your life, and that our life would be like in a fairy tale after we meet in real life? Was that also a joke when you said that I was a very special person in your life, and that you would always help me and protect me? You also said that you would never hurt me... Do you really know what emotional pain is? Do you even know what emotional attachment is? What about your favorite statement, "Be true to your word, be true to your friend?" Do you really live according to that statement? Were you just making fun of me all that time? Why did you tell me all those wonderful things? Why did you shatter me emotionally like this? Why were you so cruel to me? What did I do to you to deserve something like this?

Do you remember our last telephone conversation? Instead of apologizing to me or explaining anything, you did not even accept all your lies and fake stories. Instead, you even said that I was supposed to know everything because I am smart. Well, you made a very good point. I was not smart enough to use the "Reverse Phone Search" service to find out your true identity in the very beginning. I should have done that. It is my terrible mistake, and I have to live with this now.

Do you remember how you said that you were a man of honor for whom words had more value than life, that you would never hurt me, deceive me, or disappoint me? Do you remember how you wanted to revenge against all my enemies? You also said that you would never make anyone feel emotional pain because you knew very well how terrible it was. You said that you would never hurt anyone without a reason. You always told me that I helped you a lot because I talked to you. There were a lot of wonderful things that you used to tell me...

Daniel, what you did to me has killed me. I am completely dead inside, and I do not know how to live my life now. I could never expect anything like that from you. I just do not understand why you did that to me. Why did you betray me? Why did you kill me? What did I do to you? I liked you so much. I have never liked anybody as much as I liked you. I have never treated anybody as well as I treated you. I fell in love with you. You were my first real love, and I cannot forget you now...

Sometimes emotional attachment can be much stronger than physical attraction. It is true that I have never seen you in real life before the 05/09/2009 meeting; however, I have become very attached to you. I do not understand how that happened... Maybe we talked to each other too much, but I really liked it. The fact that I fell in love with you without even seeing you in real life proves my point that for me one's physical appearance does not mean anything; I only care about a person's inner world, inner beauty. I just wanted to meet a good person... I will always be true to my life principles and moral standards.

I was so happy when I met you; I thought that I was so lucky. I considered myself the happiest person in the world. I could not even think that for you all this was just a game. You were just playing the role of a beautiful and wonderful A. Thoreau. I did not know that Aaron Thoreau was not your real name; I did not know that you were not 36 years old; I did not know that you never lived in Nashua, NH; I did not know that you have a beautiful daughter who is almost my age. How would you feel if some man hurt your daughter the same way you hurt me? I think you would want to kill that man. How do you think my parents feel now? I did not know that Aaron Thoreau does not exist in real life. It was like being shot in the heart when I realized that you are not real. It looks like when I was so happy, you were just making fun of me. Why did you do that? Did you enjoy that so much?

When you saw me in real life, I am sure you understood everything. I am sure you understood that I never told you a word of lie. I really liked you a lot, and I even prepared a present for you. I really wanted you to like my gift. You saw everything... I can imagine how much you laughed at me and at my present when you went home. Maybe you told your friends about me and my gift, and you all laughed at me. I agree that it is probably very funny and stupid - for everything you did to me, I gave you a present; you received a gift from me for ruining my life!

By the way, I totally do not understand why you agreed to come and meet with me in real life. You hid so much from me; you lied about everything; you faked your identity. Even at the meeting and after the meeting, you continued to play your meaningless and wicked game. Why did you decide to reveal your identity in such a cruel manner? Maybe you wanted to be cruel... Don't I deserve to know the truth or to get some sort of explanation after you understood that I was real? Don't I deserve that for everything I did for you?

To be honest, your disappearance does not make any sense to me too. Don't you think it was much better to disappear before our meeting in real life or to say that you met somebody else and just stop talking to me before we met? Daniel, why did you come to that meeting? What was the purpose of our meeting in real life? Was the purpose of that to ruin my life? Do you remember that a day before our meeting you said that our life would be wonderful together, that we just had to see each other once in real life, and everything would be okay? What was the meaning of those words? I do not understand... Where you just making fun of me all that time?

Do you remember how you said before our meeting that everything would be wonderful in our relationship, and that every woman needs a man, and every man needs a woman, and that you really wanted to see me in real life? Do you remember how you promised to make me forget depression and sadness and to make my life like a fairy tale? Why did you make all those fake promises to me? You knew that you were not real, and I did not know that. You made me believe every word you said. You made me have full trust in you. You made me fall in love with you. Why did you do that? Were you not supposed to make my life like a fairy tale? Your words to "make my life a fairy tale" have become the biggest joke in my life. My life had become a terrible nightmare because of what you did to me!

Why did you make all those wonderful promises and why did you tell me all those beautiful words when you knew very well that it was all a lie? Why didn't you tell me the truth? You had plenty of time and opportunities to do that... Maybe I would understand you; at least I would try to understand you. Why didn't you want to be yourself? Why did you need to change your name and your identity in order to talk to me? Trust me, your real name is not worse than your fake name. Why did you need to tell me that H. D. Thoreau is your relative?

You did not need to hide from me your real name, age, family, and everything else. You did not have to hide from me anything. Despite everything, I would still want to be with you if you had the inner beauty. I told you many times that a person's outer appearance does not matter to me. I only care about the inner world and inner beauty of a person. You could have told me the truth after our meeting in real life. You could have told me everything when you became 100% sure that I was real, and that I never lied to you. Trust me; there was no need to play that game with me.

Maybe you wanted to tell me everything, but did not know how to do that, or maybe you were afraid that I would not be able to understand you and forgive you. Maybe you did not think that I would accept you the way you are. Maybe you did not want to hurt me and wanted to stop that evil game, but it was too late. Maybe you did not think that I would take you so seriously. Maybe you did not want to continue to lie to me but did not know how to stop everything. Oh my God, Aaron! I just want to believe that you did not intend to hurt me; that it happened accidentally. I just want to believe that it was never your intention to break me, to destroy all my dreams and hopes, to take away my life. How could A. Thoreau hurt Rebecca intentionally?

I do not know why you did that to me, and I do not know about everything that happened in your life. I can only imagine what you had to go through in your life. I just believe that there was a reason for you to act that way with me; there has to be some reason for what you did to me. I know that you do not trust people, especially women. Maybe some woman hurt you so much that you decided to revenge. However, why did you decide to take revenge against me if I was not the one who hurt you? I just do not understand why I should pay for other people's mistakes. There has to be some reason and some explanation for all this...

You know, my life was not so wonderful either. I was hurt so many times by so many people… You know what Jeff did to me. However, I found comfort in you... Unfortunately, sometimes our life is much worse than we think. Sometimes our life hurts us so badly that we want to disappear, to run away somewhere and hide. Sometimes we want to run away from ourselves and from our reality. Sometimes our reality is just unbearable, and our pain is above and beyond human comprehension. I cannot even describe in words what I felt when I saw you in real life, and when I understood that you lied to me.

I remember you used to teach me that positive thinking always helps, and that we should always try to think positively and laugh at things, which make us cry. I guess your teachings are not valid in all life situations… I think your wonderful teachings cannot be applied to all life situations and circumstances. Should I laugh now instead of crying? Maybe you can teach me what one should do when life kills him/her. Maybe you can tell me what one should do when he/she is dead inside. Maybe you can teach me how to continue my life now after being betrayed by a person I loved so much.

I do not know what to do with my unending emotional pain now. What happened to me is just above and beyond any human comprehension. What Jeff did to me is nothing in comparison to what you did to me! This time I am not just hurt by life; I am killed forever! I do not even think that anyone can bring me back to life again. The unbearable emotional pain and the indelible memories will haunt me forever. Even after I die, I will still remember you!

Ending this letter, I would like to say that despite everything, I am ready to forgive you and accept your true identity. I am ready to accept you the way you are, with all your inner flaws and outer defects. I am just too attached to you; I mean to Aaron Thoreau. Unfortunately, I do not know Daniel Gorski... My emotional attachment to you is much stronger than any physical attraction. My emotional attachment to you has killed me; it has destroyed me completely.

In one of our telephone conversations, you said that it is necessary to have physical attraction in order to be with someone. However, as my example proves, physical attraction is not always necessary in order to love someone. Sometimes emotional attachment can be much stronger than physical attraction. I still believe that emotional attachment can be the most important thing. If I was wrong in everything else, there was one thing that I was right about. You are indeed not like everybody else; you are unique, and you will always be a mystery for me. You used to say that I feel you and understand you very well; however, now I know that nobody can feel and understand you well. It is just impossible to understand someone like you. Unfortunately, I do not understand you at all. You have a very mysterious soul.

By the way, do you remember how you promised to think about a better place for our second meeting? Didn't you know that there would be no other meeting? Why did you make that promise if your intention was to disappear forever? If you ever build a house in the White Mountains, if that is indeed your dream, you will definitely be a dark mystery in the White Mountains. I agree with the title of your book.

To be honest, I do not believe that you were just playing with me. I do not believe that you enjoyed hurting me. I just do not believe that you wanted to destroy me when you were saying that we would have a wonderful future together. I just do not believe that the purpose of your game was to kill me. I do not believe that you agreed to meet with me in real life because you wanted to ruin my life. I do not believe that; I cannot believe that; I do not want to believe that.

I really want to know who you are, and what made you treat me so inhumanly.

Why were you so cruel and ruthless with me?

I just want to understand who my mysterious friend from New Hampshire is.

As Henry David Thoreau says, "It takes two to speak the truth: one to speak and another to hear." Please tell me who you are in reality, and why you did what you did. Please tell me why you lied to me about everything. Please tell me the truth; I am more than happy to hear you.

Now I may seem really stupid and crazy; however, I am still ready to accept you the way you are. Despite everything, I will be happy to be with you. I am still waiting for your call, and I really want to talk to you again. I really want to hear your very beautiful voice again. I miss you so much. I just want you to be my A. Thoreau again. I promise I will forget everything that happened. We can start everything all over again. I trusted you so much; I was ready to die for you, but our meeting in real life destroyed everything. Our meeting killed me. My dreams and hopes are buried in the place where we met. My dreams and hopes are buried in the place where I met my love in real life. Only you can revive them; only you can make me alive again. My heart and soul are dead because of you, but you can bring me back to life. Only you can save my life now. I know that without you, I will cry for eternity. My life has no meaning without you. Please tell me who you are, and I will forget everything. Please be honest with me. I will accept you the way you are. Please tell me who you are in reality and why you did that to me. I need to know why you did that to me.

As Henry David Thoreau says, "May we so love as never to have occasion to repent of our love."

Aaron, please help me understand everything. You are the only one who can help me. You helped me forget Jeff. Now please help me understand and forget what you did to me.

If you want, we can definitely choose a better place for our second meeting.

I promise, it will be a warm and beautiful place. You will not be cold at our second meeting.

Aaron, I forgive you for everything.

Please come back to me. I miss you a lot.

I miss you so much. I have never missed anyone as much as I miss you.

Rebecca

September 22, 2010: Boston, Massachusetts (MA) – Boston University

Elizabeth continues her speech…

ELIZABETH

Rebecca never sends this letter to Aaron because she is too afraid not to receive a response from him or to receive a disappointing response. She hides this letter in her bedroom closet. Rebecca calls Aaron multiple times again, but he does not respond to her phone calls. Aaron continues to ignore Rebecca.

When Rebecca sees Aaron's profile with fake beautiful pictures under his real name on a different dating website, she creates a fake profile in order to verify the information that she discovered on different websites. Rebecca has no other choice but create a fake profile and pretend to be someone else in order to talk to Aaron again and try to understand something.

Rebecca is very surprised that Aaron created a profile under his real name. Aaron deleted the profile of A. Thoreau from the dating website where

he met Rebecca, and he created a new profile on a
different website. The name on his new profile is
Daniel Gorski. Thus, the character of A. Thoreau
disappears forever without living a trace. A. Thoreau
dies.

ELIZABETH (CONT'D)
My daughter was so upset and hopeless,
when Aaron continued to ignore her,
that she created a fake profile in order to talk to him.

Rebecca's Fake Personality

After four months from the day of their meting, Rebecca accidentally
finds Aaron's profile on a different dating website. This time, Aaron
is registered under his real name – Daniel Gorski. He posted his
beautiful fake pictures. Rebecca also registers on that website under
a fake name in order to talk to Aaron and find out the truth.

Rebecca pretends to be Stephanie, who is 26 years old, and who is a
school teacher in Providence, Rhode Island.

This is what Daniel told Stephanie about himself...

STEPHANIE
Hi Daniel,
I accidentally saw your profile on this website, and I really liked your
pictures. Maybe we can be friends. Can you please tell me a little
about yourself? By the way, who is that beautiful little girl in your
profile picture? Is that your daughter? (*Rebecca has never seen that
little girl before, and she has never seen the woman that is with Daniel
in some of his pictures*).

DANIEL GORSKI
Hi Stephanie,

This is not my daughter; this is the daughter of my friend. She just loves me a lot. I have lived in New York for 20 years. I do not have a family; I mean I had a family a long time ago. Where are you from? Can you send me your pictures?

STEPHANIE
Hi Daniel,
I live in Providence, Rhode Island (RI). My parents live in Providence too, but I do not live with my parents. I live alone. I just emailed you some of my pictures.

Rebecca sent Daniel some pictures of a beautiful young girl.

DANIEL GORSKI
Thank you very much for the pictures! I live in Manhattan now. I have a townhouse in Hudson, state New Hampshire. I go there sometimes. I came to the United States from West Ukraine. I work as a property manager in one of the big companies in NY. By the way, I know very well your city in New England. I have a daughter, she is 15 years old, and she lives with my ex-wife in Houston, Texas. If you do not mind, let us talk on the phone. This way, we will get to know each other better.

STEPHANIE
Hi Daniel,
Do you have any brothers or sisters? I think that you are a very interesting person. I would like to know more about you. Please tell me more about yourself.

DANIEL GORSKI
Hi Stephanie,
I only have my mother here. I do not have any brothers and sisters. My father used to work in the military; he lives in Ukraine now. The first 17 years of my American life, I lived in NY. Then I decided to move to NH. I was just tired of living in the same city and doing the same work. It is so good to live in NH. If my mother was not

sick, and if the economic situation in the country was better, I would never move back to NY.

However, I cannot complain now. I have a good job and a good place for living. Moreover, I can spend enough time with my sick mother.

My townhouse is still in Hudson, NH, and I am not going to sell it. NH is my favorite state in the county. I have been in all other states except for Alaska. I love NH very much, and after some time, I will definitely go back there again. Of course, NY is dear to my heart too. I have many opportunities here, and a lot of people know me.

STEPHANIE
Hi Daniel,
I want to ask you something…
How old are you, and who is that little boy in one of your pictures? Is that your childhood picture?

DANIEL GORSKI
Hi Stephanie,
I turned 36 on January 1, 2009. That little boy in that black and white picture is not me; it is the best friend of my father. They went to the same military school together. He is like my father's brother. Our families always were very close to each other. This is how we lived. We were like relatives.
Please write to me; I will be waiting for your response.

STEPHANIE
It is very cold in New Hampshire. Do you like the cold weather in NH?
By the way, I do not have any brothers and sisters. I had a younger sister, who died in a car accident many years ago. My mom is still very sad and depressed. She still cries because of what happened to my poor sister.

DANIEL GORSKI
Regarding the cold weather in NH, it is true that the weather is very cold there. It is colder in NH than in any other state in New England, but it is nothing new to me. I am used to the cold weather. The first seven years of my life, I lived in Siberia.

What happened to your little sister..., of course, it is a big tragedy. Your mother will always remember that. Your sister will always be in her memory. Unfortunately, life takes away the most important things. Our life takes away those who are very dear to us, and we cannot do anything about that. I lost too many important people in my life, the most important people. However, we have to think about the future, and we must enjoy every minute of our life while we are alive. You never know what will happen tomorrow.

STEPHANIE
Hi Daniel,
Are the two dogs in your pictures your dogs? By the way, I am sorry for asking, but why do you have red spots on your arm? Also, can you please tell me about your favorite music and movies?

DANIEL GORSKI
Hi Stephanie,
These dogs are not my dogs. I accidentally met them at one of the farms in New Hampshire. Regarding the red spots on my arm, I was born with them. It is a birthmark. What kind of music do I like? My most favorite music is the songs of one band called *Blatnoy Udar* (Criminal Strike). This band performs in the former Soviet Union; their songs have a special meaning for me. One day I will tell you why these songs are so important for me. What kind of movies do I like? It is important for a movie to be interesting and to have my favorite actors. That is all.
Please tell me more about yourself. I am waiting for your response.

STEPHANIE

I am a school teacher in Providence, RI. I teach Art History. I like my job a lot, and I like my students. My students are excellent. I have always wanted to be a teacher. This was my dream. I am so happy that I work as a teacher. It is no nice when your work is also your dream.

Daniel does not respond for the next several days.

DANIEL GORSKI
Hello Stephanie,
I am sorry for the late response. I will try to make sure that nothing like that happens again. I just had a lot of things to do at work. To be honest, I started to get used to your letters, and I missed your letters a lot. How are you? How is everything in school?
My mother was a history teacher in school all her life. I am very interested to see you in real life. I would like to meet you in real life. I understand that you may need some time... You are a very interesting and well-rounded girl. One day, I will tell you all the truth regarding why I like European songs, and what connections I have in Europe. I just cannot tell you everything right now; it is too early. Please do not be mad at me because of that.

DANIEL GORSKI (CONT'D)
What are you going to do this weekend? Are you going to go anywhere or will you stay at home? How do you spend your free time, and what do you like to do in your free time?
Do you have any close friends here?
Please write to me. I look forward to hearing from you soon.

STEPHANIE
Hi Daniel,
I do not have a lot of free time, but when I have free time, I like to go out with my friends. I like music, and I like to dance. I do not have many close friends, but I have a few very good friends, and I really like spending time with them. What about you? What do you like to do in your free time? Do you have many friends?

Daniel does not respond for the next several days again.

DANIEL GORSKI

Hello Stephanie,

I am sorry for the late response again. I just had a very busy week at work. I do not really have time for anything these days, but it will not be like this always. I missed reading your letters and talking to you online. If you do not mind, let us start talking on the phone. This way, it will be much easier and more comfortable for me to talk to you. I think it will be more comfortable for you too. I am not sure what a better way to ask to talk to you on the phone would be. Here is my telephone number (*Daniel writes his NY cell phone number*). If you trust me, you can give me your phone number, and I will call you first. However, if you want to call me first and see what kind of a person I am, and if it is worth talking to me, please do so. I understand everything...

I am waiting for your response.

Rebecca cannot call Daniel...

DANIEL GORSKI

Hello Stephanie,

I do not understand why you do not want to talk to me on the phone. I just need to hear your voice. I just need to make sure that you are who you say you are. I have some reasons for doubt... I have nothing to hide. I can talk to you on the phone. Why can't you do it too? I need to know whom I am really talking to. You have to persuade me that the pictures you sent me are your real pictures. If it is not a secret, where were those pictures made? Why did you decide to write me? What did you find so attractive in me? How long have you been on this website? Would you like to meet me in real life? Where would you like to meet me? Please call me, and we can talk about everything on the phone.

September 22, 2010: Boston, Massachusetts (MA) – Boston University

Elizabeth continues her speech...

ELIZABETH

When Daniel starts doubting and insists that they talk on the phone because he does not have time to write messages online, Rebecca ends their online conversation. She ends their online conversation forever. Daniel ignored Rebecca's phone calls, but he was looking forward to talking to Stephanie on the phone.

He would be very happy if Stephanie called him.

It was even more painful and shocking for Rebecca to realize that Aaron liked to talk to all young girls. Aaron liked to pretend to be a wonderful and beautiful person, and he liked to talk to females. He was more honest with Stephanie than he was with my daughter.

Rebecca did not expect to confirm that Aaron has a daughter, and that he never lived in Nashua. She did not think that Aaron would tell that to someone. Becky was very surprised that Aaron did not hide his daughter from Stephanie. He just did not tell the truth about his daughter's age, and he lied about his age too.

My daughter wanted to find answers to the following questions:

Would Aaron indeed agree to meet Stephanie in real life?

Why did the songs about prison and betrayal attract him so much?

Was Aaron in prison too just like his favorite singer?

Why did he listen to these very sad songs about a
boy whose mother died?
Is Aaron's mother alive?
What is the special meaning of these songs?
Why are the songs of *Blatnoy Udar* so special for
Aaron?

Now Rebecca's pain is indeed unbearable, now she
lost every hope that Aaron will be back, now she
really wants to end her life. She does not want to
continue living because her existence has become
too unbearable.

Rebecca understands that Aaron does not feel any
remorse. He does not even feel sorry for ruining
her life. Aaron probably does not even think about
Rebecca and their meeting in real life. Maybe he
forgot everything. Aaron has changed his biography
a little, and now he is ready to make another girl
fall in love with him. Now he is ready to destroy
someone else just like he destroyed Rebecca. My
daughter understands that the character of Aaron
Thoreau died forever. A. Thoreau will never be
back.

ELIZABETH (CONT'D)
After my daughter met Aaron in real life,
she changed so much. It was a different Rebecca.
I could not recognize my own daughter.
She was always extremely sad and depressed, and
she was crying all the time.
My dear daughter was in tears all the time.
Becky could barely go to work.
She missed many days at work, and
she was about to get terminated.
Becky did not want to do anything,

and she did not want to see anybody.
I have never seen my daughter so upset.
In August 2009, Rebecca got into a car accident.
She told me that when she was driving, she was
crying,
and she did not see a car to the right side approaching
her.
Rebecca crashed into that car.
My daughter was so upset because of Aaron that
she did not see the car to he right side of her.
She was taken by ambulance to the nearest
emergency room.
Doctors said that it was a miracle that my daughter
survived that car accident with minor injuries.
I still do not know if Rebecca crashed on purpose
because she did not want to continue her life…

ELIZABETH (CONT'D)
September 22, 2009 has changed my life forever.
In the morning of that day, I had a strange feeling,
and I did not want to leave Becky alone at home.
However, my husband and I were invited to a
friend's house for a barbecue.
I wanted to stay, but Kevin persuaded me to go.

Becky was very quiet, and she looked
very sad all morning.
She was listening to Aaron's favorite songs
"The House of the Rising Sun" and "Losing My Religion."
Then Rebecca watched a movie about one girl's love story.
The movie had a happy ending, and Rebecca said that
she could have children too if Aaron was real, or
if Daniel agreed to be with her.

Rebecca's birthday was coming up.
September 23 is my daughter's birthday.
She said that she would like
to invite Aaron to her birthday.
I told her that it was not going to happen since
Aaron was not real.
Becky became very upset, and
she said that he would live in her heart forever.
She told me that she would never be able
to forget Aaron, even after she dies.
The character of A. Thoreau would always
be alive for her no matter where she was.
I did not like what she said about Aaron…

Elizabeth continues her speech. She cannot
hide the deep sadness in her eyes.

ELIZABETH (CONT'D)
Maybe Rebecca was right…
The mystery of Aaron Thoreau
will live forever in the White Mountains.
My daughter was too naive to understand
that Aaron was too good to be real.
Aaron was too good to be true.

ELIZABETH (CONT'D)
These were Rebecca's last words before Kevin and I
left the apartment: "I really want to see
the White Mountains in NH.
My true love is in the White Mountains; my true
happiness belongs to the White Mountains.
The dark mystery lives in the White Mountains.
The love of my life lives in the White
Mountains in New Hampshire.
My heart and soul belong to the place where my true love lives.
I have become so attached to Aaron; I cannot live without him.

I want to be with my mysterious friend from
NH who has a very beautiful voice.
Maybe I will see the White Mountains some day…"

"Mom, I think I understand the meaning of those
beautiful pigeons that I saw fly
over our heads when I was with Aaron in the park.
These were not pigeons; these were my dreams and
hopes, which left me forever."

ELIZABETH (CONT'D)
I will never forget the afternoon of that day.
It has changed my life forever.
We came home earlier because, all of a sudden,
I felt bad - I had a migraine.
When we entered our apartment, I heard the
song,
one of my daughter's favorite songs, and
the last song of Freddie Mercury "Mother Love."
I ran into Becky's room; she was in her bed.
My daughter was sleeping.

As I looked at her, I saw that she had cut off her
beautiful, black long hair,
which was very strange to me.
I looked down and saw that strands of her long
black hair were left on the floor.
I thought Becky would never cut her hair.
I also heard the final part of the song called
"Mother Love" by Freddie Mercury:

"My body is aching, but I can't sleep.
My dreams are all the company I keep.
Got such a feeling as the sun goes down,
I am coming home to my sweet Mother Love."

When I came closer to Becky, I saw her cell
phone in her hand.
The last dialed number was Aaron's number...
I also saw an envelope on her desk.
Inside was the letter that she wrote Aaron, and
that she was going to send him,
but was hesitant to do that.
I have already read that letter to you...

I tried to wake my daughter up, but I could not
do that;
Becky would not wake up.
At that time, I did not know that Becky
would never wake up again.
At that time, I did not know that
I lost my dear daughter forever.

Later doctors said that Becky took too many sleeping
pills,
and that it was impossible to save her life.
My daughter killed herself by taking 20 sleeping
pills.
She committed suicide because of everything Aaron
had done to her.

Later I understood that the final part of the
song that I heard when I entered Becky's room
was probably describing what my poor daughter
felt
when she was dying.

My poor girl was so disappointed in life and in love
that she wanted to hide somewhere; she just wanted
to have her mother love.

I could not even hug and kiss my dear Becky before
she...

Elizabeth stops talking. She cannot hold her tears
anymore, and she starts crying.

ELIZABETH (CONT'D)
My daughter was always honest and decent.
She liked to help people, and she never
hurt anybody.
My daughter lived according to the highest
moral values and principles.

Rebecca died hoping to talk to Aaron.
Maybe she would not kill herself
if he answered the phone.
Maybe my daughter would be alive now
if Aaron answered the phone that day...

I wanted to hurt Aaron so much;
I even wanted to kill him.
I wanted to give Aaron Becky's letter personally.
However, my husband Kevin stopped me.
I wanted to call and speak with my daughter's killer.
I even called Aaron once and said that I would like
to speak with him.
Aaron replied that he would be happy
to talk to me later because he was a little busy at work.
Aaron was happy to talk to my daughter too.
He was happy to talk to her for seven months.
I never called Aaron back....

ELIZABETH (CONT'D)
Rebecca should have met Aaron in real life
after talking to him for a couple of weeks.
She should have checked his identity on

one of the websites before talking to him.
She should have not trusted him.
Rebecca should have not been so naïve.
I should have allowed Becky to meet Aaron
in real life in the very beginning, although
I am not sure if Aaron would agree to meet
my daughter in the very beginning.
My daughter's inability to meet Aaron in
real life sooner gave Aaron the opportunity
to play his role, the role of A. Thoreau.
My daughter's inability to meet Aaron sooner
gave him the opportunity to destroy her
and to kill her.
I lost my daughter forever because of certain
mistakes that my daughter and I made.

After my daughter died, I thought that I died too.
I thought that my life stopped forever.
I loved my daughter so much!
She was indeed a wonderful person.
However, if my daughter's story can teach someone
an important lesson;
If Becky's story can help someone avoid the mistakes that
she and I made.
If her story can help save somebody's life,
I will be very happy.
If Rebecca's story can teach others a lesson and
help them live a better life and
not become a victim of online predators.
I am sure she will rest in peace.
My daughter always liked to help others.
I will try to tell her story to as many people as possible.

Elizabeth's Final Words

A wonderful English poet and writer John Masefield said the following about love, "Love is a flame to burn out human wills. Love is a flame to set the will on fire. Love is a flame to cheat men into mire." Nietzsche, one of the greatest philosophers, once said, "Love is blind. There is always some madness in love. But there is also some reason in madness. Whatever is done for love always occurs beyond good and evil." Maybe he was right, maybe love does not know what is good and what is evil, maybe love is indeed above and beyond everything, maybe love is indeed blind. My daughter loved someone who did not exist in real life. When she understood that the love of her life was fake and everything was a terrible lie, it was too late...

The summer of 2009 was not a good summer; it was raining almost every day. After Becky and Aaron met in real life, it started to rain. These were probably the tears of my daughter...

Aaron killed my daughter, and he was never punished for that. He has destroyed my and my daughter's life in so many different ways that can never be repaired. He has deprived my daughter of her life, and he has deprived me of my happiness. Aaron hurt my daughter on so many different levels, and Becky could not live with that unbearable emotional pain. He made my daughter's existence too unbearable. I want my daughter's story to be a lesson for all of you. I want you to understand that Aaron is not the only one; there are many such "Aarons" online.

Please be extra careful when you meet someone online, no matter how honest, decent, wonderful, and incredible that person seems. If you are interested in someone, please try to meet him/her in real life as soon as possible. Also, do not hesitate to check their identity before talking to them on the phone and meeting them in real life. One must be very careful when trusting someone else. Please remember that all beautiful words and wonderful promises should be proved with real life actions. It is a very famous and a very true statement that "Actions speak louder than words." The irreversible tragedy that happened to my daughter; the unspeakable cruelty that she had experienced, the deep and unbearable pain caused by the betrayal, and the forever lost hopes and dreams – all this contributed to my daughter's death. Rebecca wanted to find a person with a beautiful soul, but she found a person with no soul at all. Rebecca trusted Aaron without a doubt… Inside my heart and soul, Rebecca will always remain a pure and naïve girl, who is full of hopes and dreams, and who wants to find her happiness. She will always be alive in my heart, my beautiful girl. I hope my daughter's story becomes the unforgettable lesson for those who use dating websites and for those who abuse them. I am sure this story can teach you what mistakes not to make, what people to avoid, and how to be happy. The more careful you are, the less likely you are to become a victim of your innocence and kindness; the less likely you are to become a victim of online predators. I hope this story helps you to be more careful when it comes to online dating, and I hope it helps prevent the online predators from ruining the lives of honest, pure, innocent, and naïve people.

Please never stop doubting if there is any room for doubt. What happened to Rebecca is only one example of the harsh reality of our everyday life, the reality that can become your reality any time if you are not careful enough. I made a mistake too in not allowing Becky to see Aaron in the very beginning. I blame myself for what happened to Rebecca too, and I will have to live with this pain all my life.

We shall never forget that there are a lot of people who do not live according to the statement, "Live the life you have imagined, but please, do not hurt others." There are many people who play wicked games with hearts and minds, and who enjoy ruining the lives of other people. However, our dreams can come true if we choose the appropriate means for achieving them and take all the necessary actions and precautions for self-protection. Otherwise, beautiful fairy tales can turn into detrimental nightmares, and our dreams can lead us to self-destruction. There are many people online, who have fake pictures and fake identities. Some people may even use a famous last name in order to attract other people's attention. Please be careful when you meet someone online. Please be careful and cautious.

Despite everything he had done, Rebecca loved Aaron, and she forgave him for everything.

My daughter was more afraid of losing Aaron than of being unhappy with him. Rebecca forgave Aaron for pretending to be a different person, for pretending to be a perfect man. My daughter wanted to find someone special, but instead she found Aaron. However, despite everything he had done to her, Rebecca did not want to hurt or offend Aaron. She never even mentioned to him that he had fake pictures, and that in reality, he was a severely disfigured person. My daughter did not want to embarrass Aaron or make him feel uncomfortable.

Aaron was the love of her life, the weakness of her soul. Aaron was Becky's first and last love. He was my daughter's true love and happiness. My daughter was ready to accept Aaron the way he was. Becky did not care about Aaron's outer appearance, and she was waiting for his phone call until the very last minute of her life. However, Aaron never called Becky, and he did not respond to my daughter's last phone call. Maybe Rebecca would be alive today if Aaron responded to her last phone call on September 22, 2009.

Maybe love is the biggest weakness of all human beings, but love is also the greatest and the most wonderful feeling that human beings can have. Then maybe it is not our weaknesses that we must avoid, but certain types of emotional attachment should be avoided. As one of the greatest American philanthropists and television hosts Oprah Winfrey says, "Think about any attachments that are depleting your emotional reserves. Consider letting them go." Simone Weil, a French philosopher, says that "Attachment is the great fabricator of illusions; reality can be attained only by someone who is detached." An American writer Norman O. Brown says, "Love without attachment is light." However, is love without attachment possible?

Rebecca's strong emotional attachment to Aaron shattered her emotionally. My daughter died emotionally before she died physically; her heart stopped beating long before her physical death. A. Thoreau was indeed my daughter's biggest weakness, a weakness that she could not avoid or let go. Becky's love for Aaron was her biggest weakness. Aaron broke my daughter's heart in pieces; he broke her life forever. He deprived my dear daughter of her life. Maybe Aaron was right when he said that the year of 2009 was very important for him, and that he had to accomplish a lot in 2009. If one of his intentions was to kill someone, he definitely succeeded in killing my daughter.

Daniel Gorski lived the life he had imagined; he lived the life he had dreamed. However, my poor daughter paid a very high price for his imagined life. Becky exchanged her life for Daniel's illusion. He must have understood very well what H. D. Thoreau meant when he said, "The price of anything is the amount of life you exchange for it."

Daniel's illusion, his imaginary reality was too expensive…

A. Thoreau killed my daughter, but her soul is alive, and it will always be alive. Becky's soul will live forever. Her soul forever belongs to a place where all dreams come true, and where all dreams are destroyed at the same time. Her soul can be found in a place, where she was extremely happy once. Becky's dreams and hopes are forever buried in a park in Lynn, MA next to North Shore Community College. There she will be eternally happy and hopeful; there she will be eternally young and beautiful; there she will always be waiting for her mysterious friend from New Hampshire; there is the end of a beautiful beginning; there is the end of my daughter's story; there is the end of my daughter's life.

Who knows, maybe Rebecca's soul indeed lives in the White Mountains in New Hampshire…

I do not know if H. D. Thoreau was right when he said, "There is no remedy for love but to love more." Maybe that statement is correct…

I agree with him that "Love must be as much a light as it is a flame." H. D. Thoreau was definitely right when he said, "It is best to avoid the beginnings of evil."

The memories of my heart will never disappear; they will stay in my heart forever.

Maybe Aaron was too good to be real; maybe he was too good to be true...

My daughter was definitely too naive and too honest to survive in this very cold and cruel world.

Rebecca indeed had a very pure soul and kind heart. She never even mentioned to Aaron that his pictures were fake because she did not want him to feel embarrassed. Rebecca never told Aaron that he was a very disfigured person in real life.

A river of lies always turns into a river of tears, and a river of tears may result in somebody's death. My daughter was a victim of injustice and a victim of her naivety.

Rebecca once told me the following about her love for Aaron, "My love for Aaron is bigger than the universe. It is more important than life, and it is longer than eternity. My love for Aaron is brighter than the sun, higher than the sky, deeper than the ocean, and hotter than the fire. I am so afraid of losing Aaron that sometimes I wish I did not love him." My daughter loved Aaron too much, and she had a pure soul and a kind heart. Aaron broke her soul and heart beyond repair. Aaron broke my daughter's spirit forever; he broke her life. Aaron deprived my daughter of her life.

In conclusion, I would like to tell you what an American fiction writer Jonathan Safran Foer says about love, "I am so afraid of losing something I love, that I refuse to love anything. In the end, everyone loses everyone..."

M daughter was looking for true love and happiness, but she found misery and death.

Rebecca was only 23 years old when she died on September 22, 2009.

My daughter was supposed to turn 24 on September 23, 2009.

Thank you all for listening.

Class is dismissed.

As the students leave the classroom, they hear the words of that very sad song again, the song that was playing in the car outside the University. The students heard the same song when Elizabeth started telling the story of her daughter. This is "Flowers" by Rozz Williams:

> "This is my favorite sad story,
> Forget me not or I will forget myself.
> I have got quite a few things that I am afraid of…
> That is how they found me last time, dead."

CHAPTER 17

A. THOREAU IS BACK

Two Months Later

November 22, 2010: Hartford, Connecticut (CT) – Leah's Apartment

Two friends, Leah (22) and Angela (24), want to find their true love, and they are searching for a nice and interesting person on a dating website.

LEAH
Hey Angela, look who is online.
It is a friend of Ralph Waldo Emerson.

Angela smiles.

ANGELA
What friend?
Henry David Thoreau?

Leah laughs.

LEAH
Well, his first name is not Henry,
but his last name is Thoreau.
His first name is an abbreviated "A."
He is 35 years old, and he lives
in Riverside, New Hampshire.
He has a very beautiful picture posted.

His eyes are so beautiful and so mysterious.
I have never seen such beautiful and interesting eyes.
I am going to send him a message.

LEAH (CONT'D)
Hi, how are you?

November 22, 2010: Hudson, New Hampshire (NH) – Daniel's Townhouse

A. THOREAU
Hello. Do we know each other?

LEAH
No, we do not know each other.
However, I would like to get to know you.

A. THOREAU
Why are you so interested in me?
What did catch your attention?

Leah laughs.

LEAH
Wow! He wants to know why I am so
interested in him.

LEAH (CONT'D)
I just think you are a very interesting person.

A. THOREAU
Are you not afraid to fall in love with me?

Leah smiles, thinking that it was a joke.

LEAH
Oh no, I am not afraid of love.
You have to be an extraordinary person to
make me fall in love with you.
Trust me, you must be special to make
me love you.

Leah and Angela laugh.

LEAH (CONT'D)
I do not like too many people
on this dating website.

A. THOREAU
Well, I do not like too many people as well.
I do not really talk to anybody on this site.

LEAH
Do you have a girlfriend?

A. THOREAU
No, I do not have a girlfriend.

LEAH
Were you ever married?

A. THOREAU
No, I was never married.

LEAH
Maybe we can be friends.

Daniel smiles.

A. THOREAU
I would love to have such a young, beautiful,
and smart friend.

However, only time will tell if we can be friends.

A. THOREAU (CONT'D)
Are you in Connecticut now?

LEAH
Yes, I live in Hartford, CT.
What about you?

A. THOREAU
You live very close to me.

LEAH
Where do you live?

A. THOREAU
I live in Nashua, NH.

A. THOREAU (CONT'D)
Could you please show me Hartford
when you have time?

LEAH
Yes, of course.
I can show you Hartford any time.

LEAH (CONT'D)
What is your first name, and
why is your last name Thoreau?

A. THOREAU
My name is Aaron.
H. D. Thoreau is my relative.
One day, when we know each other well,
I will tell you my life story.
One day, when I know you better,
I will tell you everything about my life.

A. THOREAU (CONT'D)
What do you like to do in your free time?

LEAH
I play the piano, and
I like to dance a lot.
Now I take dancing classes.

A. THOREAU
You are a very talented girl.

LEAH
What do you like to do in your free time?

A. THOREAU
I like to fly airplanes.
When I have free time,
I fly an airplane with my flight instructor.

Leah smiles.

LEAH
Wow, you are a very talented person too.
I would definitely like to have a friend like you.

A. THOREAU
I can feel, we will be very good friends.

A. THOREAU (CONT'D)
Would you like to talk to me on the phone?
I think it will be easier for us if we talk
on the phone.

LEAH
Yes, of course!
What is your phone number?

A. THOREAU
This is my cell phone number.

Daniel writes his NH cell phone number, which he had never disconnected.

LEAH
Thank you, Aaron.
When can I call you?

A. THOREAU
You can call me any time you want.
Please call me whenever it is a
good time for you.

LEAH
Okay, great!
Then I will call you now.

Daniel smiles.

A. THOREAU
Okay, I am waiting for your call.
I look forward to talking to you
on the phone.
We will definitely find many interesting
subjects for our first conversation.

Leah smiles.

LEAH
It will definitely be an interesting
conversation.
I also feel that we will become
very good friends.

A. THOREAU
I am sure this will not be our last
telephone conversation.

Leah smiles again.

LEAH
You are definitely correct about that.
I think we will talk a lot, and not only
on the phone, but in real life too.
I think you are a very interesting person.
I would like to meet you in real life.

Daniel smiles again.

A. THOREAU
Thank you, Leah.
I will be happy to see you in real life too.
You are a very young, beautiful, and smart girl.
I like intelligent people.
I feel we can have a wonderful relationship.
We will definitely meet in real life, and
I will definitely show you a very beautiful place in NH.
I will show you my favorite place in NH, the White Mountains.
I love the White Mountains of New Hampshire!

Leah smiles.

LEAH
Oh my God, will you really show me the White Mountains?
I would really appreciate that.
I always wanted to see that wonderful place in New Hampshire.

Daniel smiles too.

A. THOREAU

Of course, I will definitely show you the White
Mountains in New Hampshire.
Please remember, I never say anything for the sake of saying it.
If I say something, I mean it.
If I promise something, I do it.
I am always honest about everything;
I am always honest with everyone.
I have always lived according to a great
statement by H. D. Thoreau:
"Be true to your word and be true to your friend."

~END~

AFTERWORD

A wonderful American actor, film director, and screenwriter Woody Allen says, "To love is to suffer. To avoid suffering, one must not love. But then, one suffers from not loving. Therefore, to love is to suffer; not to love is to suffer; to suffer is to suffer. To be happy is to love. To be happy, then, is to suffer. But suffering makes one unhappy. Therefore, to be happy one must love or love to suffer or suffer from too much happiness." However, it is possible to love, to avoid suffering, and to be happy if appropriate measures are taken to protect oneself from possible misfortune and tragedy. A remarkable American novelist and professor Albert Guerard says, "Doubt until you cannot doubt no more. Doubt is thought and thought is life." One must doubt until there is no more room for doubt. If one of the main characters had a little doubt until the very end, she would be alive today. Rebecca lost doubt, and she lost her life.

In his famous speech *The Perils of Indifference* Elie Wiesel, one of the greatest writers, professors, and Nobel Laureates in the world and a Holocaust survivor, says the following about indifference, "What is indifference? Etymologically, the word means "no difference." A strange and unnatural state in which the lines blur between light and darkness, dusk and dawn, crime and punishment, cruelty and compassion, good and evil. Indifference reduces the other to an abstraction. To be indifferent to that suffering is what makes the human being inhuman. Indifference, after all, is more dangerous than anger and hatred. Indifference elicits no response. Indifference is not a response. Indifference is always the friend of the enemy, for it benefits the aggressor – never his victim, whose pain is magnified when he or she feels forgotten."

Elie Wiesel also says, "Of course, indifference can be tempting – more than that, seductive. It is so much easier to look away from victims. It is so much easier to avoid such rude interruptions to our work, our dreams, and our hopes. It is, after all, awkward and troublesome to be involved in another person's pain and despair. Yet, for the person who is indifferent, his or her neighbors are of no consequence. And, therefore, their lives are meaningless. Their hidden or even visible anguish is of no interest. Indifference reduces the other to an abstraction."

According to Woody Allen, "Events unfold so unpredictably, so unfairly; human happiness does not seem to be included in the design of creation. It is only we, with our capacity to love that give meaning to the indifferent universe." In addition, our capacity to help gives meaning to this world. It is my responsibility now to tell this story to as many people as possible and to help prevent this tragedy from happening again. I do not want this to happen to anybody else. I cannot and do not want to be silent when I can speak. I cannot and do not want to be a bystander when I can help people. I cannot and do not want to stay indifferent when I know I can make a difference. I hope this story will not leave anyone indifferent. We shall never forget that indifference is the worst enemy of humanity. This is the story of my friend Rebecca.

To all those who have been hurt: "Please find the strength to continue your life and try to overcome sadness and emotional pain. Please try to overcome your weaknesses and remember, our offenders do not deserve our life. Also, please remember, silence and indifference can kill."

- Kristi